EVERYONE CONSID
AMERICAN INNOCE

NO ONE WANTED H

Worldy-wise Charles L............ .... clear to Abigail that she was entering a society where honesty was the only unforgivable sin.

Cynical and jaded Lord Reginald Longford showed his ardent delight at the prospect of introducing Abigail to the secrets of the boudoir.

His mother, Lady Longford, made sure that Abigail learned how fearsomely uncomfortable looking fashionably beautiful could be, and how low on the ladder her position as a wife would be.

Even Lord Longford's ravishing mistress went out of her way to enlighten Abigail about her future husband.

But if everyone was so eager to teach Abigail so many different things, she also was ready to hand out a few startling lessons to those who knew so much about life and so little about love. . . .

THE
AMERICAN BRIDE

THE AMERICAN BRIDE

by Megan Daniel

A SIGNET BOOK

NEW AMERICAN LIBRARY

TIMES MIRROR

SIGNET TRADEMARK REG. U.S. PAT. OFF. AND FOREIGN COUNTRIES
REGISTERED TRADEMARK—MARCA REGISTRADA
HECHO EN CHICAGO, U.S.A.

SIGNET, SIGNET CLASSIC, MENTOR, PLUME, MERIDIAN AND NAL BOOKS
are published by The New American Library, Inc.,
1633 Broadway, New York, New York 10019

First Printing, September, 1983

1 2 3 4 5 6 7 8 9

PRINTED IN THE UNITED STATES OF AMERICA

In loving memory
of my father, Milton Meyer

Chapter One

For a young lady brought up amid the quiet, shady hills and meadows of Pennsylvania, the sights, sounds, and smells of the great harbor at New York were overwhelming. The tang of salt air mingled with the stronger aromas of sun-dried hemp ropes, pitch, bales of tobacco ready for shipping, rotting garbage in the gutters, and everywhere the smell of fish. Fresh fish and rotting fish and dried, salted fish. It was a distinct change from the smell of horses, with which the young lady was more familiar.

But she did not mind any of it. Not a bit. For Miss Abigail Dawson had never been happier in her life. Or more excited. She relished the busyness and the stench and the swarms of people all about her on a bright but chilly morning in late January in the year 1819. She didn't want to miss any of it.

"Ho there!" echoed a gravelly voice. "Swing to larboard!" A winch creaked, and a heavily laden cargo net eased its way up and over to one side of the *Abby Anne*, the neat little packet about to head off into the Atlantic for her maiden crossing to England.

"Heads up!" came a second shout as another net, empty and sagging, was lowered to the deck.

Adding to the cacophony was the rustle of the ironshod wheels of scores of heavily laden barrows as they rolled over the wooden planks of the pier, almost, but not entirely, drowning out the gentle lapping of the water of the East River as it licked at the sturdy piles. Peddlers all along South Street hawked their wares. Passengers chatted and made their way up the gangplanks. Horses

7

whinnied, and the occasional bark of a dog sounded. In short, everything was as it should be.

"Oughtn't to stand there, girlie," came the voice of a husky stevedore with a huge trunk perched on his shoulder as though it weighed a few ounces.

"Oh! I am sorry," came the reply from the pretty pixie of a girl as she stepped quickly out of his way. Her head was a riot of glossy black curls beneath her capuchin hood, and her emerald eyes were very wide in her oval face.

Abigail Dawson was about to embark on her first real journey, and a momentous one it was to be. She was not at all used to traveling, except for the road that ran between her father's New York townhouse and her uncle's horse farm where she had lived almost the whole of her young life. True, there had been the one visit to her antique of a great-aunt in Boston, but that had been years and years ago, when Abigail had been a mere child. And now, *now*, she was about to go to London. She was about to be married. She was about to become a countess!

The excitement bubbling within the girl added an extra bloom to her already glowing skin, which was perhaps a little too brown for fashion—Abigail was wont to spend much of her time out of doors, and she *would* forget her bonnet—but it was a very pretty face nonetheless. The sun, inching its way higher over the river and bathing the scene in bright yellow, sparked little golden lights in her deep-green eyes, and the liveliness of her smile gave her face an animation that one could not easily resist.

She was well wrapped up in a long cloak of black merino edged in rabbit, and her small hands were buried deep in an oversized fur muff. A traveling dress of camel-colored kerseymere trimmed in black velveteen peeked out from under the cloak, and well-cut half boots of morocco completed a toilette that stated for all to see that Abigail Dawson was a young lady of means.

On a nearby ship she could glimpse large, rough-textured bags being unloaded, the word "coffee" lettered on their sides. Farther along the dock a small group of young women, their clothes garish and their hair a palette of improbable reds and yellows under brightly beribboned bonnets, called and waved to the sailors hanging over the rails of the ship just maneuvering up to a pier. The sailors whistled and waved back.

Horses' hooves clip-clopped nearby as a hackney cab rolled to a stop. The driver jumped down, and a good-looking gentleman emerged from the carriage. The two of them began unloading the luggage strapped to the roof and the boot.

A mangy dog loped past, barking ferociously and heading for the gangplank of the *Abby Anne,* where a very short, very wide lady in a plum-colored pelisse and trailing shawl was trying to coax an obviously recalcitrant pug to follow her aboard. A smartly dressed ship's officer sent the mangy mutt scurrying away with the threat of a kick and smiled up at the struggling lady. But the pug was not to be coaxed. "Really, Archibald!" cried the lady in a sort of *basso comico,* well suited to her stout frame but surprising nonetheless. "You are far, far worse than the most incorrigible child." She bent over, a slow, careful process that set the forest of ostrich plumes on her bonnet to dancing, and snatched at the dog. Once down, it looked as if she would have trouble righting herself again. She began to gather her breath to make the attempt but was interrupted by a voice even more *basso* than her own.

"Coming, my dear. Coming. Just wait right there." A tall middle-aged gentleman with formidable side-whiskers of iron grey and an abundant stomach rumbled up the gangplank, setting it to rocking violently. He lifted the wriggling pooch from the lady's grasp, then took her by the elbow, firmly but surprisingly gently, and lifted her to a standing position. It looked like a well-rehearsed move.

She tweaked the dog on the nose, reached up to right her listing bonnet, then smiled at her husband. "Thank you, Mr. Stackpoole." He offered her his arm with a stately nod, and the pair of them proceeded up the gangplank like royalty. Archibald had no choice but to accompany them.

Abigail could not help but giggle at the scene. Another laugh, this one decidedly male, echoed from behind her. Looking around, she caught the eye of the gentleman from the hackney cab standing amid his luggage. The pair of them shared a small moment of gaiety and understanding.

Abigail could not but notice how exceedingly pleasant he looked, with his ready smile as quick as her own, and his warm, friendly eyes. And the sound of his chuckle was warm and real as well, she thought, neither forced nor arrogant.

He gazed at her for just a moment, admiration obvious on his face, then offered a small bow and a nod of good humor before turning to speak to the hackney driver. She saw the driver nod. The gentleman strode off down the dock, obviously in search of a porter to help get his baggage aboard.

Abigail turned away to see to the progress of her own rather immense number of trunks, valises, and portmanteaux. She was not, of course, on her own on the New York Dock. Such a thing was unthinkable for any well-brought-up young lady, which Abigail certainly was. A tiny Negro maid was scurrying about, checking the strapping on this valise, checking the lock on that trunk, bullying the stevedores, all of them at least twice her size, who were employed in taking her young mistress's luggage aboard.

"I tole 'em, Missy Abby, to be extra special careful with that brown trunk," she piped up in a voice even smaller than she was, like a reedy little note blown from a very small flute. "It's the one's got your momma's wedding dress in it."

The maid's dark-brown eyes were sparkling almost as brightly as her mistress's green ones. She was a year or two shy of Abigail's ripe old age of eighteen, though her assertive personality made her seem older, and she had a tendency to mother Abigail like a hen with one chick. She was dressed much as her mistress in a warm and pretty cloak of good merino, but without the luxury of a fur lining. A frilly bit of a mobcap, glistening white, perched uselessly atop her fuzzy black hair.

Abigail turned to the maid and reached out a dainty white hand to squeeze one the color of rich mahogany. The two girls looked at each other, then broke into excited giggles. "Oh, Betsey," said Abigail, almost in a whisper. "Thank goodness you are coming with me. I think I'd die else."

"Not coming with you! Well, where else would I be goin', I'd like to know?" It was a reasonable question. Betsey had been with Abigail Dawson for the whole of her young life. Her mother had served Abigail's mother and had died in the same carriage accident that had taken the young Mrs. Dawson's life when Abby was but three years old. The two girls had grown up together, and Betsey was much more than Abby's servant. She was her best friend.

Betsey was not a slave and never had been. Abigail's father did not approve of that barbaric institution. Betsey's mother and every other Negro who had ever served Rupert Dawson had been freed the same day they were lucky enough to be bought by him. Consequently, they inevitably served him faithfully, as did their children. He paid decent wages and treated them well. He had even apprenticed some of the boys and helped to set them up in trade. Betsey was a perfect example of the loyalty thus engendered.

"Where's that lazy no-'count Jacob got to, then?" Betsey said, then let out a squeak as she felt an unmistakably masculine hand pinching her little brown shell of an ear.

"I ain't lazy," answered a very large, very dark young man as he flashed her a very white grin. After glaring at him a moment, she pointedly turned her back and flounced off to see to the loading of a final trunk. He watched her go, still grinning.

"Really, Jacob," said Abigail with a laugh, "you oughtn't to bedevil her so. You are going to see an awful lot of each other when we get to London."

His grin grew larger. "I know," he said happily.

"Poor Betsey," Abigail returned with another laugh. Then more seriously, she asked, "Have you seen to Mr. Adams?"

"He's aboard, Missy Abby, all tucked up in his own box an' all with plenty of oats and a whole bushel of apples. I got me a bed made up right by him."

"And you'll be able to walk him on deck? The poor sweet is going to hate being cooped up on the ship so long."

"Ain't so sure I'll like it myself," said Jacob, who had a

profound mistrust of anything to do with the sea. "But the horse'll stand it, an' so'll I, I reckon."

"It won't be so bad, Jacob. It's only for about a month, you know. And besides, the *Abby Anne* is brand-new."

"You mean this boat ain't never sailed anywheres before?" he asked with a comically rueful expression.

"Don't let Poppa hear you calling it a boat. She is a ship. And you know very well that Poppa has the best ships anywhere."

Mr. Rupert Dawson did in fact own some of the finest ships afloat, and the three-masted, square-rigged *Abby Anne* was the newest and the best. Dawson was a keen businessman—which explained the fact that he had, in something under a quarter century, amassed what was possibly the largest fortune in New York State if not the entire nation—and when it had become clear at the end of the recent war with England that his countrymen were eager to indulge themselves in the long-denied pleasure of a trip to the "motherland," he had decided he would be the one to take them. Long involved in the shipping of goods on all the seas of the world, he saw at once that what was needed was a new and specialized service geared to the needs of the passenger who could afford to pay for a comfortable passage. He knew they would willingly pay a premium for comfort, speed, and reliability. Thus the Red Bird Line was born, a line of swift packet boats that sailed on a regular schedule, whether full or not, and with no regard for the weather. It was a true innovation.

Despite the dire predictions of his cronies that Rupert Dawson's whimsy had taken him too far and he was likely to lose his shirt, the idea was a success almost from the start. In answer to the doom-sayers, Dawson grew more wealthy than ever.

And now here was Mr. Dawson himself, striding across the pier to beam down at his pretty Abigail, his only child. "Well, poppet," he said in the muted roar that served him as a voice, "let's get you aboard. I expect Lydiard will be along shortly. There's a little something in your cabin I want to show you." His large, ruddy face was full of pride and affection as he looked down at the girl. "Just the two of us, eh?'' He turned to the Negro groom. ''Jacob, see that Betsey gets aboard and finds her cabin, will you?''

He gave a toothy grin in reply. ''Yessir, I'll do that.'' Abby tried to give him a warning look, but he only laughed.

She turned back to her father and gave a little bounce of anticipation. She knew him very well. When he offered her a gift it was likely to be both extravagant and perfect. ''What is it, Poppa? What have you done?''

''Come along then and find out,'' he said with an air of delighted mischief, and shepherded her up the gangplank and onto his ship. They crossed the white holystoned deck to a steep stairway, all mahogany and polished brass, and descended to a short hallway with individual cabins, or staterooms as they were coming to be called, opening onto it.

The first thing Abigail noticed about her little cabin was the flowers. The room all but throbbed with the mingled scents of roses and freesias, clove pinks and honeysuckles, set in a huge arrangement that managed to be charming despite a certain garishness. The basket all but covered the top of a pretty rosewood bureau built into one corner. The colorful magnificence was reflected in a pair of gilt-edged mirrors set into the wall. On the high and comfortable-looking feather bed sat a second arrangement, a profusion of daisies and buttercups surrounded by ferns and tied with peach-colored ribbons. The card propped up in front of the arrangement said simply, ''We will miss you. With love from Uncle Roger and Aunt Sylvia.''

''However could so many flowers be found in January?'' asked Abigail as she breathed in the scent.

''Hothouses, of course. You can find anything you want, you know, if you want it badly enough. But look here at the other.''

She grinned at his impatience. The larger arrangement had no card visible. She looked up at him with a twinkle and began searching among the mountain of blooms.

She quickly found what she was looking for, a square, flat box covered in grey velvet. She squeaked with pleasure as she pulled it from the depths of a fern. She opened it and was silent.

Finally she breathed out a long sigh. "Oh, Poppa!"

"You're a lady now, poppet, hard put as I am to believe it, and you'll soon be even more. Time you had a lady's baubles."

"Baubles! Oh, Poppa," she repeated and lifted the "baubles" from their bed of crimson silk. There was a pearl choker, three strands wide and perfectly matched with a large teardrop pearl hanging from the center, a pair of dainty pearl eardrops, and a hair ornament shaped into a tiara. The pearls were tiny and profuse and gave the tiara the look of an exquisite piece of glowing lace.

Mr. Dawson immediately found himself wrapped about with a girlish pair of arms and with a kiss being placed on his cheek, and he was a happy man.

One might be forgiven, while watching such an affecting scene, for thinking that Abigail Dawson was a spoiled young lady. But such was not the case, at least not in the commonly accepted sense. It was true that Abby, as her friends and family called her, had never known want, but neither had she been senselessly indulged, her every whim catered to.

It would have been an easy matter for Mr. Dawson to do just that. He had a naturally generous disposition. But he was also a man of innate good sense. Having built his reputation and his fortune on fair dealings and good economic management, he was careful to instill in his only child the value of a dollar. Her pin money was limited, and she had been expected to spend it wisely.

There was one gift, however, perhaps the greatest of all, that Rupert Dawson had been determined his daughter should have. At great cost to his own happiness, he had given Abby a family. He was wise enough to realize, soon after her mother died, that his hectic, business-oriented, and essentially masculine style of living was not the proper milieu for a young girl. And so, though the separation nearly broke his heart, he had sent Abby away to live with her maternal uncle in the hills of Pennsylvania.

Her Uncle Roger specialized in the raising of horses and children. Six children, to be exact, and Abby easily became the seventh. The family included Aunt Sylvia, a gaggle of servants, a passle of dogs, a meowing of cats, two goats, and a pet raccoon. It was a busy, noisy, somewhat disorganized, and altogether happy household.

Here Abby became, in one important respect, very spoiled indeed, and it made her particularly vulnerable as she prepared to step out alone into a larger world. She had never known anything but total acceptance, total friendship, warmth, and affection from everyone she met. She liked people instinctively and assumed they would like her. And they always had, not because she was heiress to a great fortune, but simply because she was Abby, warm, impulsive, gay Abby, with a quick smile and a totally engaging enthusiasm for life.

It was this basically trusting nature that made Abigail view her trip to England to marry a man she had never met with optimism. She could have no notion of the differences between the simple country folk who inhabited the Pennsylvania hills and the dandies and hostesses of London's *haut ton*. She knew only that a long-cherished dream was about to come true.

"Thank you, Poppa," she said with great simplicity and utter sincerity as she flung off her cloak and clasped the choker around her neck—though pearls with kerseymere were perhaps not quite the thing. "They will be the most beautiful pearls in all London."

"Ah, they'll have to vie with my princess for that title, don't you know. And they'll lose." He beamed and set the tiara among her curls.

She pranced over to the mirror and held the pearl drops to her ears. She turned her head this way and that, marveling at the beauty of the pearls, which glowed a deep ivory. But when her gaze focused on her face with its high, rounded cheekbones and slightly pointed chin she frowned. "Do you think Lord Longford will find me pretty, Poppa?"

"If he doesn't he's a nodcock, and if he was a nodcock, he wouldn't be marrying Rupert Dawson's daughter. No, sweet. I've picked you out a good man, a smart man, and he'll see right off what a pearl he's got in you."

"I hope you're right." She reached into her muff for the

miniature she'd carried about for weeks, ever since learning of her betrothal. Gazing at the face she had practically memorized, she saw the aristocratic-looking gentleman, dressed in the kick of fashion. His shirt points were high and starched, his neckcloth a wonder of the valet's art. His fair hair was dressed *à la* Brutus, and blue-grey eyes looked out over a long, straight nose and full, almost sensual lips. It was a handsome face, and Abigail was more than halfway to being in love with him already.

"Don't forget," said Mr. Dawson, gesturing at the miniature, "Longford's got one of those of you. Went into raptures over it. He's promised to get Mr. Lawrence himself, or Sir Thomas as I should call him, to paint your portrait. Said no one else would do for the lovely Countess of Longford."

Abigail looked back into the mirror. "Countess of Longford," she sighed, then let out a giggle. "How odd it seems. Will Janey and Pru have to curtsy to me when they come to London?" she asked, referring to her two young cousins, who were really more like sisters.

"Can't say," he replied, seeming to consider the question with a gravity that was belied by the twinkle in his eyes. "I may have to curtsy to you myself. Have to ask Lydiard about that."

"Oh, Poppa. I wish you were coming with me."

"So do I, princess, but it can't be helped. If I'm to pay for this wedding of yours, I've got to tend to my business here first. I'll be in London in plenty of time to hand you over to his lordship at St. George's."

"But it would be so much more, well, comfortable to have you there. Everything will be so different."

"That's why you'll have Mr. Lydiard. And of course there's his lordship's grandmother. The Dowager Countess, she's called. She'll help you find your way. I'd be no earthly good to you. What do I know about how a lady should go on in Society? No, no. You'll be better off with Lydiard. Good man. Trust him with my life. Or my daughter. I'll wager he'll be the best teacher you could want. You know I'd never trust you to his safekeeping else."

"I know, Poppa. What is Mr. Lydiard like?"

"Oh, you'll like him. Women do, I don't doubt. Been

working for me more than a year. He could probably run my business himself. I can't tell you his story because I don't know it. Never asked him, you see. I didn't need to. It's clear as the nose on his face that he's a gentleman, and from the contacts he's got among the *ton*, it's clear he knows his way about there, too. Said he wanted to learn the shipping business, and that was enough for me. He's a man of honor and a man of sense. That's what I know about him. That's all I need to know."

"I can hardly wait to start learning all about the *ton*. But won't you be sorry to lose him, Poppa?"

"Damned sorry. But thank the Lord his decision to go home to England came when it did. When I knew I couldn't go along with you on the *Abby Anne*, I was at my wit's end, I can tell you. Then up he comes with his resignation. Timing, you know. Timing is everything in this world. Funny, his last bit of work for me will be his most important." He stroked her hair, ruffled now because she had removed the tiara. "Never have I sent off a more precious cargo," he said almost to himself.

Abby smiled up at him fondly.

Chapter Two

The cozy meeting of father and daughter was interrupted by a knock at the cabin door. Mr. Dawson reached it in two short strides—even the most luxurious cabin on the *Abby Anne* was not exactly of grandiose proportions—and when he opened it Abigail saw the very gentleman she had noticed on the dock, the handsome one with the friendly eyes and the warm, pleasant laugh. He looked at her in some surprise.

With his entrance the tiny cabin seemed to overflow with life and health and energy. It poured out of him and embraced the air about him, Abby thought.

"Ah, Lydiard," boomed Mr. Dawson, shaking the gentleman's outstretched hand. "Come in, man, come in. Come and meet your charge." The two young people stared at each other as they were introduced, a not unfriendly stare. Finally Abigail, being a well-mannered young lady, managed a curtsy.

The gentleman bowed and smiled. "Miss Dawson," he greeted her in a warm, rich baritone.

"I thought you would be older," she blurted out without thinking. She quickly blushed and gave a self-conscious little laugh. "Oh dear, how rag-mannered you must think me. I do beg your pardon. How do you do, Mr. Lydiard?"

"Very well, thank you," he said with twinkly eyes. "And you needn't apologize, Miss Dawson. You are rather, well, *different* from what I expected myself." He shook her hand. His voice had the clipped, cultured tones of the English upper classes, so much more musical and exciting to Abigail's ears than her own American drawl. His handshake was firm and friendly, and Abigail liked him at once.

As for Charles Lydiard, he was not sure exactly what he had expected to find in the daughter of Rupert Dawson, but he was very much taken aback as he looked down at this chit of a girl.

It was not just her natural, unsophisticated beauty that struck him, though she was quite the loveliest thing he had seen in years with her raven-black curls and those huge emerald eyes that so dominated her face. But no one could help but smile at the life just bubbling inside her. She looked so young, so eager, so *fresh*.

He supposed he had thought she would be harder, more seasoned. He had expected ambition to show on her face. And he realized now that he had been picturing a large raw-boned girl with a horsy laugh and brusque country manners. He could hardly have been more wrong. He felt a moment's chagrin as he smiled down at her—she was so very petite—and wondered if her father had the least idea of the lion's den he was sending this little lamb into. It would not take too many days, or nights, in the drawing rooms and ballrooms of the English *ton* to wipe all that obvious eagerness and those impulsive smiles from her pretty pink lips.

Rupert Dawson was beaming down at the girl. "Well, Lydiard. What do you think of her? What do you think of the future Countess of Longford? Will she do?" His laugh said clearly that he had little doubt that she would.

Abby laughed as well, and neither of them noticed the shadow that crossed Mr. Lydiard's face. "Really, Poppa!" cried Abigail. "How unfair of you to put the poor man in such a spot. You know very well that I will *not* do, not at all. Not as I am now, at any rate. I've so much to learn before I'll make a proper countess. That's why Mr. Lydiard is here. To teach me." She turned back to the young man. "Isn't it famous, Mr. Lydiard? A countess! My cousins are green with envy."

The shadow lifted slightly from his face under the power of her ingenuous smile. "I imagine they always have been," he answered somewhat enigmatically.

"I can't tell you, Lydiard," said Mr. Dawson, "what a relief it is to hand this little magpie over to you. She's been with me three days now and has asked me every possible question about London and about his lordship at least a dozen times. Now it's your turn."

"I shall be pleased to tell her what I can about both, sir."

Abigail clapped her hands in delight. "But do you mean that you actually know Lord Longford?"

Even her smile could not keep him from frowning now. "I know him," he said simply and a bit grimly.

"But that's famous! Poppa, you did not tell me so. Oh, Mr. Lydiard, you must tell me *all* about him. Is he truly as handsome as his miniature suggests? And is his house in Piccadilly *very* fine?"

"He is generally accounted a good-looking gentleman," said Charles stiffly, then added with a hint of sneer, "At least the ladies seem to find him so. As to his home, it is thought to be one of the finest addresses in London."

"Capital," she exclaimed. "Did you hear, Poppa? I

shall be mistress of one of the finest houses in London."
The girl turned those incredible green eyes on Charles, and
he felt something deep inside him, a hard, cold knot of
very long standing, loosen just a little. "And you must
teach me *everything* about the *ton*, and London and . . .
and . . . well, everything!" Before he could answer, her
enthusiasm carried her along in a rush. "I do hope you
won't be terribly 'tutorish.' " She wrinkled her pert nose
in distaste. "I have only recently wriggled out from under
scores of tutors and governesses and music masters and
such. But then, I was never so eager a pupil for them as I
will be for you. For you see, I intend to make a *very* big
splash in London." She looked up at him earnestly a
moment and added, "Do you think I shall?"

Though very near to being beguiled by her openness and
eagerness, the question brought Charles back to his own
reality. That deep place within him began to clutch up
again as it always did at the thought of the London *ton*.
Another degree of hardness settled around his mouth.
"The future Countess of Longford could not do otherwise," he said, unmistakable cynicism in his voice.

Mr. Dawson frowned now, too, but Abigail chirped on.
"And I shall have my own carriage—a high-perch
phaeton—to drive in the park of an afternoon, and I shall
buy my gowns from all the most fashionable Bond Street
modistes." She offered a dimply smile. "You see, Mr.
Lydiard, I already know a great deal about London."

"I can see that you do, at least those things important
for a woman of the *ton*."

"Yes, but I must learn more. Things will be very
strange at first, I know. There are bound to be differences
in what is expected of a young lady on a Pennsylvania horse
farm and one in a London ballroom." She gave an unself-
conscious laugh at herself. "Poppa calls me his princess,
you know, and now I have my own fairy tale to live, even if
my Prince Charming is only an earl. Is it not a Cinderella
story? And *you* are the fairy godfather." Her tinkly laugh
sounded again, and the knot in Mr. Lydiard loosened again
by at least an inch. The girl had a very odd effect on him.
"I promise you will find me an eager pupil. I shouldn't like
to seem a bumpkin, though I am sure I am one now. But

then we shall have *weeks* at sea for you to turn me into a perfect princess."

Mr. Dawson placed a fond hand on his daughter's shoulder. "I'm sure real princesses never chatter so," he said, pinching her chin with affection. "And I'm sure Mr. Lydiard would like to see his own cabin."

"And *I* am sure you wish to speak with him privately and remind him I am but a child and a precious burden and that he is to take very good care of me and keep a very close eye on me, too." There was no rancor in her words. She knew her father very well and loved him even better. "Go along then and ply the poor man with all your odious instructions. Betsey will be along directly to help me unpack. But you must promise to come back before we sail."

"The king never lets his princess go off without a goodbye kiss," promised her father. The two gentlemen took themselves out the door.

It was but a few steps along the lushly carpeted corridor to Mr. Lydiard's cabin, similarly appointed to Abigail's, though perhaps a touch less lavish. When the two gentlemen were ensconced in the small room and Mr. Dawson had unceremoniously poured out two glasses of fine aged brandy from a cut-glass decanter set into a perfectly fitted hole in the top of the sideboard, the older man tuned a serious face to the younger one.

"It was clear when I first told you about this marriage, Lydiard, that you'd no liking for Longford. I asked then and I'm asking again now, have you aught to say against the man?"

It was true that Charles Lydiard heartily disliked Reginald Olney, fourth Earl of Longford. It was also true that he had what he considered good and sufficient reason for his dislike. But the reasons were his own, and he'd been uncertain that he had the duty, or even the right, to share them with Rupert Dawson. That was before he met Abigail. Now he was less certain of his decision to keep his opinions to himself. He studied the burly Dawson a moment, wondering how much to say. "Have you met his lordship, sir?"

"Of course I have. Do you think I'd give my Abby, my

only child, to a fellow I'd never laid eyes on? Took me to
dine at White's, just as if I was a nob myself. Capital fellow, I found him." His voice held the slightest note of
defensiveness.

"How did you come to meet him?" asked Charles, trying to school his expression to one of noncommittal
blandness.

"Sir Albert Stromleigh made the introduction. Known
him for years. Buys his horses from my brother-in-law in
Pennsylvania, ships them over in my ships. Prime cattle
Roger raises. Stromleigh had a feeling Lord Longford
might like one of Roger's fillies I took over last year."

"And did he?"

Mr. Dawson gave a hearty laugh. "Aye, he did. And he
ended by settling on another filly as well, the finest Roger
ever raised, though I sired her myself. Abby's the primest
bit of all."

At mention of Sir Albert Stromleigh, much became
clear to Charles Lydiard. He knew the fellow, a smooth
talker with a jocular air who could ingratiate himself to
anyone when it was in his interest to do so. But he was a
fellow for whom blood was all, whether in horses or people,
and the bluer the blood, the higher the esteem in which Sir
Albert held its possessor. His own title being of the
lowest possible, his main goal in life was to insinuate himself into the topmost echelons of Society. He was always
at their disposal. By advancing their interests, he
advanced his own.

And what better way to put the Earl of Longford in his
debt than by putting his impoverished lordship in the way
of an extremely wealthy wife, even if her blood had not
the tiniest tint of azure to it? So what if the girl was innocent and lovely and far better at heart than his lordship
deserved? She should count herself lucky for a chance to
buy her way into the finest Society the earth possessed.

Charles could almost see the scene at White's, Sir
Albert and Lord Longford both smiling with benign condescension on the bedazzled American tradesman, happily
taking his money at faro and whist, allowing him to drink
a little too much brandy, and casually mentioning a soirée

at Carlton House they'd recently attended, or a presentation at the Queen's Drawing Room.

Charles had long held Mr. Rupert Dawson in great admiration, but he recognized in him a typical example of a strangely American phenomenon. He had always found it odd that a country with such an admirably egalitarian system of its own should hold the aristocracy of the "mother country" in such absolute awe.

But there it was. Mr. Dawson, like so many of his countrymen before him, had obviously been bemused, his usual good sense knocked completely askew, by the dazzle of nobility. Charles knew it would do little good to try to undazzle the man, not with the specter of a countess's coronet on his daughter's head before his mind's eye.

But Mr. Dawson was waiting for an answer, and now he repeated the question. "I'd be obliged if you'd tell me if you've anything to say against the Earl."

"I'm afraid you have the advantage of more recent acquaintance with his lordship," Charles finally said. "I've not laid eyes on the fellow these four years at the least."

"Will he make my Abby a proper husband?"

Charles conjured up the image of the girl's face. Her enthusiasm for the marriage was obvious; her ambition to become a great lady of the *ton* was clear. Who was Charles Lydiard to judge what kind of marriage would be best for her?

With only the slightest hint of sarcasm, which he was unable to stifle, he gave Mr. Dawson the answer the man clearly wanted to hear. "He will make her a countess, sir, and that, I am certain, will make Miss Abigail a very happy wife."

"Aye, that it will," said Mr. Dawson, still thoughtful. "Never seen her so taken with an idea in my life. It's what she's always wanted, you see, to go to London and make a splash. I'm afraid I'm in the habit of giving her what she wants."

"She will make a very big splash indeed, sir."

"Aye, she's a pretty thing. And the Earl's got the goods to make her accepted anywhere. But I want more than that for her, Lydiard. I want her happy." He gave

Charles another long look. He wanted this for Abby almost as much as she wanted it herself. His own marriage had been blissfully happy. He wanted that for her too. "Would you let one of your sisters marry Longford?" he asked suddenly.

"I would prefer they did not, sir."

"Why not?"

Choosing his words carefully, he said, "I find his lordship a bit too worldly for my taste. And my sisters are gently bred."

"So is my Abby!"

"I meant no disrespect for Miss Dawson, sir, I assure you. I can see she is a fine young lady. I only meant that in my experience American girls are more resilient than their more sheltered English sisters. They tend to live their lives much more in public and to be more pragmatic in their outlook." He gave a warm smile. "Indeed, it is quite their most endearing charm, to my mind."

"Ah, we do breed up a fine race of females, and my Abby's got 'em all beat to flinders. She's no milk-and-water miss, like some of your English girls. His lordship'll be getting a fine gem in return for his title. I'll not deny it'll please me mightily to be able to say 'my son-in-law, the Earl.' And Abby's in higher gig than I've ever seen her." He walked to the tiny porthole of the cabin and looked out a moment toward the teeming river. "She's all I have, you know. I'd spend every penny I've ever made to see her happy."

Charles took a swig from his brandy glass and looked thoughtfully at the man he had grown to both like and respect. Unless the Earl of Longford had drastically changed his stripes, he was likely to cost his father-in-law a pretty penny indeed. And obviously he had not changed, else why would he have sunk to the level of linking his name to that of an American tradesman? The Longfords were ever proud, and the Earl must have come to a sorry pass indeed to have agreed to this marriage.

But the Dawsons would undoubtedly be getting their money's worth. The Longford name would give Abigail a position in English Society that she could not hope to gain in any other way. Charles sighed, a sigh of resignation. No, he would say nothing more of his feelings toward the Earl of Longford. It had all happened so long ago.

He put on a smile, that smile that seemed to fill his whole face, and refilled the brandy glasses. "Shall we drink to the future Countess of Longford, sir?"

"That we shall!" said a beaming Rupert Dawson, and the pair of them drained their glasses.

Chapter Three

When Mr. Dawson finally went to bid his daughter farewell, leaving Charles alone in his cabin, the young man sank into a chair to think. After nearly four years of running away from a bitter past—and quite successfully, he had thought—it was now rushing in upon him inexorably. It might have been a mistake to decide to return home to England. It was almost certainly a mistake to take on the job of escorting this young girl to her soon-to-be-husband.

Longford! The mere mention of the man's name still had the power to cause Charles Lydiard to tremble with hatred and suppressed anger. Would he never be free of the damned blackguard?

The history of their acquaintance went back several years. It had begun innocuously enough at Oxford, where they had been nodding acquaintances, his lordship being some two or three years older than Charles. Then he had simply been Reg Olney, or Lord Reginald if one wanted to be perfectly formal, which Lord Reginald usually did. He was more or less the bane of his noble father's existence, a second son with the tastes and proclivities of an heir to the huge fortune that would go to his older brother. God

knew how many times the old Earl had had to bail poor
Reggie out of the slough of his own excesses.

Fortunately for Lord Reginald, and most unfortunately
for the Longford family line, his elder brother was killed in
the Peninsular campaign. His father died of heart failure
within the week, perhaps from the realization of what
would now become of his family, his fortune, and the
estate he had so carefully husbanded and enlarged. Lord
Reginald became the Earl of Longford.

His father's fears had been well founded, for in a world
of gamesters, rakes, and profligates, Longford was soon
out-gaming, out-raking, and out-profligating them all. He
and Charles Lydiard occasionally met—they did, after all,
belong to the same small world of the English upper
class—but they had little in common and had never considered themselves friends. Charles felt little admiration
for the Nonesuches of Longford's set, but neither did he
have reason to hate his lordship and all that he represented. Not yet.

And then Charles met Daisy. Sweet, pretty Daisy of
the straw-yellow curls and the melting blue eyes, Daisy of
the innocent smile and the vulnerable welcome. Daisy,
whom Charles wanted more than anything to marry and
live with happily ever after. (Oh, but he *had* been a romantic young man! He laughed a hard, brittle laugh at the
memory of himself back then.)

Daisy Hollings had not been of Charles's world. She had
never had a governess or gone to a Queen's Square Semi-
nary for Young Ladies. She spoke no French, and the only
songs she knew were hardly suitable for genteel drawing
rooms. Her father was a shopkeeper, quite a prosperous
one and newly respectable, but a shopkeeper nonetheless.
Charles met her at the lending library, struggling over a
copy of the *Times*. Daisy had long been involved in a soli-
tary attempt to improve herself. In her fresh naiveté, not
knowing that a young lady did *not* speak to a strange gentleman to whom she had not been properly introduced, she
turned those big blue eyes of hers up to him and asked if he
could tell her please what Quatre-Bras meant and why was
it so very important to everyone. Charles was captivated
on the instant.

To most "gentlemen" of the *ton*, Daisy would have quite naturally been put into the role of *chère amie*. But Charles was far too honorable for such a liaison with a girl he loved as much as he loved Daisy. He intended to marry her. His family accepted both his decision and his fiancée with complaisance. They had a long history of marrying as they liked, however unfashionably, and Charles had no need to marry wealth when he had quite enough of his own.

But the rest of the *ton* was appalled at such a shocking *mésalliance*. Charles was a gentleman of wealth and position. He was heir to his uncle, Viscount Cumberley. Such a gentleman simply did not marry a shopgirl, or the daughter of a shopkeeper, which came to the same thing.

Charles would have quite happily turned his back on them all and retired to his uncle's estate in Kent, there to sink into a comfortable squirage with Daisy at his side.

But Daisy wanted desperately to become part of a bigger world, to become a "real lady right the way through." She wanted the jewels and horses, the pretty gowns and prettier compliments that were part of that world. So Charles stayed in London to brazen it out. He squired her to Vauxhall Gardens and the Opera. He drove her in the park and escorted her to those *ton* parties where he was certain they would be admitted.

Daisy was such a fresh, pretty thing, rigged out in the new clothes Charles had helped her to choose, and so voluble in her wonder at all the new sights and riches she was seeing, that many of the young men were captivated by her charms, just as Charles had been.

One of those so captivated was the Earl of Longford. He plucked Daisy like the helpless flower she was.

There are all kinds of flower lovers in the world. The serious florist will labor over his arrangements to achieve the most artistic design. He will change the water regularly to ensure the longest possible life for the bouquet. The dilettante will simply clip the blooms wantonly and fill every possible bowl with as many flowers as possible to enjoy while their beauty and fragrance are bright and pungent, knowing they can easily be replaced with fresh-cut flowers when the colors fade and the petals show sign of wilting. There are far fewer true gardeners, those who nurture a plant so that it may bloom over and over again, giving many years of beauty and pleasure. Charles was a gardener.

Having transplanted Daisy to the hothouse of the *ton*, he hovered over her anxiously, trying to help the tender roots sink into their new soil and take firm hold. But Daisy's roots did not prove strong enough for the friable soil of the English upper crust. Longford came along, a dilettante flower lover of the shallowest sort. The more delicate the bloom, the more eager he was to pluck it at the moment of perfection and enjoy its fleeting beauty for as long as it lasted. Poor little, innocent little Daisy was all too easily plucked.

Looking back, Charles knew he should not have been surprised. To an innocent and unschooled girl like Daisy, the hothouse glare of the *ton* must have been dazzling. All the excitement had turned her pretty head. Longford's flowing compliments and extravagances were so much headier than Charles's gentler but far more sincere praise.

And so Daisy fell from grace. One afternoon, she drove to Richmond with Lord Longford. Evening fell, and Charles began to fear for her safety. She did not return for a week; neither did the Earl of Longford.

When the pair finally returned to London, there was, of course, quite a scandal. But all the degradations malicious tongues could utter fell upon Daisy's head; not one word of censure attached to Longford's name. The fact fairly turned Charles's stomach. Ladies happily whispered behind their fans that they had always known Daisy Hollings was no better than she should be. What could Charles Lydiard have been thinking of to introduce her into their select circles? The man should be grateful to Longford. He had had a narrow and lucky escape from a shocking entanglement.

Their callousness, their clannishness and blind class chauvinism, made Charles seethe with resentment fueled by grief for his ruined Daisy, who absolutely refused to see him.

It never occurred to Charles, then or later, that those hateful gossips might have been at least partially correct.

For some time before throwing herself on Lord Longford's protection, Daisy had begun to realize that a quiet, peaceful life in the country with quiet, loving Charles was apt to be a dead bore if it didn't stifle her completely.

Longford recognized something in her that Charles had never seen, perhaps because he did not want to see it. The girl was ripe for adventure, ready to kick up her heels, to take some risks. They were, in some respects, kindred spirits. She was ready to abandon innocence and boring propriety, to throw off the prim sprig muslins Charles had insisted were "suitable" in favor of the more dashing silks and satins in red and gold and dramatic black. She wanted to dance at masquerades and laugh at risqué jokes and be adored by a score of fashionable gentlemen.

What Charles was too blinded by love to see clearly, a rake like Longford could perceive, and act upon, with alacrity.

And so Daisy was easily stolen away. After her little adventure to Richmond, which she had enjoyed enormously, Longford set her up in a little house of her own in Hans Town. Charles never saw her again.

Unable to consider that Daisy had been a truly willing participant in her own downfall, Charles was filled with hatred for the Earl of Longford, callous rake, despoiler of innocent maidens. He was filled with revulsion for a society in which such things were commonplace, in which wealth, family, and position held total sway with no nod to goodness or affection. He had to get away.

He might have joined the army, perhaps in hopes that a French cannonball would put an end to his misery. But the year was 1815. Bonaparte had just been thoroughly routed at Waterloo; the country was at peace once more. Soldiers were being discharged by the hundreds.

So he headed first to the West Indies, where his uncle the Viscount had several plantations that would one day be his. Then he moved on to North America. He studied cotton growing in Georgia, tobacco farming in Virginia, and the mining of coal in Pennsylvania. He ended up in New York, where he spent some time in a brokerage house before moving on to Rupert Dawson's shipping offices.

He had no need to work at anything. His inheritance from his father was comfortable; the one to come from his uncle was enormous. But he found working at and learning about a number of businesses stimulating and a good antidote to his unhappiness. He was happy in America, or at least content, until a growing homesickness and sense of responsibility to his family made him realize it was time to go home.

The image of Daisy Hollings had all but faded from his memory. And now here was another girl to bring back the memory. Abigail Dawson was both like and unlike Daisy. She looked quite different, but she had the same innocence of the world and the same eagerness to be part of it. And it was Charles's responsibility to hand her over to that destroyer of innocence, Reginald Olney, fourth Earl of Longford.

Ah well, he sighed, looking about the tiny room that was to be his home for the next few weeks. At least the fellow had promised to marry the girl this time. He would follow through with it; he could get his hands on the Dawson fortune no other way. And Charles would see that little Miss Dawson was prepared to take on both Longford and the *ton* far better that Daisy had been able to do.

It was the least he could do for Rupert Dawson. And for Abigail. And perhaps even for himself.

Chapter Four

At last the moment arrived for the *Abby Anne* to weigh anchor and lay on sail. A brisk wind scooting down the East River filled the fore-topsail. The giant red bird painted on it seemed to be taking off. The graceful little ship moved away from her moorings right on schedule. The newest packet of the Red Bird Line was on her way to England.

Abigail came up on deck to wave a fond goodbye to her father and her homeland. He returned the wave. Abigail could clearly see the tears running unashamedly down his tanned, rugged face. Her own eyes and cheeks were far from dry, even though she knew she would be seeing him again in a short time when he traveled to London for her wedding.

His big solid frame grew smaller and smaller, and still Abby waved. She waved long after the ship had sailed past the tip of Long Island and headed for the Narrows, blocking him from her sight. She knew she was performing a cliché; she didn't care.

"I shall miss America," said Charles Lydiard beside her.

"Will you?" she asked. "But you are going home. Are you not eager?"

"Eager to see my family, yes." His smile when he spoke of them was his most genuine and warm. "I'm sure I shall find my sisters shockingly grown up in my absence, and my mother with a few more grey hairs than she had when I left. And I shall be glad to see my home again. It is in Kent, you know, a blindingly lovely country."

She gave him a thoughtful look. "I think I hear a 'but' in your voice."

He smiled. "Very perceptive, Miss Dawson. I must confess to some reticence to rejoin English society. I have found the less rarefied air of American more to my liking, and the people refreshingly natural."

"But have you not found us shockingly provincial?"

"Yes. Delightfully so."

"Certainly we cannot compare to the English *ton*, the finest, most select Society in the world."

"Tell me, Miss Dawson. Just how much do you know about this august and select Society you seem so eager to join?"

"Well, not as much as I shall know, of course, but I read all the London journals." She began cataloguing the vast extent of her thus acquired knowledge. "I know that any gentleman worth his salt has his coats made by

Weston or Stultz. He has his boots from Hoby's and his hats from Locke's. I can name all the Lady Patronesses of Almack's''—which she proceeded to do—''and I know that Mrs. Drummond-Burrell is thought the hardest to get round and Lady Jersey, whom they call Queen Sally, the easiest. I've read all about Mr. Brummell's feud with the Prince Regent, and now the poor man has had to go off to Belgium because he's lost all his money, which really is too bad, because I so wanted to meet him. Oh, and I can describe the gown Princess Alice wore to the last Drawing Room.''

"I see," he said with grave seriousness, but a smile was lurking behind his eyes and tugging at the corners of his mouth. "It seems you've scarce need of a tutor, Miss Dawson. You seem remarkably well prepared."

"Pooh!" she declared matter-of-factly. "You know I am no such thing. You must teach me to waltz beautifully and flirt my fan and all sorts of fashionable chit-chat and, well, you know."

He sighed. The trace of a smile deserted his face. "Yes, I know."

They stood a moment in silence, gazing out on a sea already turning orange and red; the short winter days made for early sunsets. Abby discreetly studied the gentleman beside her. She was able to study him in greater detail than she had earlier. She very much liked what she saw. As ever, her father had chosen well.

Charles had removed the simple topcoat he'd worn on the pier. Although his style was perhaps a bit sober for Abby's taste, she could see that he was well dressed. His fawn whipcord pantaloons were smoothly fitted, and showed off a pair of powerful thighs and shapely calves. The coat covering his broad shoulders was of a rich brown tweed. His camel waistcoat was simple over a pristine muslin shirt and simply tied neckcloth.

Abby considered how much smarter and more dashing he would look in a frilled shirt and cuffs or in one of the wasp-waisted, swallowtailed coats she had seen sported about the streets of New York. But she realized that such a costume might not be quite the thing for a man in his position, besides being horrendously expensive. As an employee of Rupert Dawson, Mr. Lydiard's position almost surely depended on a somewhat less flamboyant style. And his pocket most likely demanded it. It was a pity.

But Abigail was not disappointed in Charles Lydiard. No indeed.

"Well," he said at last, "if you will excuse me, Miss Dawson, I think I'll go below. I had little sleep last night, and I suspect," and his warm smile returned in full force, "that you had even less."

She laughed a reply. "Scarcely a wink, in fact. How could I?"

"How indeed? I suggest you take the opportunity to rest. I understand the captain has planned a gala dinner this evening to welcome us aboard. I shall see you then."

"I expect you're right, though I don't feel the least bit tired. When I was a child and didn't want to rest, my Aunt Sylvie would tell me that I need not do so if only I would lie on my bed and count slowly to one hundred. I don't think I ever got beyond fifty, and I don't expect I shall today either." They began strolling back toward the cabins.

"Your aunt sounds as if she understands children."

"Oh, perfectly." Her happy laugh rang out again. "Almost as well as Uncle Roger understands horses."

They reached the steep stairway and began to descend, Abigail's hand automatically taking the arm that he automatically offered. The rising wind caused the ship to give a little lurch as they descended, and she fell lightly against the solidity of his broad shoulder. His arm instinctively came around her shoulders to catch her should she fall. He was amazed at how tiny and delicate she felt in the circle of his arm, like some vulnerable little bird with glasslike bones, easily crushed. A surge of protectiveness toward this little creature poured through him as she turned those amazing green eyes, so full of trust, up to his.

"Oh dear," she said with her birdlike chirp laugh. "It seems it will take me a while to get used to the movement of the ship. I already fell *up* these stairs once today, in an ungainly sprawl of skirts and petticoats."

"Very unladylike," he said with a smile, reluctantly removing his arm now that she had regained her balance.

"Yes, but no one except my maid saw, and she already knows I'm not a lady."

"And she won't tell."

"Gracious no! *All* my secrets are safe with Betsey."

"Can such a young lady have so many secrets?" he teased.

"Oh, you would be amazed, sir," she returned with a dimply smile that would definitely have been coquettish in anyone more worldly than Abigail.

"Then you are fortunate to have your Betsey."

"Oh yes, I couldn't go on at all without Betsey, who is probably waiting for me right now, eager to tuck me up for my nap. Sometimes she's worse than my Aunt Sylvie."

"Till dinner then, Miss Dawson."

"Till dinner, Mr. Lydiard."

Abby did indeed fall fast asleep well before she could have reached the count of one hundred had she been trying. She was refreshed and looking pretty as the proverbial picture when she entered the dining parlor at eight o'clock. She was also starving. She was used to keeping country hours with dinner served promptly at four, and her empty stomach had been growling a noisy protest at the change in schedule.

Betsey rigged her young mistress out in a charming dinner gown of peach-colored muslin with short puff sleeves and a gathered bodice. A cameo on a velvet ribbon of deep burnt orange adorned her long white neck, and similar ribbons fluttered from the high waist of her gown. Her hair had been brushed till it shone like obsidian, her curls piled atop her head and confined with a ribbon. The smiles gracing the gentlemen at the table as she entered were more than mere politeness.

The large round table was nearly full when she came in; only three seats remained unoccupied. It was immediately clear that the company was a select one, accustomed to the sort of luxury the *Abby Anne* offered but nonetheless delighted to find it in so unaccustomed a place.

It was not a large group. The ship offered only a dozen

first-class cabins and on this maiden voyage only eleven of them were filled. Each member of the group nodded politely at Abigail as she entered, masking their rampant curiosity about her and each other. They were, after all, destined to see a great deal of each other during the forthcoming weeks.

Charles Lydiard held Abigail's chair, gave her an encouraging smile, then reseated himself on her left. On her right was a middle-aged gentleman who was the ship's captain. His coat was very fine, its deep blue expanse of wool set off by gold buttons and handsome epaulets.

"Miss Dawson, I welcome you to the *Abby Anne*," he said in a voice clearly used to and comfortable with its own authority. "I trust you will have a pleasant crossing aboard your namesake. I can tell you she's the finest thing on this ocean."

"I can see she is, Captain Hargrave, and, according to my father, she has the finest captain."

He accepted the compliment without demur, clearly pleased but not at all surprised by it, for it was the simple truth. "Between the two of us, the *Abby Anne* and I will get you to England safe and in record time."

A white-gloved steward offered Abby a glass of sherry just as the last pair of passengers entered the room. It was the same Mr. and Mrs. Stackpoole Abby had seen boarding that morning, though they were now minus the stubborn dog, Archibald. Mr. Stackpoole helped his massive wife ease herself into a chair, then took a seat opposite Abby. She caught Charles's gaze, and they exchanged a quick conspiratorial grin.

"Well," said Captain Hargrave in a voice almost jolly. "We are all here, and I hope we are all hungry. Allow me to make the introductions."

Next to Mr. Stackpoole sat a canonical-looking gentleman. His coat was very new and very black; his neck bands were very new and very white. The balding patch nesting in the center of his fading brown hair was very pink, and his smile was very friendly. He was the Reverend Mr. Benton.

To the reverend gentleman's right was a woman somberly clad in a gown of midnight blue, cut high in the neck and trimmed in grey. She wore no adornment other than a small brooch of carved ivory. She couldn't have turned thirty yet, Abigail guessed, but she had a serenity and calmness about her usually found in an older person. From her accent it was clear that the young woman was both English and a lady of Quality. Her name was Viola Wyngate.

As the introduction process moved around the table, Abigail was made known to the Misses Brough. A matched pair of Boston Brahmins, the two ladies were twin spinster sisters "of a certain age." Americans both by birth and by temperament, they were going, somewhat against their better judgment, to visit a younger sister who had been traitorous enough not only to marry but to marry an Englishman.

Then there were Sir Geoffrey and Lady deForest. Their nods to the group were perfectly correct but could hardly be thought warm. There was an edge of condescension in their manner that Charles Lydiard recognized at once. They were perfect examples of the English upper classes.

The final passenger at the table was another gentleman, quite young and made to look even younger by the dandified apparel and manner he affected. As his name was pronounced, Mr. Ronald Dimmont raised an elaborately chased quizzing glass to one eye to survey the established company. He subjected Abby to a prolonged study and ended with a smile that he clearly hoped held a trace of a sophisticated leer. It held, instead, much more than a trace of the inexperience of youth. Charles Lydiard could not forbear smiling. Mr. Dimmont, at the age of twenty, was much like himself at that age. The only other person at the table the Captain introduced as his first mate, Mr. John Welsh. He was youngish and good-looking, and had, despite his good manners, a sort of American insouciance that was charming.

They were served an excellent meal. It was clear that the chef had made an almost superhuman exertion. Of course, it was not every day that Captain Hargrave had the only child of the owner of his ship as a passenger, but he was also inordinately proud of the *Abby Anne*. He intended her service to be as fine as her sailing, and if this night's meal was a good example, he would not fail.

Course followed delicious course, beginning with a savory soup rich with butter and cream and thick chewy clams. There was codfish, gently boiled and surrounded by tiny russet potatoes, followed by roast wild turkeys with chestnut stuffing, bright-red crabapples, and a macaroni pie heavily crusted with melted cheese. Mashed parsnips and a compote of stewed fruits came with a sugar-cured and baked ham. There was fresh-baked bread and sea biscuits, pickles and curried nuts, jellies and sweet creams, and the most delicious blackberry tart Abigail had ever tasted. Throughout the meal the goblets were kept well filled with champagne by a small army of stewards.

It was abundantly clear that the passengers of the Red Bird Line, each of whom—except Abigail and Charles, of course—had paid a very hefty two hundred dollars for their crossing, would get their money's worth.

Abigail ate so heartily that Charles Lydiard was both amazed and amused. In his experience, young ladies picked daintily at their food, trying a taste of this or a morsel of that but scarcely taking in enough to keep a bird alive. He had always wondered how they managed to stay healthy. Clearly he needn't worry that his charge would succumb to malnutrition during the voyage.

The conversation flowed as easily as the champagne. Everyone was in a happy, excited mood. They had not yet had time to be bored by the ever-present view of the sea or the undiluted continuity of each other's company. There was much oohing and aahing about the grandeur of the ship and its appointments, and about the clever design of the table, which had a small railing to keep things from sliding off and a depression to keep each plate and glass steady. They commented on the convenience of sailing on a fixed schedule, and the reasons each of them had for making the trip.

Mr. and Mrs. Stackpoole, it turned out, were embarked on a dual-purpose expedition. Mr. Stackpoole was a businessman with numerous associates to see in England. In addition, the couple planned a tour of the major capitals of Europe to celebrate twenty-five years of wedded bliss. Mrs. Stackpoole loudly stated her intention of visiting every fashionable *modiste*—and, one would assume, every *corsetière*—in Paris, London, and Rome. Her husband's mission, more in the nature of a holy crusade really, was to show the Old World that the upstart Americans had earned the right to join the ranks of civilized societies.

"They think us a lot of backwoods bumpkins, you know," he harumphed as he slurped up some raspberry jelly. "But we will show them that we are a people of refinement and taste, will we not, my dear?"

"Oh decidedly, Mr. Stackpoole," bellowed Mrs. Stackpoole. "Decidely."

Miss Wyngate revealed that she was returning home after several years as governess to a New York family with eight daughters.

"Yes, that's right," she said calmly. "Eight. Of course, the two youngest were still really in the nursery, so I had minimal responsibility for them, though it was often difficult to remind them of that fact," she finished with a chuckle.

She seemed remarkably unscathed by the experience. A small legacy from an aunt made it no longer necessary for her to earn her living by her wits. She was refreshingly unashamed of both her previous penury and her recent favorable change in circumstances. Abigail was struck by the serenity of her manner, a sort of calm self-possession that could not but attract.

The American Misses Brough and the English Sir Geoffrey and Lady deForest discovered a similarity in the reasons for their travel. The deForests were returning from a visit to their eldest daughter, married to a Virginia planter, and their first grandchild. The Brough sisters, after several years of refusing to leave Boston despite their sister's repeated entreaties, had finally given in to the lure of their never-seen twin nephews. Such is the power of the newborn.

Mr. Benton was on his way to an international ecclesiastical conference, and young Mr. Dimmont was going to join a cousin preparatory to embarking on the Grand Tour.

None of the passengers, of course, could fail to be impressed by Abigail's reasons for making this journey, though a few of them tried hard not to let it show. Lady deForest's eyes quite lighted up at the word "countess," and she looked at Abby with new respect. No one in London could have too many titled friends.

Ronald Dimmont, who thought it too, too gauche to be awed by anything at all, ostentatiously stifled a fashionable yawn at the news, but his eyes were alight with envy all the same. Mr. Stackpoole stated that he couldn't see why a nice American girl had to go off and marry an Englishman when there were so many fine American fellows about, but he did allow as how perhaps an earl *might* be something of an exception.

The Brough sisters frowned on behavior so like that of their self-willed sister, but Miss Agnes was heard to remark to Miss Emily that it would be nice to be acquainted with *Lady* Longford. Miss Wyngate and Mr. Benton both smiled their congratulations, while First Mate Welsh gave a vaguely disappointed grin.

The Captain began to outline the ship's amenities. Tea would be available at all times in the parlor, he said. Or the passengers could have it in their staterooms should they prefer. They need only ring for a steward. Areas of the deck had been especially set aside for their pleasure, although it was perhaps unlikely they would choose to spend a great deal of time there at this season of the year.

The outboats, they were told, provided not only an extra degree of safety should they meet with some emergency—an extremely unlikely occurrence, he reassured them—but also stall space for a cow, a number of sheep, and several chickens. They were thus assured of a continuing supply of fresh milk, eggs, and mutton.

"However, I feel I must warn you that water is something we must keep a close watch on," Captain Hargrave continued. "There is a limit to how much we can carry, and I'm afraid we haven't yet learned the trick of making it ourselves. We've all we'll need for drinking, of course, and for watering the animals and such, but I'm afraid you ladies will have to forgo the luxury of a hot bath until we reach England."

The Misses Brough blushed furiously to hear such a delicate business referred to in their presence, and by a gentleman! Lady deForest gave a genteel, long-suffering sigh. The Captain twinkled a smile and went on. "However, for the hardier among you gentleman, I've rigged up a device for my own use that you may try if you're of a mind to. I warn you, it's not for the namby-pamby, but I've got myself the prettiest little seawater showerbath you ever saw up near the bowsprit. I promise you, nothing sets a man up better for the day.''

Abigail thought the idea intriguing and privately resented being thus summarily excluded from the invitation merely because of her gender. But perhaps she would find a way to wheedle permission from the Captain after all.

Several of the gentlemen voiced a desire to try out the contraption, though Mr. Dimmont's only reaction was an eloquent shudder at the idea that he would entertain anything so barbaric.

Finally the Captain rose from his rounded armchair, insisting that the gentlemen could forgo their brandy and cigars this once, and the company retired to the smallish but very comfortable parlor. They sipped fine Souchong tea from delicate china cups and relaxed on comfortable chairs upholstered in rose silk damask. It was all so terribly civilized that except for the gentle rolling of the ship that set the hanging lamps to swinging slightly and the constant flap and creek of sails and spars over their heads, one might easily forget one was at sea.

When the company did finally break up, each passenger was well pleased with his decision to sail on the newest ship of the newly famous Red Bird Line.

Chapter Five

When Abigail retired to her cozy cabin she was far too excited to sleep. After trying unsucessfully to interest herself in a book, she finally gave up the attempt. The swaying of the hanging lamp was distracting, and the elegant little room seemed too confining for the excitement bubbling inside her.

Picking up a warm shawl, she headed up onto the deck. Perhaps the sea air would quiet the spiraling images in her mind, clearing it enough for sleep to creep in.

She walked past several crew members, smart in their Red Bird uniforms, and they favored her with admiring smiles. As though drawn by the home she had left behind, she made her way to the quarterdeck and across to the taffrail to where she had waved goodbye to her father a few hours earlier.

She stared down into the dark water, watching the silvery wake trail off behind them, pointing a path toward the country of which she was so pure a product and which she might not see again for many years.

She pictured in her mind the carved and gilded figurehead gracing the bowsprit of the *Abby Anne*. It was an elaborate carving of Amphitrite, loveliest of the Nereids. Abby had loved it from the moment she first saw it. The goddess strained forward, gazing into the future, eager to reach it and undaunted by what it might hold.

It was just how Abby wanted to feel, did feel in fact much of the time. But there were moments, and this was one of them as she stared at the pinpricks of light in the sky and the barely discernible horizon where America had

41

long since disappeared, when she felt just the tiniest bit
afraid.

Looking out at all that water and all that sky, Abby
felt suddenly quite alone in the world. She pulled her cash-
mere shawl closer. She had been so surrounded and insula-
ted all her life by her family, and now she was in the middle
of what had suddenly become a very much larger world,
with no one but the chattering Betsey and the grinning
Jacob to connect her with home and everyone and everything she loved.

Of course there was Mr. Lydiard, but he was the link
with her future as a woman of the world, not part of her
past as a pampered child. She marveled at how neatly her
life had divided itself into two halves. Most of her
girlfriends had had the opportunity to grow gradually into
womanhood, almost without noticing they were doing so.
But in Abby's case there was to be no such easy transi-
tion. The Atlantic Ocean represented a clear line cutting
her life in two just as surely as it divided the old "motherland" of England from its recalcitrant child to the west.

She would undoubtedly have much to learn about her
new world. She was strangely comforted by the thought
of Mr. Lydiard nearby. He emitted such strength, gentled
by his pleasant smile. She could not be so terribly afraid
with him to guide her.

As though her thoughts drew him, she heard footsteps
and turned to see the gentleman himself approaching.
"You could not sleep, Miss Dawson?" he asked with concern. "I hope you have had no trouble finding your sea
legs." He searched her face for signs of the distress of sea-
sickness and was relieved to find none. He was struck once
again by her freshness, her naturalness. The moonlight
turned her cheeks to alabaster; her curls riffled lightly in
the breeze that kept the sails straining against their
yards. Her green eyes were glistening, and he saw a tear
gathered in the corner of each ready to spill over and roll
down the expanse of alabaster. "But what is this, my
dear?" he said softly, reaching up a finger to flick away
one of the tears. "You are crying."

To his surprise, she laughed. "Yes. Isn't it silly? I'm
afraid I do it on the slightest pretext, though I do try not

to. Just now I was simply wondering when I should see Pennsylvania again and feeling just the tiniest bit homesick for my aunt and uncle and my cousins. And I have scarce been away from them a week!''

''But you have never been away from home before. It is natural you should be a bit ill at ease.''

''I suppose you are right, though I am very happy about going, of course. As to your question, no, I am pleased to say I've not experienced even the tiniest symptom of what my aunt so delicately calls *mal de mer*.'' She laughed again, and he felt himself smiling wholeheartedly at the free, natural sound of it. Her tone became confiding as she added, ''I think I am really afraid to, you know, for my Aunt Sylvie sent a veritable trunkful of infusions and decoctions and tisanes against the dread malady. I'm certain they are enough to *make* one ill. I shall dump them all overboard, then write to tell her how wonderful they were and that I was feeling perfectly wretched until I used them up, whereby I experienced a miraculous improvement and arrived in London in the pink of health.''

To her delight, he threw back his head and laughed the laugh that already had the power to warm her right through. ''As I trust you will do.''

''Oh, I am never ill. No thanks to Aunt Sylvie's remedies.'' She gave him a mischievous grin. ''Do you think it too horrid of me to lie to her so?''

''I think it can be called a fib in a worthy cause,'' he said gravely.

''Yes, and perhaps I need not fib entirely, you know, for Jacob was not looking at all the thing this afternoon. I think I shall take him a tisane, poor thing.''

''If it is as awful as you suspect, he'll not thank you, I'll wager. Have him pop round to my cabin. I have something of my own that is not in the least vile and is highly effective.''

''Why, thank you, Mr. Lydiard. That is kind of you.''

''Unlike you, I'm afraid I know only too well the humiliating effects of *mal de mer*, though luckily I seem to have outgrown the tendency. I can assure you they are not the least bit amusing. We cannot have Jacob neglecting your horse while being sick as a dog himself. That is a beautiful animal, by the by. One of your uncle's, I imagine.''

Her face lit with enthusiasm. ''Yes. That is, Mr. Adams was born and raised on my uncle's farm, but he is really mine. I chose the sire and dam myself, some of the best blood in my uncle's stable, and I was beside the mare when the foal dropped. I've practically raised Mr. Adams single-handedly.''

Halfway through this matter-of-fact discussion of horsebreeding, Mr. Lydiard was choking on a combination of laughter and astonishment. ''My dear Miss Dawson, I must counsel you to watch your tongue. The fans that would drop in any London drawing room should you let it be known that you were present when the 'foal dropped.'! It is not a subject commonly discussed among young ladies, or even old ones if it comes to that.''

''Why not? Any girl brought up in the country must have done much the same.''

''Not any English girl, I assure you. Besides, you will not be in the country, but in London, where everyone makes it his business to pretend he has forgotten the country exists and where doing or saying anything *natural* is a definite *faux pas*.''

The smile had disappeared from his face, as it had a habit of doing when he talked about the *ton*. ''It is a lesson you will have to remember if you want to fit in, as I assume you do.''

''I do. I want it more than anything.'' He could not help but hear the determination in her voice. His frown increased, and she noted the hardness that settled around his mouth and the coldness that entered his eyes.

''Well then, you have several lessons to learn. If you cry as easily as you say, you must endeavor not to become upset. Constant tears will never do.''

To his surprise she laughed again. ''Oh, I don't have to be upset, you know. I'm afraid I scarcely need a reason at all. Poppa calls me his watering pot. Why, when he took me to the theatre the other night to see Mr. Power's performance I began crying during the applause. Have you ever heard anything so silly? I was mortified, but really I couldn't help it. When the cheers and bravos rose up to meet him, and he just stood there on the stage so simply, it seemed so . . . so . . . I don't know, so *wonderful* that anyone could be loved that much by all those people. I was so *touched*."

Mr. Lydiard was finding himself experiencing an odd mixture of emotions talking to this straightforward and altogether disarming girl. He wanted to shake her shoulders and yell at her never to change, never to become like "them." He longed to reach up and brush away the dusky curl that had fallen over one eye, and he felt an almost overpowering desire to kiss the pink lips that smiled up at him with such trust. Instead, he turned away. "That will never do, you know, not for a lady of the *ton*," he said.

"No, I don't suppose Lord Longford will like to have a watering pot for a countess," she said with a giggle.

Whatever tender emotions the girl might bring forth in him, the name of her betrothed effectively quelled them. His voice grew brisk and cold. "Quite," he snapped. "We must break you of the habit. A true lady never allows her emotions to show so clearly, whether they be happy or sad. To do so is seen as hopelessly common. Indeed, I sometimes believe that the members of the *ton* have no feelings to hide. You will do well to remember that if you wish, as you so obviously do, to join their exalted ranks."

There was no denying the sneer in his remarks now. She did not understand it, but she felt inexplicably as though she had been slapped. "Everyone has feelings, Mr. Lydiard," she said quietly. "It's what makes us human, after all."

"Human?" he said with a mirthless laugh. "My dear girl, you are on your way to join the greatest zoo on earth." He turned and stared off into the empty grey-black sea. "In any case, you will learn to curb your emotions. It is part of my job to see to it that you do. You will recall that I am to 'tutor' you, as you put it, in all things English. We shall begin tomorrow after breakfast."

She wondered what on earth she had said or done to make him angry, to make his voice so chilling that she almost shivered. "Yes of course, Mr. Lydiard. I am eager to begin."

"Yes, I am certain you are. In the meantime, I suggest

you return to your cabin. It is not seemly for you to remain
on deck by yourself after dark.''

"But surely . . .'' she began, but was stopped by the
black frown that had completely overtaken his face.
"Very well. I bid you goodnight then.''

"Goodnight, Miss Dawson,'' he said with a nod and
turned away once more. He heard her slippers patter
lightly on the smooth deck as she walked away. "Do not
forget to send Jacob for the medication,'' he added. He
heard the footsteps stop for a moment, and then they
faded away.

He knew he had hurt and confused her—it had been
written plainly on her face—and he felt grimly pleased
with himself. She was entirely too open, too trusting, to
survive long in London. Once among the snapping turtles
of the *ton*, she would be quickly devoured unless she managed to grow a thick shell of her own, and that quickly. He
knew he had just taken the first step toward putting that
shell in place. The knowledge gave him neither pleasure nor
peace.

He treated the sparkling stars overhead to a fierce
scowl.

Chapter Six

The company at breakfast next morning was noticeably
thinner than on the previous evening. Captain Hargrave
and Mr. Welsh were occupied with the sailing of the ship.
Mr. Dimmont was missing too, but whether from indispo-
sition or merely from an unwillingness to do anything so
unfashionable as appear in public before noon no one knew.

The sisters Brough had sent a request for a little thin gruel and some sarsaparilla in their cabin.

"Poor things," murmured Mrs. Stackpoole, if the deep vibrato in which she spoke could ever be called a murmur. "And barely enough flesh between them to keep a body warm in summer," she added, savoring a perfectly broiled mutton chop and spooning up some of the eggs laid fresh that morning.

As neither of the Misses Brough, though far short of Mrs. Stackpoole's considerable heft, could be considered lithe, Abby was hard pressed to stifle a giggle. Looking at her own reed-thin wrist as she raised her coffee cup, she could only wonder what Mrs. Stackpoole must think of her.

"Mr. Lydiard must send them some of his tonic," she suggested, buttering a fresh-baked muffin and piling thick strawberry jam upon it. "Jacob, my groom, was feeling perfectly wretched last night. But he declares that he feels *almost* human again this morning."

"I'm glad to hear it," said Charles Lydiard, striding into the dining room. "I was afraid he would toss himself overboard. Said he felt as if he was going to die, but was afraid he might not."

Everyone laughed, the sort of nervous laugh that comes over one who knows he has had but a narrow escape from a similar fate and may not be out of the woods yet.

Lady deForest, nibbling at a piece of toast and sipping her tea in the approved genteel and ladylike fashion, plied Abigail with questions about Lord Longford, his estates, his family, and his connections at court. She seemed most disappointed to discover that Abigail hardly knew more than she did herself. The lady's position was on the very fringe of the *ton*, but she was determined to improve it. Ingratiating herself with a soon-to-be countess might prove helpful.

"Perhaps I may be able to assist you with a little information, then," she said with her most gracious smile. "I have my copy of *Debrett's* below—I never travel without it, of course—and we may look up Lord Longford's arms and lineage." She turned to her husband, who was busily worrying a slab of Virginia ham and a plate of hominy, an oddity he had developed quite a taste for in Virginia. "You see, my dear? I told you I should be glad of having it along, though you would say I could have no need of it in America." She smiled at Abigail. "If you would care to join me in the ladies' parlor . . . ?"

"Perhaps another time," put in Mr. Lydiard in a strangely brusque manner. "Miss Dawson and I have work to attend to." The scowl on his face matched his tone.

"So we do," said Abigail brightly. She had unashamedly explained to them all that Charles was to be her tutor for her entrance into Society. "I'm sure Poppa had no idea when he was building the *Abby Anne* that she would be a schoolroom." She thanked Lady deForest for her offer, then rose from the table with an enthusiastic bounce and a smile that chased away some of Charles's scowl. "Lay on, MacDuff," she said as they headed out.

Although the air held a January chill, sunlight streamed from a clear sky, bouncing off shiny water and glistening white decks. They decided to hold their first lesson in the fresh air, taking advantage of the sunshine while it lasted.

"But not until you get yourself a bonnet," said Charles sternly. "A bonnet with a wide brim. Young ladies of fashion do *not* have brown faces like country sparrows."

She ran off without demur and returned in but a moment with a straw villager propped slightly askew atop her head, its wide brown ribbons knotted in an untidy bow below one ear. He sighed involuntarily as she approached. She really did look like the veriest schoolgirl. Her frock was a simple calico of sea green with a wide ribbon sash at the waist that accentuated her extreme slimness. A shawl was tossed negligently around her shoulders. She had tied her hair at the nape of her neck, but several disobedient tendrils had escaped to frame her face.

She was whistling as she made her way across the deck. He recognized the tune as "Yankee Doodle." Lifting her skirts slightly, she hopped nimbly over some coils of rope, offering him a momentary view of a pair of pretty, slender ankles. She skipped over to him and threw herself into a chair.

He gave a look meant to be long-suffering, though a

clearly discernible smile lurked in his eyes. "Lesson number one," he began.

"Number two," she corrected, patting her bonnet.

"Number two, then," he agreed, reaching to right the crooked hat with a tender touch. "Young ladies do not whistle, certainly not in public, and in England they most particularly do not whistle 'Yankee Doodle.' "

"Oh my, was I?" she asked. "I wasn't aware of it. It is very difficult not to whistle when one is feeling particularly pleased with the world."

"Nevertheless, you must learn to bridle your musical high spirits."

"But how can I when I don't even realize I'm doing it?"

"That is just my point. You must learn to be aware of what you are doing, of the impression you are making, at every moment. You must always be on your guard against making any sort of disastrous *faux pas*."

"Oh dear. This may be more difficult than I thought," she replied with a laugh. "I'm afraid I'm rather impulsive, you see."

"I do see," he said wryly.

"Aunt Sylvie is always after me to think a bit more before speaking or acting."

"You will do well to heed her advice if you wish to be acceptable in London."

"I will try."

"Nor," he went on, "do young ladies throw themselves at the furniture like hoydens or ill-mannered children." "

She looked up at him sheepishly, a look that had an unexpected and not altogether desirable effect on him. He felt as if he were melting. He gave his head a shake. "So," he said briskly, "we will begin with movement. Stand up, if you please, Miss Dawson."

She did, promptly bouncing to her feet. "You know, Mr. Lydiard, I don't think I can possibly learn anything from someone who calls me Miss Dawson in that pompous way. Can you not call me Abby, or at least Abigail?"

"In view of my position, it would scarce be proper."

"Oh, stuff! We are to spend the next weeks in *very* close proximity. Just because you work for my father is no reason we cannot be friends. Please? If I promise not to tell anyone?''

He was not proof against her wheedling tone or her beseeching green eyes. ''Very well,'' he smiled. ''Abigail.''

''Thank you, Mr. Lydiard.''

After a brief pause he said, ''Charles.''

''Charles,'' she repeated comfortably.

The movement lesson went on through the morning until Charles was satisfied that Abigail could cross smoothly to the chair, her head held erect, could turn easily, just touching the edge of the chair with the back of her knees, and could lower herself gracefully into it, perching, as it were, on the very edge, her spine straight and her feet angled precisely to one side.

''It isn't terribly comfortable, is it?'' she said at one point.

''There is little comfort to be found in elegance. You will have to get used to that notion.''

She nodded and tried again. She was a quick student, paying close attention and mimicking his movements with a sure eye. She needed nothing more than a little practice.

By lunchtime he was pleased to note a degree of newfound grace as she took her seat at the table. She still attacked her meal with a gusto not entirely becoming in a Young Lady of Fashion, but he could not deny that the meal merited such attention. It was a delicious repast of hearty vegetable soup, cold sliced beef, ham, and turkey, fresh tomato salad lightly dressed, piping hot cornbread dripping butter and honey, and creamy rice pudding heavy with raisins and cinnamon.

Abby ate everything set before her.

There were no lessons scheduled for the afternoon, and Abby took the opportunity to explore her seaborne home. Before the sun had faded, she was on excellent terms with every seaman aboard. She could recite the manifest of the cargo of apples, beeswax, clocks, and a large load of mahogany and bird's-eye maple. It was only after the sternest look from the bos'n that she refrained from scrambling up the rigging to see what she could see.

Instead, she decided to pay a visit to Mr. Adams. She cadged some sugar cubes from a friendly steward and headed off to the surprisingly comfortable makeshift stable Jacob had rigged up.

Betsey was there before her, which surprised Abby not at all. Jacob was feeling much better now, thanks to Charles's tonic, but one would never have guessed it from looking at him. He lay on his cot, making horrid faces and groaning theatrically as Betsey clucked over him and laid cool cloths on his forehead.

"Poor Jacob," said Abby. "I had thought you so much better."

As Betsey turned away to see to her teapot, Jacob took the opportunity to give Abby a wicked wink. A guffaw of laughter escaped before she could stifle it. Betsey turned with a suspicious look, but Jacob managed a very credible groan that turned her all solicitous once more.

Abby, giving Jacob a wink and chuckling to herself, stole away. She knew when she was not needed.

Dinner that night was another marvel of the culinary art. "I declare," said Lady deForest. "It's very like being at a house party in the country." She nibbled daintily on an asparagus tip. "Yes, it feels quite like the time my cousin, Lady Rushingham, you know, had us down to Hampshire for the hunting."

"Shouldn't try taking out a gun in the morning if I were you, m'dear," said her husband, who then laughed hugely at his own joke and plunged into a dish of scalloped corn.

"No good sea air in Hampshire, I'll wager," said Mr. Stackpoole. "Not like in Boston."

His wife picked up this theme between bites of a perfectly roasted quail. "Nothing like good sea air to set up one's appetite, I always say," she rumbled. "I never feel the least bit off my food when I am near the sea." She took another hearty bite. "Archibald will like a bit of this mutton, I'll wager." The pug at her feet liked it so well he nearly took one of her sausagy fingers as well.

Mr. Dimmont, decidedly green around the gills, managed to down a forkful or two of rice.

As on the previous evening, the company retired to the parlor for tea and coffee, cards and conversation. As they left the dining room, Abby found herself beside Charles.

"What a meal!" she said with a laugh. "I am positively stuffed!"

"I imagine you are. Never have I seen a young lady enjoy her dinner more." She gave a delightfully unself-conscious chuckle that drew a returning laugh from him. "You know, I really think you must learn to curb that healthy appetite of yours."

"But everything is so delicious!"

"And everything will continue to be delicious in London. But if you think tonight's dinner was enormous, how will you manage when some forty dishes over four courses are set before you in the space of three hours?"

Her eyes widened, then she broke into giggles. "Charles, you are bamming me!"

"I assure you I am not. At every *ton* dinner, enough food is consumed to support an army, and enough is thrown out to feed half the poor of the City." His smile faded; a tinge of the old bitterness crept into his voice.

She eyed him a speculative moment. "You don't like the *ton*, do you, Charles? You think I am foolish and childish for wanting to be a part of it."

"It is not my place to have an opinion one way or the other," he said. "What is all wrong for me may perhaps be perfectly right for you."

"But why is it all wrong for you, Charles?"

"I dislike pretense, and the world of the *ton* is built on nothing else. It is an art you must strive to learn if you wish to fit in."

"But how can friendship, much less affection, flourish in such an atmosphere?"

"Friendship and affection have nothing whatsoever to do with the *ton*," he said in as gentle a voice as he could muster. "Indeed, they have no place there. They make one far too vulnerable."

Abby looked up into his face, searching for some clue to what was obviously a deep hurt. He could not hold her gaze. "Would you care for a hand of picquet?" he asked to change the subject.

"Thank you, but I have promised Mr. Benton a game of chess."

"You play chess?" he asked, somewhat surprised.

"Since I was ten. You may have your own notions about what constitute the feminine arts, Charles. To my Uncle Roger, the first is the ability to play a good game of chess."

"And did the training include the feminine trick of letting your masculine partner win?"

"Never! Oh, Uncle Roger often outplayed me—though not always, mind you, for I am quite good—but to *allow* him to do so would be unthinkable. I dislike losing, you see."

He offered a vaguely ironic smile. "I shall remember that."

She made him a pert curtsy and joined the smiling Mr. Benton. He was already setting up the cleverly designed chessboard. Each piece was pegged to fit into tiny holes in the board, thereby keeping it from sliding to the floor with the roll of the ship, ruining the game and at least one temper.

Charles was soon asked to make a fourth at whist. He was partnered by Miss Wyngate, whom he had discovered to be a charming young woman with a wry sense of humor. They set out to beat the deForests.

The *Abby Anne* sailed on into the night, tacking to starboard, tacking to larboard, laying on canvas or furling sail, but all the while heading inexorably east, carrying her passengers closer to England.

Chapter Seven

The days fell into a pattern. Charles and Abby spent their mornings in her "schooling." During the first sessions he told her what he could of fashion. Of course, the real lessons in that highly refined art would come from Lady Longford, carried out in the fitting rooms of fashionable London *modistes*. But Charles was able to explain the subtle but nonetheless important differences between a walking dress and a carriage dress, how a morning costume differed from one appropriate to afternoon, and which evening entertainments called for a demi-robe rather than a ball gown or a mere "evening ensemble."

"Dear me!" exclaimed Abby. "And here was I thinking all I had were mere dresses. Surely I cannot need so many gowns and robes and costumes as all that. Where would I wear them all?"

"You needn't worry about that. The Countess of Longford will never lack for invitations. And it would not do to be seen twice in the same gown."

"No, I don't suppose it would." Her face took on the dreamy smile it always wore when she thought of the beautiful fantasy about to become real.

They discussed the theatre and poetry and other acceptable subjects of fashionable conversation. He was surprised to discover that she was well and widely read not only in classical drama and fiction but also in history, art, and the sciences. She had a mind like a sponge, it seemed, that could pick up most any subject he introduced and add something of interest to it.

It was something of a revelation to him to find himself

enjoying intelligent discussions with a female about Shakespearean sonnets or the relative merits of corn and wheat as cash crops.

Also, she really did play a very good game of chess.

But one morning, as they were discussing Ovidian poetry, he pulled himself up short. "This will never do. You will gain a reputation for being bookish if you go on like this. Nothing could be deadlier."

"Don't English ladies read books?"

"Of course. They are considered a fashionable way of filling the few hours between promenades and parties. And it does give them at least one subject to discuss besides each other, though that is by far their favorite topic. They read romantic novels by Mrs. Radcliffe and the like or Lord Byron's poetry. Occasionally one of Mr. Scott's tales is dipped into. They do not, however, read Ovid and Homer. They do not discourse on medieval history, and they own to no more knowledge of Natural Philosophy than they do of the foaling of colts."

"Oh," she replied, giving this information serious thought. She had always found joy in discussing everything she read with like-minded people. She came from a family who all took as much interest in the treasures of the library as they did in those of the stable.

"And besides," he continued, "you will have little time for reading once the Season begins. You must, of course, read the currently popular poetry and prepare two or three stock remarks upon its merit. Lady Longford will have whatever is in vogue at the moment. Now let us go on to those French phrases considered necessary ingredients in any polite conversation."

In the afternoons Abigail was released to enjoy the company of her fellow passengers. The Misses Brough were little in evidence at first, keeping to their cabin unless the weather was exceptionally bright. Then they would sit on deck wrapped in mountains of shawls, sucking on lemons, a certain ameliorative for their trying tummies. Even Charles's famous tonic had been unable to appease them. They must simply wait in hopes of gaining their sea legs before the journey was over entirely.

Young Mr. Dimmont was also somewhat scarce, though he managed to put in an appearance at dinner each evening. He ate little, however, and the experience was obviously a trying one. The sight of all that food seemed to have a negative effect.

Abigail spent many afternoons with Lady deForest poring over the well-thumbed pages of *Debrett's Peerage*. They traced every remotest connection of the Earl of Longford until Lady deForest could proclaim with great delight that she and Abigail would soon be fifth cousins, twice removed, through the third son by the second marriage of Lord Longford's great-grandmother's second cousin. Or something like that. Abigail wasn't at all certain she had followed the whole of it.

When she was released from these heraldic researches, Abby enjoyed watching the running of the ship. A certain Mr. Watts, a steward, undertook to teach her to walk like a sailor. (It was perhaps fortunate that Charles, attempting to accomplish the opposite effect, had no knowledge of the unorthodox "lessons.") Mr. Watts had developed the ability to a high art. He could climb up to the parlor carrying a full glass in each hand without spilling a drop. He sort of crawled along, his body extended forward, his legs thrust out behind, and his hands scarce a foot from the floor. It was a wonderful show.

The days rolled by pleasantly. By the end of the first week the morning lessons had advanced to the conduct appropriate to a ball, the proper manner of accepting or rejecting a dance, and the use of the fan.

The whole thing was something of a game to Abigail, and she excelled at it. Of course, the fact that she so genuninely liked and admired her teacher helped speed the learning. She was sure Charles had become her friend.

Even in the highly developed art of the fan, she quickly grasped the possibilities inherent in a bit of carved ivory. However, in her fluttering eyes and fanciful flickings there was a sense of fun, of true playfulness, that Charles could not remember noticing in any London ballroom.

"Now I shall ask you to dance," he said in his best instructor's voice. They were in Captain Hargrave's comfortable cabin. It was more commodious than either of their own, as well as warmer. The Captain had been glad to give them use of it whenever they wished. They worked under the proprietary chaperonage of Betsey, placidly knitting in a corner.

Abigail perched daintily on the edge of a chair in the Charles-approved manner, flicked open her fan, and began looking around the imaginary ballroom, tapping her foot to the music only she could hear. Charles suppressed a smile.

He approached her with a solemn bow. "Miss Dawson," he intoned with formality.

"Mr. Lydiard! How pleasant to see you again." She closed her fan with a playful snap, then let it dangle from her wrist as she raised her hand for him to shake.

Very much to his own surprise, he did not shake the hand so properly offered. Instead, he lifted it to his lips and planted upon it a warm and very tender kiss. He held the delicate hand a moment longer, gazing down at the tapered fingers.

Then quite suddenly he seemed to come to himself and dropped the hand as if it were red-hot. He cleared his throat twice before saying in his most formal tone, "May I have the honor of this dance, Miss Dawson?"

She did not answer him. She was staring at the hand he had just kissed. Her dangling fan was quite forgotten as she gazed at the spot his lips had touched. It felt unusually warm.

"Miss Dawson," he said again. Still she did not answer. "Abigail?"

She looked up to meet his eyes, her whole face a smile. Her hand raised to her cheek, and she said slowly, wonderingly, "I should love to dance with you, Charles."

She rose to move into his arms, but he turned suddenly away. His voice took on a brisk, businesslike tone. "Yes, well, I think that is enough for today, don't you?"

Disappointment flooded her face. "But aren't you going to teach me to waltz?"

"Yes, yes, of course. Another time. There is no time to do it properly now. Tomorrow, next week," he said with a wave of the hand.

In a somewhat subdued manner they went to change for lunch.

Betsey, though she dropped nary a stitch in her knitting, missed not a single moment of this affecting little scene. It brought a thoughtful frown to her sharp eyes and furrowed her brow. This was *not* a development that boded well for her young mistress's plans.

It was that very night while brushing her mistress's raven hair that Betsey noticed a thoughtful look in Abby's eyes. She was staring at the miniature of Lord Longford that she had hung from a ribbon beside her mirror. The maid wondered what the girl was thinking, suspected that she knew very well, and fervently hoped she was wrong.

She was not wrong.

"Do you suppose his lordship is as handsome as Charles?" Abby asked.

Betsey frowned. "Well, handsome is as handsome does, like your Aunt Sylvie's always sayin'. And not knowin' how his lordship does, I couldn't truly guess, Missy Abby."

"But Charles does very well, doesn't he?" replied Abby with a grin.

Oddly enough, Betsey did not grin back. "Well enough, I s'pose. Bit stiff, if you ask me," she said and pulled the brush harder through her black curls.

"That's just because he's English. They are never so casual as American gentlemen, you know. He is all that is proper."

"So I should hope," said Betsey, anxiously adding to herself that she certainly *did* hope Charles Lydiard was a proper gentleman. "Your poppa wouldn't trust you to naught else."

"Ummm," replied Abby, staring at the miniature. "I wonder if Lord Longford is so very stiff and proper." Despite her defense of Charles's manners, she sounded as though she hoped he was not.

"Not with his wife, he won't be, Missy Abby. 'Specially not with a pretty wife." This time she did grin, but Abby did not notice. She was again lost in thought. Betsey frowned.

It was two days later, while studying the proper forms of address and the elaborate intricacies of precedence, that Abigail first found herself quite alone with Charles.

"Betsey," he said to the maid, putting an effective stop to the constant tattoo of the clicking knitting needles, "run and find Lady deForest and ask if we may borrow her copy of *Debrett's*, will you please?"

Betsey was obviously not best pleased with the request. She cocked her head to one side, looked at him, and frowned. "It's not fittin', sir," she finally said.

"Don't be ridiculous, girl," he replied. "Your mistress will be quite safe. I am her instructor, not her debaucher."

"Depends of what you be tryin' to instruct her in, don't it, sir?" she said with an impertinence that would never have been tolerated in an English maid. He found himself laughing.

"That it does," he agreed. "But seduction in any form is not on today's agenda, so you may rest easy. Besides, I could hardly do anything *too* improper in the very few minutes it will take you to get the book and return, now could I?"

"*I* couldn't say, sir."

"Of course you couldn't." He gave her a grin too engaging to be offensive. "No thanks to Jacob, I'll wager."

"That one!" she said with a snort. "Knows a pile more 'bout horses than he does 'bout how to treat a lady!"

"So he tells me," said Charles. "But he is eager to learn."

"Well, he better not come round me till after he's done learned it," she said and flounced out the door, entirely forgetting the impropriety of leaving Abby unchaperoned.

As it turned out, she need not have worried. Nothing untoward happened. She found Abigail completely intact when she returned some ten minutes later. She was chattering about a dog she once had, a silly mutt of a dog with the unlikely name of Stuart. Charles was listening with that vaguely bemused expression on his face Betsey had seen once or twice before. Her entrance seemed to bring him back to the work at hand. The lesson proceeded in proper form.

This episode, while of seemingly little importance, did

establish an important precedent. Having once agreed to the acceptability of master and pupil working alone, and seeing that there were no consequences of note, Betsey often left them to run errands or carry out her other duties or to ineffectively ward off the flirtations of the incorrigible Jacob.

Despite that odd hand-kissing incident, Charles Lydiard was obviously a gentleman. Indeed, Betsey occasionally found his manner so brusque and cold that she wondered if he even truly *liked* her Missy Abby.

In any case, Abigail and Charles found themselves more and more often alone in Captain Hargrave's cozy cabin.

Chapter Eight

Abigail, who had never had much difficulty sleeping even under the most trying circumstances, found it even easier aboard the *Abby Anne*. Eating was slightly precarious, with the movement of the ship liable to turn over a wineglass at any moment. Every movement, in fact, took a certain amount of concentration. But once in her bed, the ship became a huge cradle, rocking her into a gentle slumber and serenading her dreams with the lullaby of sounds that were the delightful backdrop of daily living.

She also woke earlier than usual and was more refreshed by her slumbers. She would rise with the dawn, perch on her bed with her feet tucked under her and a blanket wrapped about her like a red Indian, and gaze out at the ever moving sea as it lightened with morning, showing the horizon constantly tilting to and fro. The very regularity of the movement seemed conducive to thinking and planning, to daydreaming.

Her commonest thoughts on those early mornings were of her wedding. It was that which filled her mind one morning when they had been nearly a fortnight at sea. It was sure to be the most magnificent wedding London had seen in many a year. She would walk proudly down the aisle of St. George's, Hanover Square, on her father's arm, dressed in her mother's wedding gown embellished with the finest veil imagination could invent and money could pay for. The whole of the English *ton* would watch her. It would be the culmination of a long-held dream and the start of another.

It was a pity Aunt Sylvie and Uncle Roger could not be there. They were almost closer to her than her poppa. They had stood in the role of parents for her almost the whole of her life. And she did wish her cousins could be there. Except for father and Betsey, none of her family or lifelong friends would be with her on her wedding day.

No matter, she thought, brushing aside the little sadness. She would soon have a new family to love. And surely Charles would come to her wedding. He was her friend.

How good it had been of Poppa to send Charles with her. Of course, he could be horridly stuffy at times, always telling her what she must and must not do. But she did like him so. Even at his most stern and "tutorish" she could always make him laugh. She loved his laugh. It was so deep and warm and rich, like fine aged brandy sweetened with honey.

Her eyes wandered to the portrait of her betrothed. Did Lord Longford laugh easily? she wondered. For virtually the first time in this whole adventure, it struck her as strange that she was to marry a man of whom she knew practically nothing. Did his eyes twinkle when he was trying to suppress a guffaw, as did Charles's? Would he look at her in that strangely intense way that made her skin tingle? And would he laugh with her? She could not imagine being married to a man who did not laugh.

She hugged the blanket closer about her and stared at the picture of the face she now knew by heart. She stared at it until she frowned, though she was not aware of it. Then, quite suddenly, she felt she could not stay inside another moment.

The sky was now wholly light. She bounced out of bed, taking only a moment to find her balance—she truly *had* become used to the movement of the ship—then pulled a calico round gown from the wardrobe and slithered into it. Abby was quite used to dressing herself. She brushed out her curls, tied them with a ribbon, then threw a cloak about her sholders. Snatching an apple from the basket on the sideboard that was always kept filled, she bounded out the door.

Outside she breathed deeply of the fresh morning air, smelling of salt and mist and promise. She reveled in the goose bumps raised on her arms by the quick breeze and soothed them with the woolen of her cloak.

She would go and visit Mr. Adams, she decided. The poor darling must be terribly confused about this whole journey, and Abby had perhaps not spent as much time with him as she ought. Tossing the apple lightly in the air and whistling a little tune—a habit she was *trying* to control but had not yet got the better of—she made her way toward the makeshift stable.

A deep bed of hay had been laid out under the horse, and Jacob kept the stall spotless. Abby looked about and wondered where he could have got to so early, but her wonder vanished in the warmth of Mr. Adams's greeting.

The horse nickered his pleasure and nudged about her person with his soft velvety nose. "Spoiled creature!" she said with a laugh. "How did you know I've brought you anything?" She had hidden the apple in her skirt pocket, but it took the horse only a moment to find it. "Oh, you are a clever fellow, aren't you?" She offered up the treat and stroked his glossy neck, drinking in his warmth. She grew just the tiniest bit homesick from the sweet scent of the hay and the beloved, familiar smell of the horse that overpowered even the salt tang of the air.

A shriek from somewhere not far away pulled her forcibly from her homey reverie. It was neither a shriek of pain nor one of fear. Actually, it wasn't precisely a shriek at all. More of a whoop, rather like what a playful child pretending to be a redskin warrior might make. Abigail went out to discover the source of the high-spirited sound.

She hadn't far to go. Just beyond the horse stall, almost

in the point of the bow, she saw Jacob. He was not the source of the continued whooping, but he was chuckling as he manipulated what looked like an oversized pump. The louder sound was coming from behind a sort of drape, a large piece of sailcloth hung on hooks with an odd-looking contraption rigged above it. Out of this contraption seawater poured, spraying out in several directions. Below the canvas, Abby could see a pair of bare wet feet dancing about in time to the whooping. She realized she was having her first glimpse of Captain Hargrave's famous showerbath.

Before she could awake to the impropriety of her position, the whooping voice yelled, "Enough, by God!" Jacob stopped pumping and handed a large Turkish towel into the hand that appeared around a corner of the canvas. It belatedly occurred to Abby that she had best leave at once. But before she could turn away, the hand reappeared, and this time it was attached to an arm, followed by a strong bronzed shoulder, followed immediately by the glistening, dripping, and altogether beautiful form of Charles Lydiard. The towel was wrapped about his waist. Wet hair curled onto his forehead, and his bare skin glowed from the cold. He was laughing. Altogether, he was quite the most gorgeous sight Abigail had ever seen.

He took another towel from Jacob, offering some laughing comment that Abby could not hear, and began to tousle his hair dry. It was then that he noticed his audience. He froze, towel to hair, The laugh died on his lips. "What the devil . . . ?"

Her eyes were enormous in her face, full of wonder at the sight of him. Despite her years on a farm, Abigail had never seen a full-grown gentleman so nearly naked before. Who would have thought a gentleman could look like that? She could scarce tear her eyes from him.

"Abigail!" barked Charles loudly enough to bring her to her senses.

"Oh, pray forgive me, Charles! I did not know . . . I mean, I couldn't . . . you see, I . . . oh dear!"

He pulled the towel closer about his shoulders as though he could turn it into a coat and breeches by sheer force of will. "We shall discuss it later if you please, Miss

Dawson," he said with very great dignity considering the circumstances. "Please be good enough to return to your cabin."

"Yes, Charles," she heard herself reply. She was trying hard, though with little success, not to smile. She turned to skitter away, but she did just turn back for one last peek at that bronze, glistening, strongly muscled work of art. Then she disappeared from sight.

"Oh God!" he moaned, turning to Jacob. Then, despite his mortification, he chuckled. Jacob chuckled back. Charles laughed harder. So did Jacob. Soon the pair of them were in whoops, which continued until Charles realized he was on the point of freezing to death. Grabbing a heavy dressing gown, he returned to his cabin. He really must speak to that girl. But what on earth was he to say?

Abigail did not refer to the incident. She was not embarrassed—how could anything so beautiful possibly be embarrassing?—but she could see that Charles was. She would do nothing to bring him pain. He was gruffer and more demanding than ever that morning, making her practice over and over again her most elegant curtsy.

"You don't want to fall flat on your face when you are presented to Prinny, which you surely will be," he said. She thought she heard him mutter, "Though why anyone would want to meet the fat flawn is beyond me," but she couldn't be sure.

She wanted to please Charles, so she tried to picture herself in the Grand Hall at Carlton House making her bow to the Prince Regent. She knew he had once been dubbed Florizel and called the handsomest prince in all the world. She had long been excited about actually seeing him.

But staring up into Charles's face, even marred as it was by a scowl, she could summon up no image more princely, more thoroughly handsome. Even the face in the miniature, that of her betrothed, would not come to her mind at that moment. She could see only Charles, and so she made her bow to him. She did it beautifully.

The incident of the showerbath was all but forgotten, but Abigail found her eyes wandering more and more often to the solid form of this strong man who was her teacher and her friend. He could never look *quite* the same to her again.

It wasn't until well into the third week of the voyage, the weather turning inexorably greyer and colder, that Charles Lydiard sat down in his cabin to review his progress as a teacher. He settled into a chair, his feet propped on a cozy footwarmer, poured a large snifter of brandy, and opened a book.

He read exactly one paragraph.

The words on the page kept fading, replaced by an oval face with big green eyes full of eager questions and excitement. With a sigh, he set the book aside and gave himself over to thought.

He had taken on a job, and though he now regretted that he had done so, he must carry it through. Sitting there sipping his brandy and watching the heaving sea, he came to realize—or perhaps "admit" was a more accurate word—that he'd not been doing it properly.

Oh, he had taught Abigail several useful things, things that would go some little way to ease her into the stream of Society, or at least reduce the ripples of agitation and defensiveness she would surely cause. But he had been avoiding the harsher lessons he knew she desperately needed to master if she was to survive in upper-class London. It was his duty to give her those lessons, and he had been shirking it.

He had to ask himself why.

Charles had never been one to shy from self-reflection. Indeed, he had always had a tendency to be rather hard on himself. He had spent hours in recalling, pondering, and trying to understand what had happened to Daisy and how much he had been to blame for the outcome.

He could not completely acquit himself of blame. True, Longford was a skirter and a rake. Charles could not be accounted guilty for that. But so were many "gentlemen," as Charles well knew. He had brought Daisy into their world all the same, thrust her into it with no preparation, no protection other than his love. He should have recognized her weakness, a weakness stemming from inexperience as well as from ambition. He should have seen, as

Longford had done, that she was a plum only too ripe for picking.

Perhaps Daisy would have fallen in any case; Charles was not so unworldly as to deny the possibility, perhaps even the likelihood. But with no defenses of any kind, she had been a ridiculously easy mark. Her downfall had been almost an assured thing from the first night she walked into Vauxhall Gardens on his arm. Charles could never completely absolve himself of guilt.

Now, as he sipped fine brandy and thought of another girl, different in her way but just as young and innocent and just as ambitious, it seemed he was making the same mistake all over again. To be sure, the situations were far from identical—Abigail's father was in a position to offer a thicker cloak of respectability than Daisy's, and the Longford name would be a powerful protection against other would-be seducers—but the parallels were marked enough to give Charles pause.

He must prepare Abby for what she would find, and not just in the way of fashionable chitchat and gossip, graceful movement, and the knowledge of what to wear for a drive in the park. He must help her form the hard shell she so clearly needed as protection from sharks like Longford and his kind.

He was forced to ask himself why he had not yet begun the task. After much rationalizing and generalizing, all of it unsuccessful, he was forced to admit the truth. He did not want her to change. Not even a little.

Abby was so thoroughly delightful just as she was in her unspoiled youth and innocence, her exuberance for life, her determination to get every drop out of living that it offered, then wring it out for that little bit more. He couldn't bear to think of her as one of "them," the icy, wasp-tongued, jaded ladies of the *ton*.

After four years of hardening his heart against any and all female charms except those purely of the flesh—he was not a monk, after all, and had not been averse to finding his pleasures where he could—he felt his iron control slipping away. He was desperately close to falling in love with a girl who was engaged to marry the man he most despised in the world.

He would not allow such a thing to happen. He would not be hurt again, and especially not at the hands of the Earl of Longford! And he knew exactly how to protect himself. It would be ridiculously easy.

He tossed back the brandy. With grim pleasure, he felt it burn its way down his throat. He would turn Abby—whom he had come close to thinking of as *his* Abby—into a fit countess for his enemy. He would destroy everything in her that was sweet and good and natural and that made her so terribly vulnerable.

And then he need never again worry about falling in love with her. He could never fall in love with one of ''them.''

Chapter Nine

Quite suddenly, it seemed to Abby, everything changed. The weather stopped smiling, reminding them harshly that it was the end of January and anyone foolish enough to venture onto the Atlantic must be prepared to suffer the consequences.

The journey had begun with such perfect, unseasonable weather, a clear yellow sun cutting through crystalline blue air to glint off aquamarine water. But as they pushed eastward, each day the sky grew a bit greyer, the sea a bit higher, and the clouds a bit nearer.

The changing weather seemed to match Charles Lydiard's darkening mood to perfection.

Abby, unaffected by the lowering weather, was profoundly affected by a lowering Charles. She could not help but notice the change. It mystified her. She had been so certain they were friends.

She had been trying so hard to do exactly as he wished, even when it seemed to make little sense. She did it to please him as much as to become a lady of the *ton*. She had been certain she was succeeding. She had always been able to coax a smile from him, even if it was sometimes a grudging one, and he often praised her little successes.

But now everything had changed, and she had no idea why. She could think of nothing she had said or done to turn him so cold and harsh, to change him from the friendly young man he had been to the rigid taskmaster she now saw daily.

Nothing she could do pleased him. The harder she tried and the more certain she was that she was doing *exactly* as he wished, the grimmer his scowl became. Even the nature of the lessons changed. Before, they had felt almost like an elaborate game of dress-up. It had been easy. It had been fun.

But now it seemed as if Charles was trying to turn her into another person entirely. It wasn't merely her manners or her dress or her topics of conversation that displeased him. It was her thoughts, her mind, her whole personality.

He criticized her speech. "Too unaffected. More archness, more coyness." He found fault with her taste in music—"unfashionable"—and in books—"too erudite!" He even disapproved of her laugh.

"That laugh won't do," he growled one evening when she laughed at some innocuous nonsense of Mr. Stackpoole's.

"You mean I may not even laugh?" she asked a little too sharply.

"Of course you may laugh. But you may not 'Hah-hah-hah!' You may titter musically up and down the scale. You may giggle coquettishly or chuckle softly if something is really *very* amusing." When he said the words, he sounded like a man who had never chuckled in his life, nor would he wish to do anything so extraordinary.

"And I may not really laugh."

"You may not really laugh," he agreed and walked away.

Worst of all, Charles now seemed to delight in taunting her, in wounding her with barbed words about her inadequacy or her background, about having the gall to think her father's trade money could buy her into the most select society on earth.

Then he would *dare* her to cry, to let her feelings show. And berate her if she gave in to her emotions.

She struggled to understand. Was she so unacceptable that polite ladies and gentlemen would feel a disgust of her? She had always been admired and accepted, and she found this idea difficult to countenance.

Then another thought crept into her mind. It was unbidden and unwanted. It burst into her consciousness with a power that startled her and made her feel a discomfort dangerously like unhappiness.

Did *Charles* feel a disgust of her?

She was in her cabin when this horrid thought raised its ugly head and caused hot tears to prick at her eyelids. She stared through them at her face in the mirror. Stared hard.

She was not a classical beauty, she knew, but surely it was not an altogether horrid face. A little too brown, but her tan was rapidly fading under the shade of her constantly worn bonnet. And her eyes were rather nice with their dark lashes and arched brows.

No, it must be more than her looks that was at fault. It must be her behavior that had turned Charles to stone. To everyone else he was unfailingly polite, consistently cordial. He had developed a pleasant friendship with Mr. Stackpoole, with whom he played cards or argued politics in a spirit of friendly rivalry. He spent hours explaining to Ronald Dimmont the intricacies of sparring at Jackson's or betting at Tattersall's. He teased Betsey and Jacob whenever he saw them, allowing his ready smile to pop through.

He had also struck up a pleasant friendship with Viola Wyngate, and this seemed harder for Abby to accept and understand. Not that Abby disliked Miss Wyngate. Indeed, she found her a charming young woman, full of kindness and good sense. But why must Charles spend so many hours in her company, walking the windy decks, drinking tea in the parlor, or discoursing on the very books he had made Abby promise not to mention in polite company?

To one and all Charles Lydiard was a thoroughly pleas-

ant, good-humored young man. Only with Abby was he
cold and harsh, his face set in lines that etched little
parentheses around his mouth.

The tears were now rolling freely down Abby's cheeks.
She gave herself a firm reprimand. Charles did not like her
to cry.

Dashing the tears away with the back of her hand, she
gave a final determined sniff, then splashed cold water
across her swollen eyes. Her face took on a look of
determination.

She could not have said why Charles Lydiard's good
opinion was so important to her. She only knew that it
was. Desperately important. She would win his regard.
She *would*.

She would follow more exactly his every instruction, be
more diligent in schooling her mind to think in the proper
channels. She would become exactly what he wanted her
to be.

And then Charles would be her friend again. Wouldn't
he?

Charles was grimly pleased with the results of his labor.
Abigail was moving rapidly along the road toward becoming a true lady of the *ton*.

It was obviously difficult for her. Prevarication and pretense were not in her nature. Neither was it easy to school
her features to the sort of bored impassivity that was *de
rigueur* among the *ton*. She was far too full of life and curiosity and enthusiasm.

But he persevered. He hated himself for trying to
destroy something so lovely and natural and real. At the
same time he congratulated himself on every success that
made her less the Abigail he could love.

Finally there came a day Charles could no longer avoid.
He could not send the girl into the world not knowing how
to dance. It was a prime requisite for anyone with preten-
sions to fashion.

She was proficient in the popular country dances, and he
had taught her the intricacies of the quadrille. But the girl
must still learn to waltz.

The new German dance was the ultimate in sophistication, and no London ball nowadays was held without it. Charles cursed the Puritan heritage of America that had not yet allowed the graceful dance to penetrate beyond the more daring ballrooms of New York and Washington. The chit had never even seen the waltz performed, much less attempted it herself.

He would simply have to teach it to her. And he did not trust himself to hold her in his arms. He did not trust himself at all.

As they rose from breakfast that morning, Abby noticed that Charles was looking particularly grim. She had come to dread their morning lessons. She always felt like shivering, even though the iron stove in Captain Hargrave's cabin poured warmth.

They walked to the cabin in silence, Abby stealing sideways glances at him every so often and wondering yet again what she had done wrong.

"Today you will learn to waltz," he said when they reached the cabin.

"Oh, good!" she exclaimed. "None of my friends knows it. We were never allowed. I think it's one of the things they most envy me."

He looked around the cabin, suddenly realizing that they were alone. "Where is Betsey?" he asked in a tone that came out almost a bark.

"I told her she need not join us. She discovered a rent in my scarlet cloak and she wanted to mend it. Now that it's grown so cold, I shall have more need of it."

"Can't she mend it here? She's supposed to be keeping an eye on you."

"She knows very well I am perfectly safe with you, Charles. And I rather think she prefers to work out on deck." She was grinning, but he did not notice.

"It's freezing out there!"

"Oh, Betsey seldom minds the cold. And there is such a nice sunny spot near the bow. You know, next to where Jacob walks Mr. Adams every morning."

"Oh," he said, finally understanding. Then he smiled too, a very little smile to be sure, but the first of the morning. "Jacob must be learning a few manners."

"Oh, I doubt it. She really would not like him half so well, you know, if he were any the less impertinent."

"A typical woman, in fact." He was grinning now.

"Of course," she replied, happy to have brought out his smile.

The lesson began well enough. He demonstrated the basic steps, then had her practice them while he counted the beat.

"No, no, you must feel the emphasis on the first beat. And, *one*, two, three, *one*, two, three. Like that, you see?"

She tried it again, daintily lifting her skirts to peer down at her feet as they traced the pattern on the floor. She learned to turn in step, to glide, and to spin. She soon began to feel quite comfortable with the rhythm.

But one does not, she knew, waltz around a London ballroom while holding up one's skirts and peering at one's toes, however nicely turned one's ankles may be. One must have a partner to hold one.

She looked up at him quizzically. The momentary loss of concentration caused her to miss her step. "Oh dear!" she exclaimed with a little laugh. "Am I quite hopeless, do you think?"

"No, no, of course not. Here, just follow me." And almost before Charles knew what he was about, he swept the girl into his strong arms, started to hum a popular waltz tune, and began circling the room with her.

Abigail made no more missteps. Indeed, waltzing with Charles felt like the most natural activity possible. The gentle pressure of his fingers on the small of her back guided her flawlessly through the circles and glides. She could feel the warmth of it permeating the thin wool of her gown. It made her feel utterly comfortable, utterly secure, and a little breathless as well, but perhaps that was merely due to the exertion of the dance.

When she looked up into his blue eyes, hoping for one of his rare smiles of approval, her breathlessness increased and her heart speeded up to a veritable gallop. He was staring down at her with the sweetest smile imaginable curving up his mouth, the tenderest and most wistful look of longing pervading his whole countenance.

Charles's emotions were in considerable tumult. As soon as she melted into his arms, flowing with his movements as though they were one person, a great wave of tenderness engulfed him. He clutched her closer, wanting to hold and protect her and never let her become what he had been trying so hard to make her. Then she looked up at him, those incredible eyes glistening with the pure joy that was Abigail, and he thought he would melt entirely and fall away until he was nothing but a puddle at her feet.

He stopped humming; the music pounding in his head made that unnecessary. After a few moments Abigail began to hum herself. It was a simple air in three-quarter time she had learned from Betsey.

She could not have made a less fortunate choice. The tune was an old tune, popular on both sides of the Atlantic, and it had been a favorite of the unfortunate Daisy, who had hummed it incessantly. Nothing could have been better calculated to remind Charles who his partner was, to whom he was taking her, and the reason they were waltzing together in a small cabin in the middle of the Atlantic.

He stopped abruptly, causing Abigail to tread inelegantly on one of his booted toes. He was still staring at her, but now she saw none of the tenderness of a moment before. She saw something very like horror in his face. Whatever could she have done, she wondered desperately, to make him look so black?

After what seemed like a very long moment with the two of them standing there like statues, he dropped the arms that still encircled her and turned brusquely away.

"That will be enough for now, I think," he said.

"Didn't I do it right?" she asked in a very small voice.

"Yes, yes, you did it perfectly. I am sure Lord Longford will be well pleased with his bargain."

"Then why are you not pleased?"

"Dammit, woman, I tell you I am pleased! I . . ." He spun to face her and saw twin pools developing in her eyes. Her lip was quivering ever so slightly. "Oh God! You're not going to cry again, are you? You know what I have told you about that!"

"I . . . I'm not going to cry," she got out, trying valiantly to quell the quivering of her lower lip and to force back the hot moisture gathering in her eyes. "I'm not!"

"No, you most certainly are not!" he declared and undertook to stop her doing so in the only way he knew. He met her quivering lips with his own much firmer ones.

The quivering did not stop entirely. But it began to take on a very different character. It spread through her whole body till she was trembling all over. Strangely enough, she no longer felt the least desire to cry. She was, instead, filled with an inexpressible joy, a feeling of sunlight and music and warmth. She wanted to laugh, to shout for joy, to go on waltzing.

Charles knew only that he was tasting heaven.

To compound his great surprise at his own actions, Abigail threw her arms around his neck and began rather fervently to return the kiss. Locked together, they floated on a cloud as big as the ocean beneath the *Abby Anne*.

It was Charles who finally broke the overwhelming embrace. He stared at her in astonishment, working to get his breathing under control. He pulled her arms slowly from around his neck and held her at arm's length. Now he was trembling as well.

When he could finally speak, though scarcely above a whisper, he said, "I can see that there are some things I must teach you about the proper behavior of a young lady."

She seemed not to hear him. She was gazing dreamily up into his eyes, her own having taken on a sort of luminescence that was startling and ethereal and altogether captivating. "I have never been kissed before," she said wonderingly. "Not really kissed. I'd no idea kissing could be so . . . so . . ." She was powerless to describe accurately a feeling so entirely new and unique.

"So . . . ?" he could not resist asking.

"So wonderful!" she exclaimed. And to Charles's surprise she decided it was so wonderful she would like to try it again. Before he could stop her, even had he wanted to, she threw her arms about him again and pressed her warm, soft lips to his.

An eternity passed, a dreamy, floating, altogether heavenly eternity, during which neither of them was aware of the sea or the sky or the incessant creaking of the sails over their heads.

Indeed, the first thing besides each other of which they were aware was the rattling of the door handle. Charles pushed Abigail away with a guilty start just as Betsey tripped into the room. Her sharp eyes took in the scene quickly and thoroughly. Her bright smile faded. She liked Mr. Charles, but really!

"I was teaching Abigail to waltz," Charles said lamely.

"Don't look much like a fittin' dance for any proper lady I ever knew," said Betsey bluntly.

Abby turned her flushed and still smiling face to her maid. "Don't be silly, Bets. The waltz is all the crack in London. I must waltz." She beamed back at Charles. "And it is such a *lovely* dance."

Charles, suffering from extreme discomfort and the guilt of a schoolboy caught in a prank, ostentatiously pulled out his gold repeater and clicked it open to study the gilded face. "That is all for today, I think," he said. He sounded exactly as if he were addressing a classroom full of recalcitrant students, or perhaps a meeting of bank directors. "Betsey, take your mistress to her cabin to repair her hair. Some of her curls seem to have escaped their ribbon."

So they do, the maid told herself with some irony, but she dipped a curtsy at the voice of authority. Charles strode past her and out the door. She turned on her mistress with a frown to no effect whatsoever.

Abby was so lost in a dream of her own that she was hardly aware of her maid's presence.

Chapter Ten

That night, for the first time since setting sail, Abigail slept less than perfectly. She was far too busy wondering at her own whirling emotions and dizzying thoughts to do more than close her eyes. Sleep was farther away than Pennsylvania.

A line from Shakespeare popped into her mind: Olivia in *Twelfth Night* after her first look at Cesario falls hopelessly in love with him and muses aloud, "Even so quickly may one catch the plague?"

Had Abigail caught it now? And with no warning? Was she in love with Charles Lydiard? And if she was, what was she to do about it?

Abigail had never been in love. Perhaps she had not yet spent enough years on earth to have reached that happy, or sorry, state. Neither was she given to reading romantic novels of star-crossed lovers and worlds well lost for love.

Thus, in her fantasies of a happy marriage to Lord Longford she had tended to leave one or two essentials out of the picture. Oh, she was not so naive as not to know that marriage involved a certain physical intimacy, a certain physicality, that made it quite special. She had been raised on a farm, after all. Also, her Aunt Sylvia had tenderly explained such things before Abby left home and had assured her that she would find that aspect of marriage distinctly pleasurable.

But she had had no idea just *how* pleasurable such things could be until Charles had kissed her and she had not wanted him to stop. Would she feel the same about Lord Longford's kisses?

She certainly hoped she would. She even expected she would, assuming (and hoping?) that it was the quality of the kisses and not the man giving them that made the activity almost unbearably pleasant. But what if she was wrong?

If she truly was in love with Charles, she was in a rare pickle indeed. Yet if she was, perhaps she would fall out of love with him just as quickly as she fell in. Her cousin Pru fell in and out of love a dozen times a week, it seemed. Abigail had always thought her behavior decidedly silly. But she didn't feel silly now. She felt confused.

She knew she must think this whole thing through very rationally, though to be sure it was difficult to remain entirely rational when she remembered the feel of Charles's lips on her own. Her heart took to pounding and her breathing seemed to speed up dangerously, clouding her mind.

She willed her body to quieten and set her mind to pondering the question. She weighed a possible future with Charles against one with the Earl. She matched the black scowls that so often marred Charles's handsome face against the aristocratically pleasant visage of his lordship. She compared Charles's brutal taunts with the graciousness shown her father by Lord Longford.

Charles lost points on every count. On only one did Abby feel any weakness in her reasoning. The thought of never seeing Charles again once she got to London, of never again feeling those warm lips on hers, left her absolutely desolate.

She pounded her pillow in an attempt to expunge the thought. She would not fall in love with Charles Lydiard. She refused to! It would simply be too inconvenient.

Even were she not engaged to the man of her dreams, the match was clearly impossible. Charles was little more than a clerk, and a proud one at that. She might be heir to a fortune, but he thought her a silly schoolgirl at best and a social-climbing tuft-hunter at worst.

She didn't know why he had kissed her. She knew men sometimes got carried away in such matters and wanted to believe that was all it was. But she had a strong suspicion that it had been another of Charles's "lessons," another test of her suitability to enter Good Society. She had certainly failed.

Indeed, if the hard glint in his icy blue eyes all afternoon was any indication, she had failed most miserably. It was clear that Charles was seriously displeased.

Abby let out a long sigh with just a trace of a quiver. Learning to fit into the *ton* was turning out to be painfully difficult. She knew what she must do now. She hadn't the least desire to do it.

She must laugh off his kisses with an appropriately melodic laugh. She must act as though overly impetuous gentlemen tried to kiss her every day of the week. Her performance must clearly state that the kisses meant nothing whatever to her just as she was certain they had meant nothing to Charles. She would pass his test, albeit belatedly.

Saddest of all, she knew that she must never allow him to kiss her again.

Charles also remained sleepless well into that night. He didn't even attempt sleep but sat in his comfortable captain's chair staring out at the black sea and the black sky scattered with a million diamond stars now that the clouds had blown away. As the ship dipped down into a wave, the stars disappeared from view, only to reappear as the *Abby Anne* climbed up the next watery mountain.

The motion did nothing to soothe Charles's troubled soul.

How had she caught him so far off guard, this chit of a girl with no arts and no artifice? He, who had erected a bastion around his heart so sturdy that no female since Daisy had produced so much as a chink in the mortar. There had been numerous assaults on his defenses—he was a prize catch in almost any female's book—but they had been rebuffed with the skill of a seasoned general.

And now, after a ridiculously short siege, the battle seemed lost. Abigail had offered a look, a smile, an innocent laugh, and a pair of the sweetest kisses ever man received, and the heretofore impregnable walls had tumbled like Jericho on the seventh day. Charles's life was a pile of rubble about his feet.

Was he destined to spend the rest of his life falling in love with unsuitable females? he asked himself in disgust. Why could he not fall in love with a perfectly worthy and available woman such as Viola Wyngate? She was a pleasant companion. She was clever and sensible and kind. She preferred the country to the city. She even came from Kent! She would make the perfect mate.

He had not the least desire to offer her the position.

Truth to tell, he had no interest in offering that particular job to any lady save one already hired on by another employer. It was a cynical metaphor, he knew. He had always disliked cynics. It saddened him that he had become one. But the metaphor seemed most apt under the circumstances.

Abby had been making progress in her apprenticeship for her new position. Her eager kisses offered further proof that she had a natural aptitude for the work. Longford would be getting more than he bargained for. Certainly more than he deserved.

Charles's stomach lurched as the ship fell into a deep trough. He gripped the sides of the chair to steady himself. The physical action, coupled with the ghastly but no less vivid picture of Abigail in Longford's arms, brought a new determination to his mind. He would get hold of his racing emotions as firmly as he now grasped this chair. Never again would he allow a pair of thick dusky lashes to sweep away his resolve.

He must be extra-vigilant, extra-circumspect, avoiding any situation where his resolve might weaken. At least the waltz was behind them; he need never touch her again.

The realization made him almost ill with longing.

The light burned low as he sat there in miserable thought. Eventually, it sputtered out, leaving nothing but a strong smell of lamp oil to mingle with the salt air. Charles sat alone with the darkness a long while, staring out at the pinpricks of light littered across the dome of the Atlantic sky and feeling gloomier than he had ever felt in his life.

The morning lessons became a torment. Abby tried so hard to be what she was not in order to please Charles.

Charles hated her, and himself, whenever she succeeded. They both wondered what unspeakably evil sin they had committed, all unknowingly, to warrant such punishment.

The afternoons were less bad. It was true that weather and tedium had combined to dampen the gaiety of the company, but the mood was not entirely somber.

Mr. Stackpoole's geniality was so genuine that nothing short of direct attack on his native land could pierce it. His wife, likewise, was naturally disposed to contentment. Let her but have her sweets, her pug, and some civil conversation. She asked nothing more.

Miss Wyngate, though her eye sometimes fell on Charles with a vaguely curious look, never lost the air of calm serenity that made her so attractive. And it was quite against the Reverend Mr. Benton's belief to be at outs with anyone. All in all, the company contrived to muddle through.

Charles was generally able to avoid Abby during the afternoons. It was not in his nature to be idle, despite his upper-class birth. He spent a good deal of the time on the quarterdeck learning the rudiments of seamanship. His curiosity and innate intelligence, the very qualities he had responded to so strongly in Abby, led him to become quite useful in running the ship. He was relieved to have the employment. It kept him from thinking too often or too deeply.

With Charles on deck, Abby was able to relax and enjoy her chats with the Misses Brough or Miss Wyngate. She listened to Mr. Dimmont's full-blown compliments with an amused ear and pored over the fashion journals that, like *Debrett's Peerage*, Lady deForest never traveled without. By midafternoon she had nearly regained the equilibrium so badly damaged by a morning with Charles.

But then evening would approach. They could not well avoid each other's company. When the passengers adjourned to the parlor for tea, they were invariably thrown together for a part of the evening. They no longer knew what to say to each other, so they lapsed into icy correctness.

Thus the day became an emotional seesaw swinging

them each from despair to a semblance of tranquillity and back again.

One evening Charles could not remain longer in her presence. He retired to his cabin. Abby followed him out with her eyes. Her behavior did not go unobserved.

Mrs. Stackpoole watched with a frown. She reached for the ever-present sweet dish placed conveniently at her elbow and popped a bonbon into the red rosebud of a mouth blooming amid the fleshy folds of her face. From the number of sweets remaining in the bowl, it was evident that the bonbon was going to join a considerable number of its fellows. She chewed thoughtfully a moment, eyeing Abby with concerned kindness, then absently handed a sweet to Archibald, who snored contentedly at her feet.

"Shall we have our game of loo, ma'am," said Abby, coming to sit beside her. "I am persuaded you will not beat me so very badly. You are too kind." Her eyes were overbright, and she gave a laugh not entirely convincing.

The older woman looked at the young girl with a very kind eye. She reached out a black-mitted hand, a beringed paw with sausage fingers and baby-smooth skin. "Child," she said in a voice amazingly gentle and kind despite its depth, "do not fret overmuch. It will all come right. These things have a way of working themselves out."

Abby began to protest that she had no idea what the lady was talking about. But Mrs. Stackpoole's grey eyes were as kind and understanding as her voice. Abby could only whisper, "Do they?"

"Believe me, child, they do. I've been wed this quarter-century, and I know. The right solutions always manage to pop to the surface just when everything seems blackest."

Oh, how Abby wanted to believe her. But then she was not even certain what solution she *hoped* would pop to the surface. She only wanted the pain to end.

"And now," Mrs. Stackpoole went on in a louder, brisker voice, "we shall have our game. I must perfect my strategy, you know. I shall soon be playing in the salons of Paris and Vienna."

* * *

In his cabin Charles was worrying a book of poetry. It was here that Jacob found him.

So deep in morose thought was he that the knock gave him a start. Jacob stood at the door, a floppy hat in his hands and a sheepish grin on his face.

Preoccupied as he had been with Abigail, Charles could think of only one reason Jacob should be here. "Your mistress? Abigail? Something's wrong!"

Jacob looked surprised. "No sir, Mr. Charles. Missy Abby, she be just fine."

Charles's tense muscles relaxed. "What is it then, Jacob?" he asked. His voice was friendly now.

Jacob's look grew shyer still, a decidedly unusual expression for such an impudent fellow. "Well, I . . . y'see, Mr. Charles, I was . . . well, I was hopin' you might could give me a bit of advice."

"Advice?" Charles said. He realized they were still standing in the doorway. "Come in, man. Come in. I cannot imagine what sort of advice you could need from me. It cannot be about horses, not from what I've seen of the way you handle Mr. Adams."

"Oh, no, sir. I reckon I know all I need to 'bout horses," Jacob replied. "It is a filly that be the problem, but she ain't got four legs." He grinned.

"A filly named Betsey, I'll wager."

Jacob's smiling shrug confirmed this truth. "Never tried to tame a human female before. Don't reckon you've had much problem with 'em, Mr. Charles, bein' the gentleman you are. Maybe you could give me a hint how to go 'bout it."

To Jacob's surprise, Charles let out a laugh, but there was little true mirth in it. The laugh went on for several seconds. "Oh, Jacob," he sputtered at last. "The splendid irony of it."

"Irony?" Jacob was unfamiliar with the word.

"Never mind," said Charles, still fighting a desire to giggle. "You seem to be doing remarkably well with the filly on your own. She is far from indifferent to you, you know."

"Well, I don't know, Mr. Charles. Seems like I *did* know, back in Pennsylvania. But all this London stuff's made her . . . well, different. She be always goin' on 'bout bein' a fine lady's maid, an 'Upper Servant' she calls it. Like a horseman ain't good enough for her no more.''

"The irony grows," said Charles softly.

"She even told me 'bout some marchioness or tother got herself a black African footman more'n six feet tall and all dressed up in satins and such with powder in his hair.'' The nice blend of jealousy and disgust in his voice would have been comic were it any less poignant.

"My friend," said Charles, patting Jacob on the back, "I think you need a drink. I know I do.'' He poured a pair of brandies. Jacob, touched by such comradely treatment, sat gingerly on the edge of the cabin's other chair, straight-backed and elegantly covered with silk damask.

They chatted about women in general and Miss Betsey in particular. Charles felt like a fraud for daring to give any advice concerning women. But he had watched the two young servants closely. It was evident they were destined for each other.

"You know, Jacob," he said at last, "I think you ought to give Betsey a bit more credit. She's a sensible young girl, not likely to have her head turned by a bit of flash and dazzle.''

"Y'think so, Mr. Charles? She's got a good head, right enough, but how do I know she'll use it?''

"Because I've seen her using it. But she's got spirit, too. Going to London makes a big change in her status. She needs to test her wings.''

"But what if they take her right away?''

"She'll come back.''

Jacob sipped at the brandy, savoring the feel of the unfamiliar liquor in his throat. "I don't know, Mr. Charles. I'd feel a might happier if she was a horse. Y'know what to expect with horses.''

"Well, and how do you treat a horse you want to break to bridle without destroying his spirit?''

"Easy. Let him think he's gettin' his way. Play out your rope, gentle-like. When he reaches the end, give it a tug. Not too hard, but solid-like, y'know. Let him know the limits. Then rein him in again.''

"There's your answer, Jacob. Give Betsey her head.

She's not flighty, and she's not stupid. She won't go so far you can't rein her in again when she's ready. She will be soon enough.''

"Sure hope you be right, Mr. Charles. I don't rightly remember ever wantin' anything much as I want that girl. It ain't a comfortable feeling.''

Charles drained his glass in one gulp. "I know, Jacob. It's damned uncomfortable.''

Jacob left a few minutes later. Charles shook his head in wry amusement. Those two would be all right. They'd find their way to each other.

It never occurred to Charles that his advice might have certain applications to his own situation. He never thought to credit Abigail with some of the good sense he attributed to Betsey, never considered that she might also see through the ''flash and dazzle'' of London Society.

The cases were entirely different. Entirely. He poured himself another brandy.

Chapter Eleven

Both Abigail and Charles were beginning to literally count the days until their journey's end. Charles began poring over Captain Hargrave's charts every afternoon, calculating their daily progress. He learned dead reckoning and calculations of current, watched a seaman casting the log and playing out its line to gauge surface speed. He grew expert in the use of a sextant until he could soon plot their course, speed, and position almost as accurately as First Mate Welsh.

Abby was considerably less sophisticated in her questions to the Captain. She merely inquired at least once a day how much longer before land could be sighted. She knew she must sound like a tiresome, querulous child on a long coach journey asking "Are we there yet?" every half hour, but she could not help herself.

They made good speed, especially the last week or so. The winds grew stronger every day. They were sailing "at a good clip," as the Yankee sailors were fond of saying.

But halfway through the fourth week, Abby awoke suddenly from an unhappy dream in which she kept reaching to pick a pretty flower only to be savagely pricked by its hidden thorns. Her cabin was inky black; she couldn't see so much as a single star through the porthole. She wondered what it was that had awakened her. And then she realized it was a sound. One she had not heard in weeks.

It was silence.

The incessant creaking of the ship, slapping canvas, flapping ropes, water, wind, and grating of wood on wood, the entire orchestra of sounds that had accompanied her life for weeks and had engrained themselves in her very soul, were gone. An eerie silence, black and total, had taken their place.

Clouds uncovered the moon, momentarily lighting the surface of the sea. It was like a giant sheet of glass; scarcely a ripple marred the surface.

The stillness was unsettling. There seemed a touch of menace to it. She lay back on her bed, listening to the silence.

The *Abby Anne* lay becalmed in the Atlantic.

Sleep seemed impossible. The quiet was too unusual. Abby had never before encountered the calm before the storm.

Eventually, sounds permeated the walls of her cabin, but they were purely human ones. Running feet on the decks overhead. The Captain bellowing an order. His voice had an edge to it she had not heard before. He sounded worried.

Another pair of voices sounded closer. The Misses Brough had stepped into the hallway outside Abby's door.

"Sir Geoffrey told me only this morning that coming

over from England they were becalmed for a whole week," said Miss Agnes in an anguished voice.

"Well," replied Miss Emily, fairly clucking. "Certainly Captain Hargrave will permit no such thing on his ship. Such a perfect gentleman, and everything done so correctly."

"Certainly," agreed Miss Agnes. Abby smiled in the darkness. She could almost see them, pulling their matching shawls about their matching bony shoulders with a gesture of finality and toddling back to their cabin, secure in their faith in the Captain's omnipotence.

She certainly hoped they were right. To sit here in the middle of the Atlantic for another week! And every day to face Charles, trying to please him and failing again and again.

She only wanted this horrid voyage to end. She wanted to become so busy in London, so taken up with her new fiancé and her new life, that she had no leisure for pondering the meaning of a certain pair of kisses.

Her eyes were damp when she finally fell asleep.

She didn't know how many minutes or hours had passed when she awoke again. But everything had changed.

The silence had fled, buried by a howling wind that screamed around the ship with a fierceness that made Abby cover her ears. The ship that had bobbed as benignly as an apple in a Halloween bucket now flew about with crashing abandon as though trying to throw off some horrible pain deep inside. Abby was nearly thrown from her bed.

The ship dove into a deep trough, plunging down and down until Abby thought they were headed for the floor of the ocean. They hit the bottom of the watery abyss with a crash that pulled a groan from the wooden ship. Abby was thrown against the wall. The ship started to climb up in the next roller, its bow pointed skyward, trying to claw its way up the wall of water.

Abby began to feel afraid.

Water flew against her window as though trying to fight its way in to her. Lightning flashed, lighting up the heaving sea, the turbulent sky, and Abby's ashen face.

A sharp crack sounded overhead, then a thudding crash,

and shouts nearly drowned out by the thunder and the screaming rage of the sea. A spar had snapped and fallen to the deck.

Suddenly, one single thought filled Abby's mind. She wanted Charles. She might die in this storm, sliding to the bottom of the cold, black sea. She wanted Charles.

She jumped from her bed, almost lost her balance on the pitching floor, and ran from the room. She reached Charles's cabin in only a moment and pounded on the door calling his name. It flew open instantly. Terrified for Abby's safety, he had been about to come to her. He was stuffing an open-necked nightshirt into hastily donned pantaloons.

One look at her pale face, at her green eyes huge with fright, and he scooped her into his arms, crushing her to him as though he could protect her with his embrace.

For a while they forgot the raging storm, the heaving sea, even their own danger. There was nothing in the world save each other. Charles held her close, murmuring her name softly, feeling the trembling of her birdlike body through the thin cotton of her nightshift.

She laid her head on his broad chest, soaking in his strength and feeling the black hairs above the open neck of his nightshirt curling roughly against her cheek. His skin was damp with perspiration and smelled of him, a spicy scent she would forever love.

He looked down at the girl in his arms, shifting his hold so he could see her oval face gazing up into his. It seemed the most natural thing in the world to kiss those soft pink lips slightly open in her fear.

The sea heaved; the hastily lit lantern swayed wildly from side to side, casting moving yellow lights and purple shadows across their faces as they kissed. Their eyes remained open at first so they could gaze at each other in wonder, then closed to more fully savor the sensations coursing through their very souls.

For that long moment it seemed as though the storm raging outside had entered the cabin, had entered their bodies and their souls, had lit them up like the lightning flashing across the sky.

They clung together, trembling with fear and longing,

with dread and desire. His hands slid down her slender body and rested on her hips, pulling her closer. Her arms moved tighter about his neck, her fingers twining in the hair curling there. A silver ewer crashed to the floor and rolled into a corner. The tilt shifted, and it rolled back again. They didn't notice it.

When their lips finally separated and Charles pulled her close to his chest once more, he groaned. "Oh, God, Abby. Abby." She raised her face again, as though begging for another kiss; his lips lowered to hers.

The second kiss had even more power than the first. It took over their every thought, every sense, until there was no room for awareness of the rapidly worsening storm, no room for questions about intentions or worries for the future. There was only room for each other, for the feel of each other's lips.

His hands moved over her back; his body pressed close to hers. He could feel the whole of her through the nightshift, and wondered at the marvel of such beauty and delicacy and warmth. How he wanted her. How he loved her.

The helpless little ship gave a mighty jolt as it hit another trough with a crash. They were thrown across the cabin and thudded to the floor. The straightback chair tumbled over and cracked, breaking apart. The pieces slid across the floor, scratching their skin with splinters.

Drunk as they had been on the powerful nectar of fear and passion combined, the fall sobered them just as suddenly. The storm and their precarious position became terrifyingly real once more.

"Charles," said Abby in a frightened voice. "I . . . I don't want to die."

"You're not going to die!" he shouted, willing it to be so. "You're not!" He jumped to his feet, gained his balance, and helped her up. He hugged her tight another moment. Things were flying all around the cabin now: a silver-backed hairbrush, Charles's shaving box, the brandy decanter and glasses. They could scarce remain upright themselves.

Abby's eyes were huge. He grabbed her shoulders and began to shake her. "Abby! Listen to me! We must help the others."

His words penetrated her fear. Some of the terror left her face, replaced by a look of resolution. She grabbed the edge of the table to keep herself from falling. "Yes, Charles." Her voice was amazingly calm. "What must I do?"

He smiled. "That's my girl. Get the other passengers. All of them. Take them to the 'tween-decks hold. It's the stablest part of the ship, and the safest. Even if we lose all masts and spars or the decks break up, you should be safe there. There must be no panic. I rely on you to keep them calm."

"I'll do my best, Charles. Where will you be?"

"On deck. They'll need every available hand to manage the sails and lash down anything that comes loose."

She shuddered. He was going to the most dangerous place on the ship. She took a deep breath. "Very well. I shall get the others. Don't worry about us. We shall be fine." She paused "You . . . you'll see to Mr. Adams?"

"I'll do my best. Send me Jacob."

He took one last look at her, standing there like a little soldier about to go into battle. A powerful surge of emotion rushed through him. He snatched her up for a quick embrace before they went out into the raging world.

"Charles," she said softly. "Be careful." He squeezed her, and they ran out.

The storm raged louder and more fiercely than ever.

Chapter Twelve

Abby did as Charles told her. She gathered the passengers together and herded them into the 'tween-decks hold, talking casually and laughing brightly to keep up their spirits and avert a mass panic. She gathered blankets and pillows; she even discovered a decanter of brandy and one of wine still unbroken.

She was kept so busy, keeping everyone together, making certain no one was forgotten, and trying to keep herself upright on the heaving decks, that she had no leisure to think of Charles and the warmth of his kisses. Well, hardly any.

The storm raged for hours, bouncing the ship like a cork on the jagged waves. It was dark in the hold, an inky, all-encompassing darkness. They dared not light a lantern, the way things were flying about. But Abby could perfectly picture the scene around her. She could imagine each face as though the space were flooded with lamplight.

Lady deForest was nearly hysterical. Her shrieking had finally been calmed by her husband and by the soothing voice of Viola Wyngate, who now sat stroking her hand and muttering common-sensical but nevertheless sensitive reassurances. The lady's outburst had waned to a whimpering and the occasional sob, nearly drowned out by the pounding of the sea against the hull.

The Misses Brough hardly spoke. Abby was certain their eyes were wide with disapproval. Now and then, after a particularly severe spell of buffeting, one would mutter, "Oh dear," or "Most unexpected!" And once, Miss

Agnes said to Miss Emily, "I told you this was a *most* ill-advised trip."

Young Mr. Dimmont had lost his rather thin veneer of sophisticated maturity early in the storm. He huddled in a corner moaning, "Are we going to die?" Abby had to reprimand him quite sharply.

In addition to the regular passengers and the cargo, the hold was also crowded with more than a dozen servants. It became quickly apparent that keeping the group calm would be an uphill battle. When a bale of fancy dress goods fell with a loud crash, landing squarely on one of Mrs. Stackpoole's enormous feet, a young maid began to scream uncontrollably. Betsey deftly found her in the inky darkness and administered a resounding slap. The hysteria stopped.

It was clear that something must be done, and quickly, to dispel the terror that had entered the hold and grown like a solid wall around them.

Suddenly Abby's clear, light soprano sang out, reverberating through the cold, damp darkness, heard clearly above the howl of the storm. She sang a sprightly air that had been on everyone's lips for months. Almost immediately, the voice of Viola Wyngate chimed in, a rich contralto that suited her perfectly. Mrs. Stackpoole's basso was quickly joined by her husband's nondescript bellow, the pair of them making up in heartiness what they lacked in pitch.

Before long, everyone was singing, ladies and gentlemen, servants and masters, moving from one lively tune to the next, in that camaraderie born of a common crisis.

Sir Geoffrey surprised everyone with a pure, well-trained tenor so full of confidence it made even the pounding of the sea sound like no more than a tympani designed specifically to accompany him. He sang a lovely aria from *The Magic Flute*, in flawless German, to a rousing round of applause.

They continued singing until they were hoarse. They were also very cold and very wet from the constant drip of seawater coming through the beams over their heads. But the wall of fear that had surrounded them dissipated somewhat. They forgot for several minutes at a time how wretched they felt with their stomachs heaving and their bodies shivering. They even began to feel they might live through the night.

So clearly had Abigail been seeing the scene in her mind's eye, despite the impenetrable darkness, that she looked at Viola's face for a full minute before realizing that she was *really* seeing it. She looked up then and saw tiny shafts of sunlight creeping through the planking above.

It was morning! And more than that, the morning sun must have pushed away the clouds to shine so brightly!

Abby began singing a recently popular ballad.

"Mid pleasures and palaces
Tho' we may roam . . ."

Viola caught Abby's look and followed her gaze to the shafts of light. She smiled a smile almost as bright as that sun. And was it her imagination, or had the buffeting lessened with the coming of morning? Her rich contralto rang with greater strength and hope.

"Be it ever so humble,
There's no place like home . . ."

Mr. Benton also noticed the change in the violent rocking. A tiny ray of light struck his shiny pink head, which bowed as he muttered a grateful "God be praised."

"A charm from the sky
Seems to hallow us there . . .

A number of the servants stopped singing, whispering excitedly among themselves. Betsey, who had been holding Abby's hand for the past hour and more, gave it a squeeze. Both girls sang earnestly.

"Which seeks through the world,
Is ne'er met with elsewhere."

Mr. Stackpoole sang louder and even more off-key but with a new quality. It was joy. His wife rumbled out a laugh of pure relief.

"Home, home, sweet, sweet home!"

The Misses Brough looked as though they might say, "Well, it is about time," but they kept singing in their thin parchment-crackle voices. Mr. Dimmont sat up from where he had been slumped in a corner and began trying to salvage his hopelessly limp and crumpled neckcloth.

"There's no place like home,
Oh, there's no place like home!"

Footsteps sounded overhead. A hatch opened, sending a shower of seawater onto them. But sunlight also streamed through the opening and onto their thankful heads.

The storm was over!

As they filed onto the deck, blinking in the strangely bright sunlight, they were greeted by a sky of piercing blue and a vivid yellow sun. A stiff wind still blew, but it was no longer sinister. It filled the sails with friendly power and pushed the ship gallantly along.

Relief made them forget the cold, the hunger, and the general discomfort, not to mention the fear, they had suffered the past several hours. They stretched their cramped limbs and gloried in the sunshine of early March.

The deck of the *Abby Anne* was a mess. Lashings had been ripped free by the force of the wind and pounding water, sending barrels and other items careering about. They'd lost a spar on the mainsail, and the topsail had been ripped to shreds. The decks were littered with bits of rope and wood, torn canvas, ripped-up planking, and even a dead fish or two that had been heaved aboard by the angry sea. The cow had been lost, and a pair of chickens had been washed overboard. There would be fewer eggs and no fresh milk until they reached England.

But overall the damage had been slight and would be quickly repaired. Already sailors swarmed up the rigging, swaying precariously in the high winds and all but sagging from exhaustion. But their bare feet on the lines were full of confidence. They went about their business with the precision of a machine. A new topsail was already being rigged, while other crewmen picked up the litter on deck and checked the fresh-water supplies.

Things began to return to normal.

Abby looked for Charles. She looked at a group of sailors unfurling the sails tightly rolled to protect them against the storm and letting them fly. He was not with them. She looked toward the outboats where the surviving livestock was being soothed and fed. She even looked toward the bow, where Jacob was brushing Mr. Adams, who munched placidly from a nosebag. But she could not see Charles.

A cold dread struck her. What if he had been hurt? Or worse, what if he had been swept overboard? *What if Charles was dead?*

A convulsive shiver from Lady deForest, whose freezing hand Abby was still holding, made her pull her attention away from her worry, though she could not forget the cold dread.

"Come, my lady," she said gently. "I'll take you to your cabin. Your maid will be along directly and help you into dry clothes. Then you will come to the parlor and sit by the fire. We shall have you warm in no time at all." She spoke with a cheerfulness she did not feel.

The lady gave a wan smile, allowing herself to be led away. Sir Geoffrey leaned toward Abby as they passed. "Bless you, child," he murmured.

Abby went stoically off with Lady deForest. Charles would want her to. But she shivered, more from anxiety than from the penetrating cold of her wet clothing.

Where was Charles?

Soon the company, looking less bedraggled in dry clothes but still obviously exhausted, straggled into the parlor. A steward was hard at work with a bellows, blowing life into a promising fire in the big polished brass-and-iron stove. Other crew members were righting overturned tables and chairs, mopping up spilled wine, and rehanging a pair of nautical prints that had been knocked from the walls. The welcome smell of fresh coffee wafted from the galley.

And still Charles Lydiard did not appear. Abby had run to the parlor as soon as Lady deForest was safely deposited in her cabin. Now she began to pace. Finally, at the insistent clucking of Betsey, she went to change out of her wet clothes. Throwing on the first dress her hand touched, a simple calico of dove grey, she rushed back to the parlor.

Still no Charles. Her worry began to get the better of her. Now that some normality was restored, the passengers made a great fuss over Abby, crediting her with keeping them sane throughout their ordeal, thanking her profusely, bringing her coffee, and generally making a to-do over her. But she could not be comfortable.

Captain Hargrave came in to assure himself that each of his passengers was still in one piece. He looked terribly weary. His usually pristine uniform was rumpled and stained with seawater. Salt crusted his skin, and there were dark shadows under his eyes.

But he was smiling. He listened to the story of Abby's efforts and congratulated her on her level-headedness. "Though it's no more than I would expect from Rupert Dawson's daughter," he said in a kindly voice.

Abby only half heard. She had but one question. "Captain," she said, taking his leathery hand like a lifeline, "Mr. Lydiard was not on deck when we came up." He looked at her blankly. "Where is he, Captain? Where is Charles?"

Comprehension dawned in the tanned face, and his look grew kindlier still. "I sincerely hope he is in his bed. It is where I ordered him to go."

"In bed?"

"Yes. He was exhausted. He was on deck throughout the storm, lashing things down when he wasn't in the rigging helping clear a snagged line or trying to get the livestock out of the boats. Never saw a fellow work so hard in my life, not even my own crew, and it's the best on this ocean. We'd be in a whole lot worse shape now if it weren't for Lydiard." He gave a weary sigh and ran his fingers through his salty hair. "Must remember to tell your father we need at least two more deckhands. Especially for these winter crossings."

"You're certain he's all right?"

"Your father?" said the Captain.

"Charles!"

"Oh, yes, yes, certainly. Sleep'll put him to rights. I expect he didn't even bother to undress." The Captain looked as if he would very much like to do the same. "If you ladies and gentlemen will excuse me, I'll go make myself more presentable." He bowed and left the parlor, a heroic but exhausted figure.

Abby breathed again. Charles was safe. It was all she needed to hear. The last of the tension that had kept her going drained away. She sank into a chair, suddenly more tired than she had ever been in her life.

Mr. Stackpoole saw her slump. With a gentleness born of thankfulness and affection in equal measure, he scooped her up and carried her to her cabin, calling for her maid as he went.

She was soon tucked up beneath a soft down comforter, a dark cloth was put over the porthole to block the sun, and Abby let go completely to sleep nearly the clock around.

Chapter Thirteen

It was dusk when Charles awoke, or perhaps "recovered consciousness" was a more accurate description. He'd fallen asleep with all his clothes on except for his boots. He couldn't remember taking them off; a seaman must have helped him.

What a night it had been! He'd worked alongside the crew till his hands were raw from handling ropes and his eyes stung from salt spray. One thought kept echoing in his head. He'd be damned—or sent to the bottom of the sea—before he'd let anyone or anything hurt Abigail Dawson.

And they had won.

He'd been on the quarterdeck when the winds let up enough for the passengers to emerge from the hold. He had watched as his courageous girl ushered them out, speaking a word here, patting an arm there, helping Miss Emily with her shawl. Abigail had not seen him, but the sight of her was enough. He wanted to go to her, but exhaustion overtook him. His knees would no longer support his weight.

The Captain, thoroughly weary himself but more accustomed to storm-tossed sleepless nights than Charles, ordered a seaman to help Charles to his cabin.

He stirred now and let his eyes ease open. They blinked in the half-light of the fading day. Reaching for his gold repeater, he flicked it open. It was several moments before his eyes would focus on the timepiece's face. Nearly six. He had slept too long. His head felt fuzzy with it. He ached in every muscle, his hands burned, and his throat was raspy.

A lovely smell touched his nose and registered on his foggy brain. Coffee! Someone had brought a pot of coffee and set it on the oil burner to keep it hot. Charles rose with a groan and poured a large mug. It was strong and black, and it scalded his tongue as he gulped it down. He wrapped his aching fingers around the mug, savoring the heat.

The coffee brought him fully awake. The fuzz in his head began to clear. But with clarity of thought memory came like a painful jolt. He saw himself kissing Abby, holding her close, wanting her.

He had forced himself on her, had taken advantage of her fear and her trust to gain the kisses he had wanted so long. And he had very nearly taken more than that. He had abused his position of responsibility; he had defiled his promise to Rupert Dawson. He felt covered in shame.

She was such an innocent, and he was her protector, her teacher. He gave a mirthless laugh. He had taught her more than a young girl in her position ought to know.

Longford would certainly call him out should he ever learn of the tender scene played out in this very cabin with the participants still in their nightclothes. And he would be right to do so. The thought galled Charles unbearably. That the man he hated as a rival and scorned as a rake should stand in such a position of moral right over him!

He must suspend the lessons entirely. That much was clear. She had learned nearly everything he could teach her anyway. Soon they would be in England. Soon he would be home in Kent, laughing with his uncle, teasing his sisters,

squiring the young ladies of the neighborhood. Soon he
would never have to see Abigail again. He would be content. He would make himself be content.

He pulled off his salt-rimed clothes and poured tepid
water into the basin. A wash and a shave might just make
him feel human again, though he doubted he would ever
feel happy again. He lathered his bronzed skin, shivering in
the cold, rinsed, then rubbed himself hard with a Turkish
towel as though he could rub away his hurt and his shame.

Abby awoke around dawn the following morning. She
had never slept so long or so deeply in her life. Betsey
dozed in a chair, a quilt wrapped around her like an Indian
maiden.

Rubbing the sleep from her eyes, Abby stood and
stretched. It was a long, thorough stretch that went some
little way toward restoring her circulation. Betsey stirred
in the chair.

Dawn light crept in at the porthole. A cold, grey sea
was dotted with whitecaps licked up by the wind. It was a
depressing view, but Abby felt only joy with the world.
She gave no thought to why she should feel so happy. She
just did.

Betsey's eyes fluttered open, focused, and blinked. She
jumped from the chair, winced as pins and needles shot
through her left leg, which had been tucked up beneath
her, and cried, "Lord, Missy Abby! I thought you'd never
be waking up. I . . ." She was cut off by the sound of a
voice. It drifted down from somewhere seemingly far
above them.

"Land ho!"

The two girls stared at each other, then ran to the tiny
window. They could see nothing but the choppy grey sea.

"Land ho!"

"Where away?" bellowed the Captain's voice.

"Hard off the larboard bow, sir!"

Betsey helped Abby scramble into a dress and lace up
her boots, and they ran up on deck. The crew was clustered
in the bow, pointing and laughing excitedly. Jacob
emerged from his stable, still tying up his pants, and ran
to join them. Abby still could see nothing.

Captain Hargrave called to her from the quarterdeck to join him. From this higher vantage point, Abigail Dawson had her first glimpse of England.

As yet it was little more than a darker-grey smudge against the grey horizon. But it was there. The storm that had threatened their lives, blowing out of the northwest with such fury, had pushed them almost to within sight of land several days ahead of schedule.

Abby's heart and mind were full of conflicting feelings as she stared at her future home. Inexplicably, some of the joy with which she had awakened now fled. She watched the smudge grow larger. Finally green touches began to appear. The other passengers began to straggle up from sleep as the smudge resolved itself into recognizable shapes and textures. The Isles of Scilly came fully into view. Soon the craggy cliffs of Land's End and the Cornish coast would present themselves as well.

In the chatter and bustle of the passenger's delight, Abby did not see Charles come on deck. He was suddenly beside her. The excitement of sighting land had caused his own determination to stay away from her to flee from his mind.

She hadn't laid eyes on him since that delicious moment when he had made her not care about the raging storm. She blushed at the memory, but her heart glowed with the warmth of it.

She had avoided thinking about that wonderful moment. It was too confusing. It demanded decisions she did not want to face. But she was overwhelmingly happy to see Charles. Her face glowed with it.

She slipped her hand into his as they stared at the green line of hills far away. Unconsciously, Charles took it and gave it a reassuring squeeze. She thrilled to his touch.

"There it is," he said almost in a whisper. "Nervous?"

"Terribly. I feel like an actress about to step before the footlights for the first time. And I'm not even sure I know my lines."

He looked down at her and felt he would drown in the deep-green pools of her eyes. With a struggle that almost came out like a gasp, he pulled free from her gaze. He saw his hand holding hers and wrenched it away. He took a step back, guilt and pain overwhelming him, and the old familiar scowl wiped the warmth from his face.

"I shouldn't worry overmuch if I were you. Your particular audience will be well disposed to like you. He cannot afford to be otherwise."

Confusion clouded her eyes. "Audience?"

Filled with hatred for his rival and loathing for himself, he spat words at her with icy coldness. "You choose an apt metaphor, you know. Longford is known to be quite a connoisseur of beauties of the stage. I am sure he will be delighted with your performance. As I said, he has little choice. Keep in mind, my dear, that he needs you rather badly. It gives you a certain amount of leverage."

"Lord Longford? But Charles, I don't . . ." she began. It had suddenly become terribly important to say something, anything, to make him smile again. She was not even sure what she was about to say, but she never got the chance to complete the thought.

"Yes," he went on, "quite soon now your dreams of glory will be fully realized, my dear. I trust you will be well satisfied with your bargain."

Abby recoiled from the ugly words as though from a physical blow. Pain and confusion covered her face. Could this possibly be the same man who had held her so desperately close, who had murmured her name so achingly? What had happened to him? To her?

Charles was almost overcome by the sight of her. But he could not allow himself to give in. He took hold of the chin she had turned away. None too gently, he turned her to face him.

"I see that you have still not mastered my number-one lesson, Abigail. You must not be so gauche as to let your feelings show so clearly. Very bad *ton*. A man of Longford's stamp would never settle for anything so unfashionable in his wife."

Something inside her collapsed, deflated like a dead balloon. She felt a fool. She had let him trick her, *use* her. She had thought his kisses sincere. What a baby she had been!

"You are hateful!" she spat out. "Hateful and vile and loathsome! I trusted you because you call yourself a gentleman. I shall know better than to trust a 'gentleman' ever again!''

"Another important lesson learned, then," he said almost in a whisper.

She wanted to scream at him, to wound him as he had wounded her. She wanted to see him wince. But she very much feared that she had not the power to hurt Charles Lydiard. To him she was nothing but a task to be dealt with, an odious responsibility, even if she was good enough to dally with on a cold stormy night.

Abigail was left with nothing but the tattered remnants of her pride. But these were made of strong stuff. She pulled them back together. She was Abigail Dawson, soon to be the Countess of Longford. She was the daughter of Rupert Dawson, and could hold her head high anywhere.

She straightened and stopped the welling of her tears by sheer force of will. "Lord Longford will have no cause to blush for the behavior of his wife, Mr. Lydiard. I will see that he does not."

She turned and crossed the quarterdeck, her bearing as erect as that of a French aristocrat on the way to the guillotine.

Charles slumped at the rail, staring unseeingly as the panorama of his homeland grew larger on the horizon.

Chapter Fourteen

The first thing about London that impressed Abigail was the size of it. As they sailed smoothly up the river, the city seemed to spread itself out before her like a giant set of children's building blocks gone mad. Hundreds of ships

filled the harbor. There were giant Indiamen, barges piled
with cargo, fishing ketches, coasting schooners, powerful
men-of-war, ferries and brigs and pleasure boats.

Even in the cold grey drizzle there was so much to see
that Abby hardly knew where to look. At one spot on the
riverbank they spotted a group of men digging in the black
mud of the shallows, turning over rubbish, stones, and bits
of wood, looking for any treasure that might buy their
dinner.

The peal of a church bell rolled over the water, carried on
the gusty wind. That same wind pulled the dank, putrid
smell of the river up to her nose. It seemed that the
Thames was the city's garbage dump. Charles, standing
nearby, gave her an ironic smile and said, "Welcome to
London."

The *Abby Anne* inched her way up the river, tacking back
and forth to make some headway against the wind and the
current. But the little packet pushed on, giving Abby
time to take in the spectacle that was the capital of
England.

Despite the grey pall of cloud hanging over the scene,
heavy with soot that quickly turned Abby's jaunty yellow
gloves the color of mud, she was astonished at the colors
that met her eye. Brick warehouses lining the quays glis-
tened rusty red in the damp air. The greys of the paving
stones and chimneys and sky were not really grey at all but
mauve, slate, steel blue, and ocher. The whites of the
building trim and church steeples shone ecru and light
green, and pale, pale lavender. A moving spot of bright vermilion danced where the mudlarks had built a fire to warm
themselves. A bluish mist curled everywhere.

"The famous fog of London," said Charles dryly, but
Abby could hear the note of suppressed excitement in his
voice. It both surprised and pleased her. He *was* glad to be
home. "Look there, just ahead," he continued. "You can
see the Tower coming into view."

All Abby's knowledge of English history sprang to life
as the imposing collection of buildings that was the Tower
of London slid into view. The granite grey walls seemed to
echo the cries of the long-dead Little Princes. She saw the
watergate which had closed behind the Princess Elizabeth

and the lawns beyond which Jane Seymour had drenched with her young blood. The blocky White Tower lorded it over London as it had since William the Conqueror ruled the land.

Stretching beyond the river was a vast expanse of buildings great and small, flowing back from the water's edge almost as far as she could see. Hundreds of church spires poked up from the sea of buildings. Streets curled off in every direction, bumping into each other or doubling back on themselves to avoid doing so.

Even the ever-talkative Betsey was stunned into silence. Her sharp dark eyes were very round, and she was heard to emit an occasional "Oh!" Jacob gaped, speechless and more than a little frightened by the sight but greatly relieved at the notion of setting foot on solid land. A sailor he wasn't.

They sailed under London Bridge. On the right glowed the dome of St. Paul's. Far, far ahead, just where the Thames curved out of sight, sat Westminster Abbey.

Before Abby could fully take in the panorama, they edged up to a dock and her awe had, perforce, to subside in the bustle of docking and getting ashore.

The scene on dry land was one of absolute chaos. Carters, stevedores, stray cats and mangy dogs, horses, piles of cargo, loiterers, and travelers ebbed and flowed in a swirl of activity. But Charles steered the little party through the throng with a sureness that was comforting. Despite his icy formality, Abby was glad for his hand on her elbow, warming her in the chill drizzle that had taken over the sky. There was little warmth, however, in his stern face or in the harsh, grim tone of his voice as he ordered them to stay close together.

He saw Mr. Adams safely from the ship and directed Jacob to follow close behind him. Trunks and portmanteaux were put aboard a carter's coach. The driver was liberally tipped to give them good care. Charles steered Abby to a line of hackney carriages waiting not far away, and Betsey scurried after, a bandbox dangling from each arm. Jacob and Mr. Adams followed. Soon they were all on their way to Piccadilly.

Betsey chattered excitedly as they rolled over the noisy

stones. "Look there, Missy Abby," she chirped. "A pie seller! Don't they look good? Oh, and there's an orange woman. Can we have one, Mr. Charles?"

"There will be plenty of oranges where you are going. And anything else you might want."

"Look at the carriages!" said Abby. "Did you ever see so many all in one place?" The traffic was indeed incredible. Hacks and private carriages jostled to share the road with milk wagons, farm carts, mail coaches sparkling with maroon paint, drays and dog carts, crossing sweeps, riders, and pedestrians by the score.

Their progress was slow, giving the girls time to ooh and aah over every sight. They passed directly under the dome of St. Paul's, noting the many booksellers in the square before it.

"I must come and look at the books soon," said Abby excitedly.

"You will do no such thing," snapped Charles. "You will note that not a single lady of Quality is among the throng if you bother to look."

"Are not ladies of Quality allowed to buy books?" she snapped back.

"Lady Longford will take you to one of the fashionable lending libraries."

"That will be most pleasant. But suppose they shouldn't have the books I wish to read?"

"Then you shall wish to read the books they have! It is much the best way to ensure that you won't disgrace yourself with a wider knowledge than you should have."

"Oh!" said Abby because she could think of no smarter retort. She lapsed back into silence as the carriage climbed Ludgate Hill and turned into Fleet Street.

Charles's mood grew blacker by the minute, but he refused to acknowledge, even to himself, that there was anything out of the ordinary in a gentleman delivering the girl he loved into the hands and household of the man he hated so that she could become his bride. In a dutiful and very tour-guide sort of manner he pointed out the houses in the Strand that had survived the Great Fire nearly two centuries earlier. He drew their attention to Somerset

House. Betsey gaped at the giant edifice, and Abby gazed in wonder.

They passed Charing Cross and turned up the Haymarket, and both girls noticed that the neighborhood began subtly to change. There were now more shops, and they were far more elegant. The number of fashionable equipages increased, and the strollers along the pavements were expensively coiffed and gowned.

At Piccadilly Circus they could look up the new, pristine white curve of Regent Street with its sumptuous shops filled with china and linens, jewelry and haberdashery. Abigail's excitement grew almost unbearable. *This* was to be her London, this world of elegance and wealth and fashion, where everything was shiny and clean and the very best available. Even the cold, grey drizzle and the sea of shroudlike umbrellas could not dim the luster of it in her eyes.

Burlington House and Arcade. Albany. Bond Street. St. James's. They passed all the spots that had long lived in her imagination. And now she was here! She was really here!

She hugged her cloak about her, as much in excitement as in response to the cold. For the moment she was able to block out both the feel of Charles's kisses and the shame that had overwhelmed her even since their last conversation. She gloried in her own excitement and the coming attainment of her long-held dream.

"Devonshire House," Charles intoned, pointing out the imposing mansion. "Once the most important house in London. The Green Park, a onetime royal preserve." He sounded exactly as if he were reading from a guide book. Abby stole a glance at him. The grim set of his face shocked her. She had never seen him look so black.

The carriage slowed; the monotone of Charles's voice changed. He could barely suppress his rage. "We are here," he snapped. His voice was like a whip, and Abby felt its lash.

Longford House was certainly imposing, not to say intimidating. Even Betsey's chatter stilled as they turned into the wrought-iron gates of a mansion larger and more grandiose than any they had yet passed. It was fronted by a stone wall high enough to announce its claim to separateness from its more mundane neighbors but not so high as to hide from the world its magnificence. It was a four-storied Palladian structure well set back from the road with a pillared portico in the center. The whole was arranged with perfect symmetry and classical simplicity and built of a greyish stone perfectly at home in the cold drizzle. It was a totally unemotional house.

As the carriage rumbled across the cobbled courtyard and pulled to a halt before the polished oak door, Abby caught herself shuddering. Magnificent as it was, there was virtually nothing about the immense structure that said "home" to the girl who would soon be its mistress.

No softening vines grew over the glistening stone facade; no tree or hedge marred the pristine grey expanse of the courtyard. Not a single window box containing a single flower or leaf interrupted the perfect symmetry of the windows. Not even one bird dared to perch on roof or ledge.

Charles stepped from the coach, then helped Abby down. She stumbled when she tried to stand. She'd grown so accustomed to the rolling of a deck that the solid earth seemed to heave beneath her. Charles caught her, his strong arms holding her securely until she could find her footing and reestablish her balance. She could feel him trembling beneath his heavy coat. She could not imagine why.

He turned from her and studied the facade of Longford House. "That's odd," he muttered, frowning still more.

"What is it, Charles?" said Abby.

"The knocker. It's down from the door. And the shutters are closed. Surely her ladyship expects you." A very uncomfortable note had invaded his voice as he surveyed the uninviting house.

Abby was far from comfortable herself. Her first sight of Longford House had combined with the growing chill, her own weariness, and Charles's increasingly brusque manner to give her the headache and shorten her temper to an unusual degree.

"Well, are we to stand here in the rain, Charles, or are

we to go inside?'' she snapped in a very uncharacteristic fashion.

His defense was icy correctness. "Let us go inside, by all means, Miss Dawson, and meet your affianced husband.'' He strode up the three steps without waiting for her and rapped on the door with the head of his stick. He waited a moment, then rapped again, louder.

Finally, after what seemed an interminable, silent wait, the door swung open, and they were confronted by a tall young footman obviously chosen for his dashing physique. Far from the dazzling livery Abby expected to see on the Longford servants, the fellow was in his shirtsleeves. A long white apron, liberally smudged with dust, was wrapped inelegantly about him.

Charles swept into the hall, pulling Abby in his wake and saying in his most imperious manner, "Kindly tell her ladyship that Miss Dawson is here and have her trunks brought in.''

The footman just stared, first at Charles, then at Abby, then out the door to where Betsey was alighting from the coach. He looked at the baggage cart piled high with trunks that was rolling into the courtyard; he looked at Jacob, shivering in the rain on Mr. Adams's back and stroking the stallion's neck. Then he turned back to Charles. "But . . .''

"At once, man! Miss Dawson is expected.''

"No, sir. I mean, yes, sir. That is, sir . . .''

The poor fellow was saved by the entrance of a more properly attired butler. His partially buttoned coat clearly proclaimed the haste with which it had been donned, but at least it was a very proper coat, just as the butler's manner was a very proper manner for the butler of an earl.

"Sir?'' he inquired of Charles with a slight bow and just the proper questioning lift of an eyebrow. Betsey slipped silently through the door, and the footman just as silently closed it behind her.

Abby looked about her with great curiosity and awe at the notion that she was actually to rule over this place. Even the entrance hall in which they stood was immense. The marble floor was laid in black-and-grey checks that made her feel like a very small pawn on an enormous chessboard. Even the formidable butler had something of the look of the bishop in the game. He quite overpowered her. With a growing sense of dread, she wondered what the king and queen would look like.

Luckily for them all, Charles was not struck dumb at sight of the butler. Rather, he seemed almost relieved. "This is Miss Dawson," he explained in crisp tones. "You know who she is?"

"Quite, sir," said the bishop/butler with a slight bow to Abby. But he was frowning. The tiny muscles rippling over his eyebrows seemed to be the only movable parts of his otherwise rigid countenance.

"Good," said Charles. "Then you will kindly inform your mistress of her arrival."

"I am afraid that will be impossible, sir."

"Impossible? Why is it impossible?"

"Her ladyship is not in London, sir. We do not look for her until tomorrow at the earliest." He turned his disapproving frown on Abigail. "The young lady was not expected for *several* days, sir." His tone was exactly that which he might have used to a recalcitrant pup who knew very well that it was not allowed on the furniture.

Abigail unconsciously moved closer to Charles. He might be cold and distant. He might have wounded her deeply. She might even have convinced herself she hated him. But at the moment he seemed the only human thing in the room besides herself and Betsey. "I am afraid my father's new ship is even faster than we had hoped," she said in a small apologetic voice. The reminder of her father's business was not well calculated to soften the butler's face. He was very much aware of what was due to his master. He was seriously displeased that an English peer should be reduced to such straits as this—to marry into *trade*. Such debasing of the blood of "his" family was almost more than the butler could bear.

"Well," said Charles, "she is here now, my good man, and must be seen to. She is cold and tired. Send someone to prepare her room at once."

Abby looked around again. The walls were entirely bare; the furniture was draped in holland covers. No fire danced in the grate of the huge hearth.

"Must I stay here, Charles," she asked softly.

"Of course, you must . . ." he began, but something in her voice made him look at her eyes. They seemed enormous in a face gone very white. He could feel the trembling of the little hand she had placed on his sleeve.

A wave of that tenderness and protectiveness he had tried so hard to kill welled up and took him unaware. Damn Longford, he thought, not to have foreseen that they might well arrive early. What a shabby greeting for one's bride.

He covered her hand with his own; the trembling stopped. "No, of course not," he said gently. "But what am I to do with you?"

"Betsey and I could go to a hotel until her Ladyship returns," she suggested. Charles scowled. The butler widened his eyes a fraction. A more worldly girl would have known at once that she had seriously erred.

"Don't be ridiculous!" snapped Charles. "Such a course would be highly improper." He lapsed into thought, occasionally muttering to himself such things as ". . . no proper matron to chaperon her . . ." and ". . . should have foreseen . . ." But finally his scowl lightened. "I have it. I shall take you to my Aunt Lucy. Capital lady. She resides not far from here. Pray God we shall find her home."

"I should hate to impose on a perfect stranger."

"Nonsense. My aunt loves nothing better than company. Yes, that will be best, I think." He turned to Betsey. "Go and find your mistress's night case. See that she has what she will need for a day or so." To the butler he said, "See that Miss Dawson's trunks are brought in, that her horse is well stabled and her groom made comfortable."

"We were not told to expect a horse, sir," the butler said dampingly.

"Well, you have a horse in the courtyard and a groom beside it. I expect them to be well looked after."

After an almost imperceptible pause, the butler said, "Very good, sir." He was well trained in recognizing the Quality when he saw it and in catering to its whims. The

girl might be naught but an upstart American; the gentleman was clearly much more.

Charles furnished the butler with his aunt's direction,
admonished him to send word the moment her ladyship
returned, and headed Abby out the door. With a sympathetic smile at Jacob, who was looking at the house with a
woebegone expression and stroking Mr. Adams's neck in a
manner better calculated to reassure the groom than the
horse, they climbed back into the hackney.

It was with relief that Abby felt the jolt of the carriage,
heard the clatter of hooves on cobblestones again, and saw
the great hulking mansion disappear behind them as they
rolled through the gates and back into Piccadilly.

"Poor Jacob," sighed Betsey, gazing out the tiny, dirty
back window at her lonely-looking swain.

"Yes," said Abigail. "Poor Jacob." It sounded very
much as if what she meant was "Poor me."

Some fifteen minutes later Abigail was shown how
greatly a welcome may differ from one house to another.

The house in Henrietta Place was elegant and comfortable, though far from grand. It seemed almost tiny compared to the magnificence of Longford House, but its
windows were bright with flowered chintz curtains. The
first daffodils were just opening in the window boxes, and
shrubs flanked the door, which opened almost as soon as
Charles's hand dropped the shiny brass knocker.

After one small moment of stunned silence, the white-
haired butler who admitted them cried, "Mr. Charles!"
His face was wreathed in a smile of genuine pleasure.
"How very good to see you home again, sir! May I say you
are looking very fit."

"Thank you, Bellows," said Charles, shaking the butler's hand. "As are you. Is my aunt at home?"

"Indeed she is, sir, and with a house full of company."
There was a decided twinkle in his eye.

"Oh, no," groaned Charles. "Who . . . ?"

A fluty feminine voice cut him off. "Bellows, who is
it?" The voice was followed into the hall by a tall, silver-
haired, and rosy-cheeked lady in brown kerseymere and
spectacles. "Charles?" she said, stopping so short she
almost tripped over herself. "Charles! It is you! Anne!

Sophie! Come quick! It's Charles! Charles is home!'' And with that she enveloped her nephew in a hug of pure delight and affection, sending her spectacles flying and not minding in the least.

Two more ladies ran into the hall, fluttering clouds of pastel muslin about them, to engulf the young man in more hugs and cries of delight. One of them was an older, feminine version of Charles, a handsome woman of perhaps forty-five with dark hair and bright eyes now misted with tears of joy. The other was a girl of about seventeen. Her golden hair was highlighted with red, and she had the same dark, slightly slanted brows that seemed to run in the Lydiard family.

They all radiated warmth, and Abby felt more comfortable standing among these total strangers than she had felt since leaving Pennsylvania.

''Mama,'' said Charles to the small, dark woman when he was finally allowed to speak, ''what are you doing here? I thought to find you home at Cumberley.''

''And so you should have, my darling, had you come home tomorrow instead of today. I've just toddled up to Town to see Sophie settled. She's making her come-out this season, and you know how tedious I find all that. Thank God for Lucy. She is going to sponsor *all* my daughters. She honestly *enjoys* it, you know,'' she added with a laugh. ''I return to Cumberley tomorrow.'' She gazed fondly at her only son, then buried him in another hug. ''Oh, Charles, how very fine you look! Welcome home.''

He turned to the girl beside her. ''Sophie? Good God, is this truly my hoyden of a sister?''

Miss Sophia Lydiard blushed with pleasure and spun around for his better inspection. Then she gave an apple-cheeked smile certain to wreak havoc among the gentlemen. ''I am not a hoyden anymore, Charles.''

He grinned. ''I don't believe it. I'll wager you're as much of a baggage as ever under that very fashionable exterior.'' Her flirtatious smile gave way to a mischievous grin.

Abby was astounded at the change in Charles. Gone were the bitter scowls and the icy words. They had been completely replaced by that warm smile she had first seen on the New York dock. How she had missed that smile!

He gave Sophie a bear hug, and Abby was appalled to feel a pang of envy shoot through her.

"But Charles," said Mrs. Lydiard. "We are being unpardonably rag-mannered. You have brought us a guest, and such a pretty one, too." Her smile at Abby was warm and friendly. Charles made the introductions and explained the situation.

"Of course you may stay here, Miss Dawson," said Aunt Lucy, more properly called Mrs. Rustings. "Charles, you did very right to bring her here."

"I'm so terribly sorry to impose on you in this shameful way, ma'am," said Abby. "But I could not stay there. I just *could* not."

"Well, of course you could not. What? A young girl alone staying in that great tomb of a place? Unthinkable. You shall be ever so much cozier here. Now do come and have a nice cup of tea, my dear. You must be parched as well as frozen." She turned to the still-beaming butler. "See that the Rose Room is readied for Miss Dawson, will you please, Bellows? And see that her maid is comfortable. Then bring us some fresh tea. And perhaps some fruit and one of Cook's cakes and . . . oh, you will know what will make us all comfortable, Bellows. You always do."

"At once, ma'am," he replied, handing her her spectacles. Then he disappeared to see to her comfort just as he had been doing perfectly for nearly thirty years.

Chapter Fifteen

Despite repeated entreaties to remain, Charles left his aunt's house almost at once, using as excuse the need to report to Rupert Dawson's London agents. Abby knew well that the matter could easily wait. Need he make it quite so obvious how he disliked her company, even at the cost of walking away from the family he'd not seen in years?

She had little chance to brood, however. She felt instantly at home in Mrs. Rustings's house. The ladies fussed over her, plying her with questions and food and clucking over her description of the storm. "How frightened you must have been, my dear," said Mrs. Lydiard. "How glad I am you had Charles to look after you."

A blush suffused Abby's face at mention of the storm. But she pushed away her uncomfortable memories of a pair of kisses and smiled. Charles's mother clearly had implicit faith in the ability of her only son to overcome any obstacle, even a storm-tossed sea.

An immediate liking sprang up between Abby and Sophie Lydiard. Sophie was pretty, bright, and unaffected, not at all like the ladies Charles had led Abby to expect in London.

Dinner that evening was a merry affair despite the undeniable fact that Charles and Abby virtually ignored one another's presence. Mrs. Lydiard chattered about her younger daughters, her house, and her garden. Susan, her next daughter after Sophia, was to make her come-out the following year.

"You cannot know, Charles, how grateful I am to your

aunt, sponsoring the girls. I needn't put myself out in the least," said Mrs. Lydiard.

"You know I enjoy it, Sarah," said Mrs. Rustings. "It gets me out and about. Society may not be just to your taste, dear, but I adore it."

"Thank goodness," replied Mrs. Lydiard.

It was perhaps natural that Abby should misunderstand the situation. None of the family was elaborately dressed, though all showed a good deal of taste. The house was nicely but simply furnished. Viscount Cumberley was referred to simply as Uncle George. Abby had no notion whatever that there was a title that would one day go to Charles.

Thus, she assumed that Mrs. Rustings had taken on the task of sponsorship because Charles and his mother could not afford to do so themselves. The impression was reinforced by Mrs. Lydiard's next comment.

"I've become such a homebody, Charles, as you wouldn't believe. I am quite content in my little cottage, looking after the girls, poking about in my garden, and playing chess with your Uncle George." Abby could have no way of knowing that the "little cottage" was the sixteen-room Dower House at Cumberley, or that the garden she liked to "potter about in" was a formal rose garden the size of a cricket field with a hedge maze at one end, half a dozen classical fountains, and an ornate gazebo in the center.

All in all, it was quite a comfortable evening for Abby, despite the constraint between her and Charles, eerily reminiscent of those spent with her own uncle's family in Pennsylvania.

At midmorning next day came word that the Dowager Countess of Longford had returned. Abigail was expected at three o'clock. The summons struck Abby rather like a sentence of doom.

"You must call on us again soon, my dear," said Mrs. Rustings as they said their farewells. "Sophie knows so few young people in London."

"And I know even fewer," said Abby. "And you must all come to Longford House, too."

"It is kind of you to say so, my dear," said Mrs. Rustings. "But of course it is impossible."

"Impossible? But why?"

"I am not acquainted with the Countess."

Charles cut in in his teacherish voice, "Have I not told you, Abigail, that everything in London, and I mean *everything*, goes by rank? It is for Lady Longford to pay the first call or issue the first invitation if she wishes for the acquaintance." He paused. "I cannot think she will do so."

Abby bristled. "Then I shall!"

Mrs. Rustings, vaguely puzzled by her nephew's uncharacteristic black looks, said gently, "And when you are Countess of Longford, I shall be very pleased to come, my dear."

"I must confess," said Sophie, "that I should like to see Longford House. I am told it is very grand."

"*Very* grand," agreed Abby with a little shudder. She caught a look in the eyes of the two older women that seemed oddly like sympathy. It puzzled her a little.

The carriage ride to Piccadilly was short. Mercifully so, since Charles said not a word. The door was opened even before they mounted the steps. Abigail was treated to the sight of several Longford footmen in full regalia. This was more like, she told herself. Not one but three of the magnificent creatures stood at rigid attention, resplendent in crimson livery heavily adorned with silver braid and buttons. Their perfect calves, obviously a criterion for the position, were covered in white clocked hose; their feet were shod in varnished pumps. The entire image was perfectly completed by the immaculately curled and powdered wigs on each erect head.

The butler, who she would presently learn was known by the name of Crowther, showed them up a wide, thickly carpeted staircase and into a large drawing room with hangings the exact shade of crimson worn by the footmen.

"Her ladyship will be with you shortly," said Crowther and silently departed the room. Charles crossed to a window and stared out.

"Well," breathed Abigail, sinking onto a settee cov-

ered in ecru-and-crimson-striped satin. She let her eyes
cover the room. It was not a pretty room. That was far
too simple and homey a word for such elegance. Neither
was it a room that would reverberate easily to delighted
laughter. It was a perfectly proper setting for an earl, a
Peer of the Realm, and had no time for nonsense, only for
elegance.

The furniture was heavy and dark; the pictures were of
people and scenes from an earlier age. It might have been a
room from a museum of the last century. Not one modern
touch intruded. A more worldly young woman, knowing
something of the family's circumstances, might have
guessed that it showed not so much a taste for the antique
as an inability to pay for anything new.

Charles seemed to take no interest in the room at all.
Nor did he seem to take any interest in Abby. She contented herself with studying the room, though she could
never be unaware of his presence, his closeness, even the
rhythm of his breathing.

The arrangement of the furniture, the subtle mix of the
colors, every tiny arrangement of flowers or bibelots was
perfectly done. It was all so perfect that Abby was almost
afraid to move for fear of disarranging the picture. She
almost longed to squash a perfectly plumped pillow or turn
a porcelain shepherdess to face the wall. Who could actually live with such perfection?

She stole a look at Charles, certain he must be feeling
the same and wanting to share a smile. He stood rigidly at
the window staring across the courtyard. His face was set
in rigid planes. She could see the muscles rippling in his jaw
as he convulsively clenched his teeth. It was only too evident that he could scarcely wait to be rid of the burden of
chaperonage, to show Longford House and Abigail Dawson
the back of his heels and ride off into the freedom of the
park or wherever he intended riding off into.

Of course, he had been brusque and surly for weeks. He'd
been impossible the past few days. But now, at the very
moment of parting, his surliness pricked her vanity. How
dare he, a mere employee of her father, show such open
contempt for her?

"You need not have come with me, you know, as I told you before!" she snapped at his broad back.

He spun around and stared almost as though he had forgotten she was in the room. "Don't be a ninny," he snapped back. "You are my responsibility and will remain so until I see you safely into her ladyship's keeping."

"You make me sound like a horse. I am perfectly capable of looking after myself for so much as twenty minutes together, Charles."

"I very much doubt it," he replied and turned back to the window.

"Oh!" exclaimed Abby, pounding the settee in frustration. How could she ever have thought she liked him, much less . . . ? She would like to . . . to . . .

What she would like to do went unconsidered, for the door opened to admit a tall, magisterial, and entirely intimidating woman who looked to be of an age anywhere between seventy and a hundred. She swept into the room with a firm step, carrying herself like a queen or a general on the battlefield. She stopped before Abigail, who popped to her feet and dipped a curtsy.

The elegance of the Dowager Countess of Longford's person matched the elegance of her drawing room. She was dressed largely in black, as befitted a widowed lady of her years, and in the style of an earlier age. But she carried her antique gown with such authority that no one would have dared suggest she update her style.

She wore black silk lustring smoothed over a tightly corseted waist. Heavy black lace foamed into ruffles at the elbow-length sleeves. Her stiff brocade stomacher was of crimson, the exact shade Abby would learn was known as Longford crimson and which no one else in the *ton* would dare to wear. The stomacher was heavily laced in silver and black and stiffened with whalebone.

Abigail had sufficient time to study the whole effect, for the Dowager did not speak at once. So unmoving was the face surveying Abigail that it might have been a mask but for the sharp dark eyes. They missed nothing. The hair was as silver as the lace foaming over her bosom and was pulled back in a severe, dignified chignon.

Her face was cut in sharp planes. Prominent cheekbones,

a high forehead, and the same long, straight nose displayed in the portrait of her grandson, fairly shouted her noble blood. She must have been an extraordinarily handsome woman in her day. She might be still if only she would deign to smile.

The Countess subjected the girl to a prolonged and detailed scrutiny. Abby had the distinct feeling that she was somehow displeased.

When the Dowager finally deigned to speak it was not to Abigail but to Charles, who had finally turned from the window. "Lydiard," she said by way of recognition. "So you have decided to come home." Charles merely nodded an agreement. "Well, I suppose I must thank you for seeing Miss Dawson safely to us."

"It was my pleasure, Lady Longford," he answered in a voice that indicated no pleasure at all.

"I am certain my nephew will wish to thank you," she added. Charles stiffened perceptibly, and the Dowager offered the closest thing she had yet come up with that could be called a smile. "He will call on you one day soon to do so."

The Dowager returned her critical gaze to Abby. "I see we shall have much to do. We may as well start at once. Mr. Lydiard, you will forgive my not offering you tea. Time is very short. In any case, being newly returned, you will have much to do. You may safely leave the girl in my care."

Charles knew when he was dismissed. He allowed himself one last look at Abby. She thought his face softened with remembered tenderness, but the look was brief. He turned back to the Dowager. "I was certain of it, my lady. I will bid you good day." He bowed. "Miss Dawson." And then he was gone.

Abby felt one of her hands reach involuntarily toward the door. "Charles," she murmured. Then, with a sigh, she dropped her hand and turned to the woman who would soon be her grandmother-in-law.

Lady Longford sat rigidly in a straightback chair. "Turn around, girl," she commanded. Abby did. "Not precisely hopeless," said her ladyship. "Sit down." Abby sat down. "Can you speak, child?"

This really was too much, thought Abby. "Of course I can speak, ma'am," she answered easily. "I did not know I was allowed to."

A gleam came into the woman's sharp eyes, but whether of admiration or irritation Abby could not be sure. Perhaps the Dowager was not sure herself. She liked a girl with spirit. However, she could not like too much of it in this particular miss. If her plans were not to go awry, the chit must do *exactly* as she was told, with no sass and no independent nonsense. She longed to reprimand the girl, but she knew it was in her best interests, and those of her scapegrace grandson, to placate the little goose for the time being. Once the golden eggs were firmly in the Longford basket, she could be subdued without worry.

The Dowager smiled, a thin smile that scarce caused a ripple in her crepy cheeks. "Of course you may speak, my dear. This is your home now. We wish you to be perfectly comfortable. I shall order tea. Will you ring the bell, please?"

In response to this more civil treatment, Abby managed a real smile. She would be very glad of a cup of tea.

"Take off your bonnet, child," said the Dowager when Abby sat down. She studied the girl's face a moment. "Yes, it is as I feared. Winkle, my dresser, must give you some crushed strawberries for your complexion. You are far too brown. The hair will do after some cutting and styling. If this is an indication of your wardrobe, we must start on it at once. It is but two weeks before the Jersey Ball, the official opening of the Season. A pity you are so dark and slight. It would have done quite well some years ago when that silly Caro Lamb was all the rage. But fashion is running to dimpled blondes just now. Still," she went on with the slightest of tight little smiles, "I am thankful to see that you are not ill-looking. That is something."

Abby hardly knew what to make of such grudging praise. "Had you not seen my picture, ma'am?"

"Oh, the miniature," the Dowager replied with a dismissive gesture. "You know how infamously the portraitist can lie. And often does."

Abby wondered if she referred to the miniature of Lord

Longford packed away in a corner of her trunk. At least she hoped it was packed. She had quite forgotten to have Betsey see to it. How could she so far forget the attention due to her soon-to-be lord and master?

Abby was feeling smaller by the moment and wondered if she would soon disappear altogether under the claw-footed table beside her. It was with great relief that she saw Crowther enter with a heavily laden tea tray. On it were cakes, tiny sandwiches, and a silver bowl of fruit. Mindful of Charles's instructions not to be a glutton, she nibbled in as ladylike a way as she could manage. She was hard pressed not to gulp down everything in sight, out of nervousness as much as hunger.

The Countess studied her thoughtfully as she sipped tea from a delicate Spode cup. Despite a lamentable lack of curves and the outré design of her American gown, the chit carried herself well. She would not disgrace the Longford name with her looks. That was something.

Indeed, it looked as if the problem would be quite otherwise. In decent gowns and with all that black hair properly done, she was like to be a fetching little thing. She didn't simper, and she would be a novelty, something quite uncommon among the *ton*. The gentlemen would flock about her.

Lady Longford quickly reviewed the list of eligible gentlemen that could be expected in town for the Season.

There was Ringworth, a handsome devil with more charm than was good for him and deep in the basket to boot. But he was only a baron. Stronton could be a threat, but he was on the Continent, thank God, and the Duke of Pertwee, though actively looking for a rich wife, was sixty if he was a day. And gouty. Scarce likely to appeal to a green girl like the Dawson chit, be she never so ambitious.

The Dowager set her cup down with satisfaction. No, there was no better title than Longford's currently available and acceptable. The Dowager could rest easy.

Longford, the devil, would waste little time once the knot was tied getting this one with child. He'd most likely pack her off to Long Meadow, the Longfords' ancestral seat, and leave her there. She might not like it, but by then it would make no odds. Her huge fortune would be well secure. It would restore Long Meadow to its former glory. With an heir, the title would be safe. Yes, even so unsavory an action as bringing American blood and trade money into the family was made palatable by the desirability of such a result.

"Now," said the Dowager at last. "What on earth are we to do about your name?"

"My name, ma'am?"

"Abigail! Humph! Makes you sound like a serving wench. Have you another we could use?"

Abby drew herself up very straight and set her teacup carefully on the table. "As it happens, ma'am, I do not. Nor would I consent to use it if I had. I am very proud of my name. I was named after Mrs. Adams, you see."

"Adams?" said the Dowager with a look both uncomprehending and withering. "Adams?"

"The wife of one of our greatest patriots, ma'am, and a great lady in her own right. I am extremely proud to be named after her."

"Oh," said the Dowager, her tone even more withering. "An American."

"Yes, ma'am," said Abigail, simply but proudly.

The Dowager did not like that bit of fire that had flashed in the girl's eyes. She did not like it at all. The chit would have to be cowed, that was clear. The Longfords could not afford to have a chit of an American with neither family nor breeding making loud with outlandish opinions or horrid social *faux pas*. Much better she should say nothing at all.

At that moment Abby did say nothing, for the simple reason that she did not know what to say. Her betrothed's grandmother seemed in no hurry to make her feel at home. She shivered despite the fire glowing in the grate.

"Well," said the Dowager, reaching for a sheet of foolscap and a pen that had been ready laid out. "We must begin to plan our campaign. There is much to do."

Abby brightened at that. "Oh yes. When shall we begin our shopping, ma'am? I confess I am looking forward to seeing all the shops."

"You've a deal to learn, girl," replied the Countess with a superior smirk. "The Longfords do not 'shop,' as

you so quaintly put it. I have never visited a tradesman's
establishment in my life.''

"But then how. . . ?"

"They will come to us, of course. I shall tell Madame
Ruelle to appear tomorrow at ten." She made a note to
that effect. "Mademoiselle Fournet, quite a clever milli-
ner, will be summoned for eleven. In the afternoon we shall
see the bootmaker, and perhaps if there is time we can
spare a moment for the glovemaker. I shall have him come
in any case. We may get to him."

The idea that so many people should be "summoned" to
dance attendance on her, to sit around the great mansion
in hopes she would have time to "spare them a moment,"
both thrilled and appalled Abby. She was not certain she
wanted such power over other people's time.

The Dowager continued making notes and ticking off a
schedule. "The following day we can see to your under-
things, nightshifts, petticoats, and such." She looked at
Abigail's gown. "I cannot think that *anything* you have
brought with you is at all suitable. I doubt even if the
housemaids will want them, though of course we must
make the offer. It is expected."

Abby was given no chance to protest this summary dis-
missal of the entire contents of her trunks. "Scarves, reti-
cules, parasols," the Countess muttered as she wrote. "It
is a great bore. I daresay we shall have the house in an
uproar. But it is, of course, quite necessary."

Abby was disappointed. She'd been looking forward to
the bustle of flitting from shop to shop, of gazing in
windows and making comparisons.

There was, however, one errand she must see to personally and soon. "I had hoped, ma'am, to call at Child's
Bank in the morning."

"Child's Bank? Whatever for?"

"To confer with my banker, of course. I must give Mr.
Devoe Poppa's letter of credit and set up my bank account
before I can buy anything."

"What utter nonsense!" barked the lady. "Highly
unsuitable! Impossible!"

"But ma'am," began Abby, mystified.

"It is not at all the thing for a young lady in your position to have her own bank account, or, indeed, to have anything at all to do with money."

"But how will I pay my bills else, ma'am?"

That Abigail should have a large sum of money at her disposal played no part in Lady Longford's plans. It gave the chit far too much independence. "You must sign the letter of credit over to Longford, of course. It is his place to see to such things for you now. Your bills will be sent to him. You need never worry yourself over them. It is the way things are done." She saw the mulish look on Abby's face and gave a tolerant little smile. "Of course, Longford will give you an allowance. Pin money, you know. Every girl must carry a few shillings in her reticule for the odd trifle that catches her eye, for giving vails to the servants and such. You needn't worry that you will find him stingy."

The determined look on Abby's face did not fade. Her father had prepared her for just this situation. Blinded by nobility Rupert Dawson might be, but he was not so bemused as not to know that Lord Longford was as far up the River Tick as he could be without drowning. He had expressly warned Abby that she was on no account to give control of her funds over to anyone. He knew she was his true daughter, perfectly capable of managing the enormous sum herself. He had sent his lordship a very large bank draft for his own use. But the man was not to touch Abigail's money.

This Abby explained to the Countess as tactfully as she could, making it clear she would handle her own money in her own way.

"It simply is not done," said Lady Longford. "I cannot think what people would say." The woman was not at all used to having her will thwarted in this way. "I am certain Longford will not permit anything so singular." She poured herself another cup of tea as though the point was decided and the conversation closed.

But Abby was not finished. "Naturally I should wish to please his lordship in all things, ma'am. But on this matter, I fear he must be disappointed. Poppa would not like it, you see." Besting this old lady at her own game, she also poured another cup of tea and sipped it slowly. Then she pointedly turned the subject. "Do you think the weather will clear soon, ma'am? I admit I would just as soon see it rain if we are to be confined to the house. I shall not long so much to be outside."

A look that in anyone less refined would have been a glower passed from the Countess to the girl. Very well, miss, she said to herself. This round to you. But I am in control here, and you shall soon know it. Then we shall see what we shall see.

Abby was beginning to droop. "I wonder if I might be shown to my room now, ma'am," she said. "I'm afraid I have the headache a little and would like to rest."

"I hope you are not sickly. That would never do."

"Not at all, ma'am. I am almost never ill. But I have had a very long journey, and everything is so new. I am feeling just a bit overwhelmed, I think."

The Countess rose, ramrod-straight, and rang the bell. "Of course. I will have Mary show you up. You should find your slave waiting for you."

"Betsey is not my slave, ma'am! Nor has she ever been. I have never owned a slave in my life, and neither has my father."

"Oh? I quite thought all Americans owned slaves."

"You were incorrect, ma'am."

The Dowager bristled at her tone, but did not reprimand her. Not as yet. "I own I am relieved to hear it. It would be very bad *ton*, I am sure. We cannot afford that."

The butler reappeared with a young housemaid in tow. "We will speak again at dinner. We dine at eight. Longford will be present." Abby was dismissed.

Chapter Sixteen

The chamber to which Abby was shown was as overwhelming as the rest of Longford House. Heavy hangings of dark blue and gold shrouded the windows and the massive bed. The furniture was of carved ebony, and the day was so overcast that little light filtered in to lighten the gloomy atmosphere.

Abby began to wonder if she would ever feel cozy again. But Betsey was here, bustling about with her usual air of industry. She, at least, was comfortable and familiar.

The maid was as full as she could hold of new faces and accents, unfamiliar foods and routines, and the strange humors of English folk. She chattered madly away as she fluttered about preparing a hot bath, washing her mistress's luxuriant hair, then carefully combing it dry before the fire. Her chatter washed over Abby like a warm summer rain.

"Who'd have thought, Missy Abby, that a body'd need so many servants just to run one house, be it never so grand. Why, we sat down twenty to tea in the servants' hall, and that with no field hands to feed. I dursn't think what your Aunt Sylvie'd say. She'd be right ashamed to admit to half so many, and her with all that family to do for."

"Twenty!"

"Twenty. And what they all find to do I dursn't guess."

"Well, it is a very large house," said Abby a little unsurely. "And London ways are not like ours."

"That be true," sighed Betsey. "And London folk too, I s'pose."

"Have they been unkind to you, Bets?" asked Abby, ready to spring to her defense. "That I won't have!"

"No," said Betsey with a thoughtful look. "I couldn't rightly call it unkind. I don't know what I *would* call it. But friendly like folks at home, they're not. Why, they kept going on about how lucky I am to be in such a civilized country. Made it sound like back home we're nothing but a bunch of savages," she said with a snort, then applied herself to lathering her mistress's hair.

When Abigail was thoroughly rinsed and could speak once more, she said, "Do you know, I am beginning to feel that is how they *do* see us. As if we're not quite civilized." She thought a moment, then put on a bright face. "Well, we shall just have to show them they are wrong, won't we? You and I and Jacob."

"That one!" said Betsey with another snort, though she could not completely hide the smile that crept onto her gamine face. "More like he'll prove them right, Missy Abby. I had to remind him to take off that smelly leather apron he wears before coming into the kitchen." She set herself to briskly toweling Abby's skin to a rosy glow as the girl stepped out of her bath.

"That's because he likes you to remind him," Abby teased. "You do it so sweetly. And you needn't rub my skin off. I can still see your blushes."

Despite herself, Betsey giggled, and the two girls felt a bit more at home in this strange new place.

Abby fussed over her toilette that evening far more than was her wont. She was about to meet the man who would be her husband. She wished to look her best. Truth to tell, she wished to look very much better than her best. She wished to dazzle his lordship, to conquer his heart at one glance.

Before boarding the *Abby Anne*, she had given little thought to the puzzle of love. She was sure she would love her husband. How could she not?

But then Charles had come into her life with his smiles and his scowls and his kisses that put all her dreams in a muddle. And worse, having intruded himself so violently into her rosy view of the future and caused all sorts of questions to whirl about in her head, he had rudely pulled himself out again, leaving her dangling for a firm foothold on her cloud.

Now she was more grimly determined than ever that she would love her betrothed and, more important, that he would love her, be besotted by her in fact. She would show Mr. Charles Lydiard that she hadn't the slightest need of his melting kisses.

Abby was not particularly well versed in the feminine arts, but she had never been one to turn away from a challenge. With a critical eye she inspected the wardrobe Betsey had unpacked, brushed, and hung away. It had always seemed adequate before, extravagant even. Suddenly it seemed highly unsatisfactory.

After a great many false starts she finally settled on a pale-green muslin with dainty lace inserts at neck and sleeve. Dark-green velvet ribbons wrapped the tiny waist. Betsey piled her curls onto her head, adding a good two inches in height, and Abby turned to survey the effect.

"I look about twelve years old!" she moaned. "What gentleman falls madly in love with a twelve-year-old?" Betsey grinned a rejoinder and pulled out the velvet box with Mr. Dawson's gift. "Oh, Bets! Do you think I ought?"

"Why oughtn't you, Missy Abby? They be yours."

"But it's not a formal dinner. Should I not save them for a special occasion?"

"What be more special then meeting your husband that's to be, I ask you? You put these on. They'll make you feel a real lady, sure as sure."

Abby did feel her spirits rise as the pearls were clasped about her throat. Surely schoolgirls of twelve never wore such very fine pearls. She put the drops in her ears, shaking her head to set them swaying. Betsey set the tiara among her dusky curls.

Well, she might not be ready to pose for *The Ladies' Magazine*, she thought, but she did feel more the thing. She picked up a shawl of green gauze embroidered with roses and she was ready.

* * *

Abby's first meeting with the Earl of Longford was all she could have hoped for. His lordship was resplendent in an evening coat of claret velvet and a green-and-rose-striped waistcoat with large gilt buttons. The cuffs of his coat were turned back to display a rose lining matching the smoothly fitted knee breeches. His lower legs were encased in pristine white hose clocked in gold. His cravat was elaborately tied, and a half-dozen fobs dangled at his waist.

Why, he looks as grand as the footmen, Abby caught herself thinking, then had to suppress a giggle at the thought.

He looked very like his miniature, and yet very unlike. There was the long, straight nose that proclaimed his noble birth and the brown hair cunningly curled and pomaded and brushed into the Windswept. There were the hooded eyes that seemed to take in every inch of her.

But no artist could capture the strange contradiction in his gaze which was both fashionably languid and piercingly sharp. And the carefully preserved paleness of his skin, which looked so romantic in the portrait, seemed somehow unhealthy in the glow of the many candles lighting the room.

Still, he was certainly a handsome gentleman and awesomely elegant. He was leaning against the overmantel when she came in, holding a goblet of wine the exact color of his coat and looking bored to an extent Abby might have found alarming had she not been prepared by Charles. Now, of course, she knew such a pose was one of the strongest dictates of fashion. To show excessive interest in anything was very bad *ton*.

Of course, she wouldn't have minded just a *teeny* bit more enthusiasm.

She made him a proper curtsy as the Dowager introduced them. He set down his wineglass and offered her a bow well calculated to sweep a green girl right off her feet. Abby was pleased by the grace of it as well as by the show of interest she could read behind the heavy-lidded eyes. If the glitter of appreciation seemed to take in her magnificent pearls as thoroughly as it did her person, she did not notice. Or at least she did not mind. Well, not so very much.

With languid grace, he raised her fingertips to his lips and turned on a well-practiced smile. When he spoke, it was in a world-weary drawl. "I see I must learn not to take your father too seriously."

"Whatever can you mean, my lord? What did he tell you?"

"Only that you were 'a pretty thing.' No man with eyes in his head could think such ravishing beauty adequately described by such an insipid word. He would much better have called you Aphrodite."

Abby, completely unused to such fulsome compliments, felt herself blush. It seemed that she was to make a conquest of her betrothed after all. She knew that she was far from plain, but to have such a man of the world, the one man above all others whose admiration she wished to inspire, find her beautiful was heady stuff. She tossed her head and gave a tinkling laugh, both mannerisms accomplished in a way she was sure Charles must approve—and whyever must she think of *him* at such a moment!—and curtsied once more.

"I think you are trying to gammon me, my lord, for I know very well that I am not at all fashionable. But I will be. Lady Longford has promised to help me choose a new wardrobe. I shall soon be . . . what is the word? Oh yes, all the crack!"

The heavy lids raised a fraction. The chit was certainly not shy. And at least he was not to be leg-shackled to some whey-faced mare. The girl was well enough and would be better when properly dressed. He drawled something appropriate about gilding the lily.

Lady Longford emitted a small "humph." She had no intention of letting the girl be "all the crack." There was no room for even a tiny bit of dash. No breath of scandal, no hint that the chit was fast or coming, must be allowed.

To Lady Longford this whole distasteful marriage was a gamble. Her scapegrace grandson had ruined not only his fortune but every chance of marrying any respectable girl in the *ton*. He was the head of the family, and no more respectable cousins were waiting in the wings to inherit

the title. He must have an heir. Also, Long Meadow must
be restored. This American, and her father's millions, was
her last chance of achieving that desirable outcome. Lady
Longford was counting heavily on the marriage to rehabili-
tate the Rake of London in the eyes of Society.

Abby had been so nervous at meeting the Earl and so
dazzled by his elegant compliments that she hadn't taken
in much detail. But as he offered his arm to lead her in to
dinner, she peeked at him with a calmer mind and clearer
eye.

He was tall, much taller than Charles, but also a great
deal thinner. To her dismay, the image of a bare, bronzed
chest rippling with muscle and dripping seawater sprang
into her mind. She felt somehow certain that Lord
Longford was not half so beautiful under his velvet coat.
To be sure, his shoulders were gratifyingly broad and his
chest was well rounded. But there was something not
quite right about the shape. She wondered if it resulted
from the tailor's buckram wadding she'd heard was often
employed.

The waist of the coat was tightly nipped in, and the
lapels were very wide. Obviously the Earl was "all the
crack," but he looked far less comfortable in his clothes
than Charles did in his.

Though Abby knew too little of fashion to recognize it,
her betrothed harbored a strong tendency toward dandy-
ism. It explained why he got on so well with his peacocky
Regent. Of course, with that somber-hued Brummell ruling them all so long with his iron hand, Longford had been
unable to indulge fully his taste for line and color. It just
was *not done* if Brummell didn't do it. But now, heavens
be praised, the upstart son of a clerk had come by his just
deserts. He'd been forced to flee to the Continent to
escape his creditors. And those of true taste, among
whom Longford certainly counted himself, were free to
throw off the yoke of his tyrannical dictums and express
themselves once more in the splendor of their attire.

Feeling the girl's eyes on him, he looked down at her and
was caught by those large green eyes. "Had I known what
beauty grew on American soil, I should have made the trip
to fetch you myself," he said.

Abby found herself searching his eyes, which were blue, like Charles's, but much paler. A network of tiny red veins took from them any chance of sparkle, and she could see no trace of the warmth that glowed in Charles's eyes even when he was angry. She gave herself a mental shake. She *would* stop thinking about Charles Lydiard! She would stop comparing her future husband, the man she was determined to love and who was, after all, an earl, with such a nobody, a man who was little better than a clerk and whom she would almost certainly never see again.

Charles Lydiard, for all his bronzed beauty and his melting kisses, didn't give a fig for Abigail Dawson, and she, proud daughter of her father and soon to be a countess, cared even less for him!

Abby mentally snapped her fingers in Mr. Lydiard's handsome face and turned her smiles, her attention, and every little art the said Mr. Lydiard had taught her on her betrothed.

Most of the conversation at dinner came from Lady Longford and concerned Abby's new wardrobe. Visions of silks and satins, of pelisses and pelerines, were soon whirling in Abby's head.

"And I must have a new riding habit, ma'am," she said.

"You ride, my dear?" asked Longford.

"Ride, my lord?" she replied with a laugh. "You must remember I was raised on a horse farm. Back home not riding is like not breathing. I hope to ride tomorrow, in fact. Poor Mr. Adams has been cooped up so long."

"Mr. Adams?"

"My horse."

"A horse," said Lady Longford, "not at all suited to a young lady, if I have heard correctly."

"Oh, Mr. Adams is a wonderful horse, ma'am. I had the breeding of him myself. He is as devoted to me as I am to him."

Longford gave her an intimate smile. "What? Must I begin to feel jealous so quickly, my dear? And of a horse?"

Something in his tone made Abby blush uncomfortably. "It's true he's a spirited horse, ma'am, but he is very well mannered with me."

"Well," said her ladyship, "perhaps Longford will take

you for a gentle trot in the park when you are properly garbed.''

"Gentle trot," said Abby with a note of derision. "That would not suit Mr. Adams at all." Nor me, she might have added.

"Well, you can hardly think to *gallop* in London. It is not done," said her ladyship.

How often Abby was destined to hear those four words in the next few weeks! How many things she would find were "not done." But she did not know that yet. She held firm. "Surely there is a time of day when few people are about and we could have a good run."

"Nonsense!"

"I cannot think Poppa would like me to be deprived of exercise. Do you not think . . ."

"Of course, my dear," said Longford quickly. "Of course you must ride. There are few people out in the early mornings, or so I am told. They say it is a wonderful time to exercise one's horses, though I am no hell-for-leather horseman myself."

At mention of her father, Longford had jumped to appease her. He felt better about his most pressing debts with Dawson's generous bank draft in his pocket, but he must do nothing to make the girl cry off. He had no intention of whistling all those millions of grubby American dollars down the wind. "And you will look lovely doing it," he said. "We must ride together one day. Not, of course, in the morning. I shall be quite proud to accompany you during the Promenade."

"I've heard of that," said Abby. "Don't they call it the Grand Strut?"

The conversation fell into easier channels, but Abby could not feel comfortable. There was something in his lordship's gaze that made her want to squirm. She should have been pleased; she had clearly made a conquest of him. But his look felt rather like that of a hunter taking aim at a sitting duck. Or of a gourmand who has just had a succulent feast laid before him.

And then there was his touch. He touched her often throughout the meal and the hour that followed in the drawing room. It was all very casual, very innocent-seeming. A hand on her arm, a brush of her fingers as she handed him a teacup. His skin was cold, slightly damp, and she had to force herself not to recoil from it. When he sat beside her on the settee, his thigh pressed hers closer than she could like.

She chastised herself harshly for missishness. The man would soon be her husband, after all.

But when at last she was given leave to retire and his lordship chided her into giving him one of the chaste kisses that were his right as her betrothed, she found she had to clench her teeth and steel herself to the task. She had needed no such resolve to kiss Charles Lydiard.

Longford sensed her unwillingness. A glint of pleasure lit his pale-blue eyes. So the chit was not quite so compliant as she should be. Good. A woman taken was always much more satisfying than one who came too willingly. And taking this little one would be as much pleasure as duty.

Abby couldn't look at him and so did not see the disturbing expression on his face, the gleam of challenge in his eyes. She gave a curtsy and a quiet goodnight and quit the room.

Chapter Seventeen

Charles Lydiard had not intended remaining long in London. He was eager to visit his uncle and to breathe again the soft air of the Kentish countryside. He wanted to be home at Cumberley, the vast estate he loved so dearly and which would one day be his. London could never be anything but hateful to him.

How odd, then, that one day slipped into another and

still he remained in Town. Odder still, he found himself almost enjoying becoming reacquainted with a city he had once loved, then loathed.

It felt good to wander up the Haymarket reading the theater bills or popping into Fribourg and Treyer to breathe the comfortable, masculine smell of snuff and cheroots. It was comfortable to while away a morning over the *Times*, sipping strong tea and catching up on the doings of the world.

And so it was that before a week had passed Charles found himself standing before a modest but respectable establishment in Ryder Street staring thoughtfully at a sign which read: "To Let, Lodgings for Gentlemen." His feet seeming to have developed a will of their own, he found himself climbing the half-dozen steps, heard his voice inquiring civilly of the landlady the terms of the lease, and watched his hands counting out the requisite number of pounds and shillings for a month's lodging.

As he sat in a comfortable wing chair in his newly acquired parlor, somewhat bemused at his impulsive action, he tried to understand what he had just done. Why had he decided to stay?

Of course, he *had* been cooped up for more than a month on a ship that, however comfortable, was still by definition confining. It was natural he should long for the bustle of Town before settling into the quiet country routine of managing his uncle's estate.

Then too he had a responsibility to his sister. However much he disliked the social whirl, he owed it to Sophie to help make her Season a success. And to keep an eye out for rakes like Longford and his ilk who liked nothing better than to turn the head of a green girl.

He told himself sternly that the presence of Abigail Dawson in London had nothing to do with his decision. It was no longer his business to worry over her. She would soon be another man's wife. She had made her bed, and it was precisely the one she wanted to lie in. He would let her.

Then too, Cumberley was only a few hours distant. He could easily go down of a morning to see his uncle and his mother and be back in time for dinner.

Of course, to do so he would need a horse. Perhaps he'd just wander over to Tattersall's and see what was on the block.

With a last look around his comfortable new home, he let out a sigh and picked up his hat. Setting it onto his auburn waves before the looking glass hanging over the mantel, he realized his American clothes looked quite shabby. Perhaps he'd stop by Weston's on his way and order a new coat. And he might as well have a look in at White's later. After all, he had to eat his dinner somewhere.

The handsome face in the mirror grinned with wry amusement for Charles had never been much good at deceiving himself. "You're a fool, Charles Lydiard!" he said to the grinning face. Sighing again, he turned away. "Aye, that you are," he muttered and headed out the door.

Thus it was that the next morning found Charles very early in Hyde Park exercising his new mount, a huge brute of a chestnut with a spirit to match his size. The horse's shiny coat shimmered in the misty morning sun. Charles's face glowed with the pleasure of the exercise.

In the joy of his gallop he succeeded for the first time in weeks in putting Abigail completely from his mind. The big horse responded beautifully to his subtlest command. He reveled in the smell of the grass still damp with English dew; he loved the feel of the soft English breeze across his face.

Slowing to a canter, he circled the Serpentine, enjoying the sight of nannies with their charges and schoolgirls in pinafores having their morning constitutionals. To his very great surprise, Charles realized with a pang how glad he was to be home.

This mellow mood was abruptly shattered as he turned into the North Ride. For there, galloping toward him with joyful abandon, her dusky curls blowing wildly about her face, was Abigail.

Abby had reason to be in high spirits. How good it felt to be out of that house at last! She hadn't set foot out-

side its walls since her arrival. Even Mr. Devoe, manager of
Child's Bank, had come to her there.

For days the afternoon parlor had been a colorful beehive
of fashion and a convenient excuse to keep Abby from the
promised ride. "Too much to do," the Dowager decreed
whenever the subject came up.

Abby had stood at attention while velvets and satins
were draped about her. A veritable garden of percale and
dimity, muslin and mull, filled the room with shades of
buttercup and saffron, cerise, vermilion, cocquelicot, sky-
blue, and sapphire.

And then there had been the ivory silk of her wedding
gown. The Dowager decreed that Abby couldn't possibly
wear her mother's gown for the most fashionable wedding
of the Season. Strangely, Abby had not demurred. She felt
an alarming lack of interest whenever her wedding was
discussed.

As to the gowns themselves, Abby's opinion was never
solicited. All decisions were made by the Dowager, rigidly
seated in a straight-backed chair passing judgment with a
nod or a scowl. Occasionally she would utter a terse
"Tighter" or "Shorter," or perhaps a gruff "Unsuitable!"

But finally and with great relief Abby received permission to ride. She took full advantage of the opportunity.
She rode hard and long, savoring the wind in her face and
the rush of her own blood. Her face glowed a becoming
pink.

She reacted with instinctive joy at sight of Charles.
How she had missed him! She drew rein, cried out a joyful
"Charles!" and gave a beaming smile.

How handsome he looked in the brisk morning sunlight,
she thought. The auburn lights in his hair glinted as he
raised his beaver in salute. And for all the somberness of
his garb, especially compared to Longford's showy plu-
mage, she'd never seen anyone look so manly.

Doeskin breeches were molded to his powerful thighs
like a second skin. His coat pointed up the solidity of his
physique. Abby had reason to know that it housed no
trace of buckram wadding. Longford no longer seemed

quite so elegant in her mind. Instead, he seemed slightly foolish.

How wonderful she looked, thought Charles, gazing at her hungrily. His heart soared a moment before plunging with a thud. He greeted her with great punctiliousness, not trusting himself to say more. "Miss Dawson. I had not thought to see you again."

The chill of his words froze her right through. The bright smile left her face as abruptly as it had appeared. Sitting very straight on her horse, she gave a cold little nod. "Nor I you, sir. Do you remain long in London?"

Instead of answering this very civil inquiry, he looked about for some sign of Jacob. Not seeing him, he gave the scowl that had become such a part of him lately. "Where the devil is your groom? Do you not yet understand that a young lady does not gallop about unescorted like some redskin savage? Will you never learn sense? You are not in Pennsylvania any longer, you know."

Surprisingly, she found his scowls easier to deal with than his frigid civility. She relaxed into naturalness. "You need not carp at me, Charles," she said. A rather harried-looking groom rode up behind her. He was panting and wore a look of strong disapproval. "As you can see, I am not alone."

Charles had the grace to apologize then, adding, "Where is Jacob? He is not ill, I hope?"

"Oh no. Jacob is very well. Though he is not particularly pleased with London," she added with a little smile. "He says they don't know how to cook here."

"Perhaps Betsey will remedy that soon," he replied with his first small smile. "But why is he not riding with you?"

She made a sound suspiciously like a snort. "Lord Longford does not like strangers handling his horses. As though the horse has yet been born that Jacob couldn't handle! But I am sending him out this afternoon to buy a mount for himself. Then he will be able to accompany me."

Abby had her back to the groom and couldn't see his look of alarm and his scowl of disapproval. But Charles could see it, and he didn't like it. The groom had obviously heard something he didn't like. Or something his master wouldn't like.

Abby, her reserve fast melting, looked over Charles's new stallion. "And speaking of horses, who is this magnificent fellow?"

"He's called Pegasus," said Charles, surprising himself by laughing outright. "Rather a pretentious name, I know, but he is splendid and does rather ride like the wind. Found him yesterday at Tatt's."

A mischievous light crept into her green eyes. She reached one gloved hand down to stroke Mr. Adams's neck. "Care to try him against some good American horseflesh?"

Much as he would have liked to oblige, Charles knew he must decline. The scowling groom gave him no choice in any case. "It is time we were returning, miss. Her ladyship will expect you for breakfast."

Charles peered sharply at him. Was he her jailer? There was something not quite right in his attitude. Something approaching a lack of respect.

"I suppose you are right," sighed Abby. Charles noted her lack of enthusiasm. Odd, he thought, when she was exactly where she had always wanted to be. But she was smiling again as she looked at him. "I have become nothing but a dressmaker's dummy of late. Why, this is the first time I've been out of the house in days! Who'd have thought one lady could need so many clothes?"

"Did I not warn you?"

"You tried," she admitted with a dimple. "But I do hope we will soon be finished. You won't tell anyone you saw me, will you, Charles? I'm not yet fit to be seen, you know," she finished and gestured to her habit of jade-green merino, American-made and perfectly charming.

"Not fit. . . !" he sputtered, but was cut off by the groom.

"Miss?" he said. Charles thought he heard a note of warning. But Abigail just laughed.

"Very well, Robert. I'm coming. I hope to see you again, Charles. Please give my greetings to your family. They were all so very kind to me."

Before he could reply, she turned Mr. Adams and dug in her heels, sending up a cloud of dust as she galloped away. The groom, a look of great displeasure on his face, took off after her.

Chapter Eighteen

Despite the endless string of drapers and tailors and dressmakers, the days of comparing lustring with *gros de Naples* and Berlin silk with *peau de soie,* despite the hours of fittings that made Abby's back ache and the Dowager's lectures that gave her the headache, Abby was almost surprised when her mentor finally pronounced her ready for a first foray into the public eye.

It was an afternoon when she'd been at Longford House about a week. The first of her new ensembles arrived. Abby lifted one fashionable creation after another from beds of silver paper and tried to feel excited about them. They were lush and elaborate and shamefully expensive. They spilled over with ribbons and ruchings, with silk floss and rolled edgings.

But even as Betsey oohed and aahed over each gown and muttered "Gracious!" and "Lordy!" Abby found herself frowning. The dresses were too fussy or too old-seeming. The colors felt all wrong.

There was one costume, however, that was perfect, the one Abby had truly chosen for herself. She smiled in genuine pleasure as she lifted a riding habit of deep-ruby velvet from its box.

It was simply cut with an almost masculine severity. The rich color was set off perfectly by gilt buttons and a

deep revers of black satin. With it was a shirt of gleaming
white percale with a high, simple stock. Abby held the
ensemble before her and pranced to the mirror.

The rich color made her skin glow, and she instinctively
wondered if Charles would like it. Then, with a sudden
lowering, she realized that he would probably never see it.
She had ridden in the park for the past three mornings,
each day wondering if she would see him again. She had
not.

Betsey ran a finger over the soft velvet. "Now that,
Missy Abby," she sighed, "*that* be a dress!" The maid had
more than a touch of her mistress's innate good taste.

"It's not a dress, silly," corrected Abby. "It's a habit.
And I'm going to wear it this very afternoon."

Just as she spoke the words, Lady Longford entered,
unbothered by such lowly conventions as knocking on
doors. "Quite impossible, I fear," she said directly she
heard Abby's words and saw the habit.

Abby controlled a desire to snap back a pert reply and
satisfied herself with giving the Dowager a questioning
look.

"You can go nowhere today. I have invited the
Drummond-Burrells to dine. It is vital that you make a
good impression on Clementina. She is one of the most
influential Patronesses of Almack's. I have hopes of
getting you a voucher, though that may be flying too high
even for me. But we shall see. If Clementina can be
brought to approve of you, the others will follow. We shall
score an important point by giving her first glimpse of
you. And if I know Clementina, and believe me I do, every
tongue in London will be wagging tomorrow about
Longford's American bride."

The name of Mrs. Drummond-Burrell had figured promi-
nently in the society columns of the London journals Abby
had read for years. The notion of finally meeting her first
ton leader made Abby a bit nervous. And the best remedy
for that was a brisk ride. She looked longingly at the new
habit. She could still have a ride; dinner was three hours
away. She said as much to the Dowager.

"I have told you before, Abigail," began the Dowager
with what she surely thought was great patience, "young

ladies of distinction do not engage in 'brisk rides' in London. Certainly not in Hyde Park at the height of the Promenade, when *everyone* is there. All the world and his wife would see you. We would have lost our edge with Clementina.''

''I see,'' replied Abby, not really seeing at all.

''Besides, we have not a moment to lose. You must be in your best looks this evening.'' She walked briskly to the bed, where the new gowns were laid out in a rainbow. After a quick but thorough inspection, she said, ''I think the orange damask will do nicely. Elegant but not too pushy. We cannot have her think you too coming.''

Abby's nose wrinkled involuntarily. The orange damask was her least favorite of all the gowns. It was not a horrid dress, precisely. It was beautifully cut and fitted, and the shirred gauze across the front of the bodice made the most of her small bosom.

But she did wish there were fewer rosettes and swags along the hem, a bit less fabric in the skirt. And she had always hated orange. It made her feel *jangled*, like a discordant note played on an out-of-tune pianoforte.

The Dowager was still speaking. ''I shall have some crushed strawberries sent up for your face. See that you use them. Then you are to rest for at least an hour with cold compresses of strong tea across your eyelids. Winkle will be in at four to deal with all that hair.'' She then turned her imperious manner on Betsey. ''Girl, see that this gown is perfectly pressed, and order your mistress's bath for precisely five.'' Turning back to Abby, she said, ''You must be dressed and ready by six.'' She crossed to the door, then turned back a moment. ''And wear your pearls.''

And so saying, she departed the room.

Abigail spent the rest of the afternoon in the prescribed manner, though she giggled while plastering her face with strawberries and licked almost as much of the juicy concoction from her fingers as she slathered on her skin. Her ''hour's rest'' shrank to twenty minutes because she was too restless to lie motionless on her bed under tea compresses. She could see nothing wrong with her eyes, in any case, and hadn't the slightest notion what improvement the compresses were intended to effect.

The notion of expending so much time and effort on her appearance was a new one to Abby. She wasn't entirely certain she approved of it. But she did want to look her best.

Winkle, the Dowager's pinch-faced dresser, knocked on the door precisely as the dainty mantel clock chimed four. She was tall, like her mistress, and gaunt, with hollowed-out cheeks beneath Puritan eyes. She dressed always in crisp black that crackled when she walked. Abby had never seen her smile.

All appearances to the contrary, Winkle was not *Miss* Winkle but *Mrs*. Winkle. There was, however, no Mr. Winkle currently residing in the world. Her husband had been her husband for something less than six months, and that well over forty years before. It had not been a particularly noteworthy or ecstatic half year, and the young woman had not grieved overmuch when the young man went to America as a foot soldier to help quell the colonial rebellion. She had mourned his death at the Battle of Lexington in the proper manner while scarce bemoaning the loss of his person in the depths of her heart.

She spent the rest of her life in black because it suited her, and she much appreciated the extra degree of respectability that came with the title of widow, especially war widow.

She did, however, harbor a strong resentment of the people and the nation that had deprived her of the income her husband might have earned in his lifetime. The loss of it had driven her back into a life she had always despised, a life of service to her superiors.

This history, among other reasons too numerous and too deep-seated for her to dare to explore, gave Winkle sufficient excuse to dislike Abigail. It was, in any case, an emotion quite in tune with the dresser's basic nature.

Abigail winced as a fine-toothed ivory comb was pulled roughly through her hair. Scissors snipped and clouds of black hair floated to the floor. As the pile grew, Abby began to be worried.

But whatever her personal feelings about upstart Americans in general and Abigail Dawson in particular, Winkle was something of a genius when it came to the dressing of hair, a genius who had had precious little scope for her talents in recent years. And with such glorious hair to work with, she could not bring herself to do less than her best. Neither could she bring herself to do it gently. Abby's eyes were soon watering from the pulling.

When the girl was finally allowed to turn to the mirror, she could scarce credit what she saw. Her raven's-wing curls had been trimmed and thinned, fluffed and feathered to create a delicate, almost transparent cloud about her face. In all the paintings of the saints that Abby had ever seen the halos were of gold, but there was no denying the effect Winkle had created was a seeming contradiction in terms, a glistening black halo.

"Oh, thank you, Winkle," she breathed softly. "It's beautiful. I can hardly believe it's me."

Her only reply was a sort of snort as the dresser gathered up her combs and her brushes and her scissors and left the room.

At exactly five minutes before six, Lady Longford sailed into the room. Betsey was just putting the final touches to Abby's toilette, draping a Norwich silk shawl about her shoulders and handing her a pierced-ivory fan.

Abby could not feel comfortable. Her gown fitted so snugly she was afraid to breathe too deeply. And the orange color did indeed make her nerves jump. Her magnificent pearls could not truly be said to enhance the overall effect, warring as they did with all the gauze rosettes at her neckline.

But Lady Longford seemed not to notice. She had Abby revolve before her while she looked on with a critical eye. After changing the long white gloves Abby had chosen for a pair of yellow ones and replacing the fan with one of brightly painted silk, she pronounced herself satisfied and escorted her young charge downstairs.

Longford was before them in the drawing room, already drinking from the wineglass Abby had begun to consider a natural extension of his hand. Englishmen certainly seemed to drink a great deal of wine. Or at least Lord Longford did.

She had seen a great deal of his lordship during the past week, yet she still could not feel completely comfortable in his presence. She felt that his supreme arrogance probably came with being a Peer of the Realm, but it was coupled with a sort of fawning on her that never rang true. And she did not like the way he looked at her. She felt almost naked before him, and it alarmed her to admit that she had no desire ever to have her future husband see her in that natural state.

Through heavy-lidded, almost sleepy eyes, he was giving her that look now. "Aphrodite must be fairly beating her breast with jealousy on Mount Olympus this night," he oozed as he took her hand, then turned it over to kiss her wrist. It went through Abby's mind that she was glad she was wearing gloves.

His lordship was an incredible sight in a coat of russet plush over an acid-yellow waistcoat and pantaloons. His neckcloth was an elaborately tied Oriental, stiff with starch—to his lordship's mind, starch was the one decent innovation of Brummel's—and creased to perfection but somewhat constricting the movement of his perfectly coiffed head.

"How insipid of me to compare you to that rather mundane goddess of beauty, my dear," he murmured close to her ear. "Your loveliness is of a greater and, fortunately for your betrothed, a much more human kind. One would not want to kiss Aphrodite, after all, while I wish very much to kiss you. That and much more."

His eyes raked her in an alarmingly intimate way as he spoke. Abby felt herself grow warm. To her own surprise, she also felt a wave of feeling very like revulsion at the thought of his arms around her. She simultaneously recalled the lovely and very *un*revolting feeling of Charles's arms about her, Charles's lips on hers as they were locked in each other's embrace in a tiny cabin on the *Abby Anne* while the storm raged about them.

The memory made her blush grow more intense. Longford laughed, a pleased and distinctly lascivious chuckle. He reached up a hand to tweak a feathery curl and run a finger over her cheek. As his hand dropped, it brushed ever so lightly against her left breast. Not much there, he thought, but she wasn't a bad little piece. And he had seen spirit flash in those green eyes, a spirit it would be a distinct pleasure to subdue. Yes, he mused, getting himself an heir on this little pullet was like to prove far more enjoyable than he had at first thought.

Abby was relieved to see Crowther enter to announce their guests.

It seemed to Abby that dinner went on forever. Once again, Charles was proved right. The quantity of food was enormous. Even at such a small party, with only five of them at table, they were presented with both turtle soup and Hessian soup. There was crimped turbot in oyster sauce, a rack of lamb, a haunch of venison, and grenadines of duck. A pair of pigeon pies in buttery pastry followed asparagus dressed with a Parmesan sauce. There were turnips mashed with potatoes and seasoned with mace, a noodle pudding heavy with raisins and brandy, a marrow pudding, a timbale of rice, and a dish of India pickles. It was all finished off with tiny cakes in spun-sugar baskets, cherry tarts, and water ices of black currant and pomegranate. By the time a bowl of fruit and a wheel of cheese were set on the table, the company had been sitting there for upwards of three hours. Abby was so stuffed she could barely see, even though she'd had but a taste of each succulent dish.

Longford ate somewhat less than did Mr. Drummond-Burrell, but he consumed a great deal more of the wine that flowed continuously throughout the meal. And he filled Abigail's glass more often than she could like. Even before the fruit was served, accompanied by a sweet Madeira, she was feeling a bit light-headed.

It was not merely the quantity of food and wine that surprised Abby, nor even the pomp and elegance with which it was served. What did amaze her was the quality, or lack of it, in the conversation. Of her four companions, not one of them seemed to have an opinion on anything of significance. She had expected to be plied with questions about America, asked her opinion on relations between the two countries.

Instead they chatted at tedious length about the Prince

Regent's latest peccadillo, of which there seemed to be quite a few, of the disgraceful way the effects of the recently demised Queen were being split up by her children, and of the impending birth of a child to the Duchess of Kent. They discussed who had been seen at the latest Devonshire ball and what they had worn, with whom they had waltzed, and in whose bed they had most probably ended the night.

Where was the sparkling wit, the bright banter? Abby wondered. Where were the charged discussions of politics? She was sitting at table with some of the leaders of British Society, one of them a member of the House of Lords, and they were discussing in excruciating detail the cut of Lord Petersham's newest coat!

The level of the conversation was no higher when the ladies adjourned to the drawing room. Mrs. Drummond-Burrell and the Dowager discussed Abigail as though she were not in the room.

"Well, Clementina?" said the Dowager.

"Oh, I think she will do, Hortensia. Not a beauty, certainly, but well enough. You wouldn't want an Incomparable. Just pretty enough and just fashionable enough is what you want."

"Precisely what I thought."

"The gown is perfect. Wouldn't do to rig her out like a first-season deb. Your choice, I imagine."

The Dowager merely nodded acknowledgment.

Abby looked down with distaste at the orange damask. The pattern seemed to swim before her eyes. Her head was buzzing.

"I must say, Hortensia," continued Mrs. Drummond-Burrell, "if anyone can pull the trick off, it is you."

"Of course," said the Dowager matter-of-factly, "I only hope that by so doing I do not open wide the floodgates."

"I fear it is bound to happen sooner or later." Abby hadn't the least idea what they were talking about. "What with the price of corn and the drop in land values and ground rents, I see little choice but for many others of our kind to do the same. Deplorable, of course, but inevitable, I fear." She sighed. "In any case, I think your first move must be Sally Jersey's ball. Everyone will be there, of course. You could have no better opening."

"Naturally, I agree," said the Dowager. "Longford is escorting us. With me along, Sally cannot very well turn him away."

"Quite."

Abby was more mystified than ever. She had said not a word, since there seemed to be little need and less opportunity. The last words of Mrs. Drummond-Burrell before the gentlemen rejoined them were, "I am glad to see she is a quiet girl."

Lady Longford gave Abby a look that said clearly that she had better remain a quiet girl.

The evening wore on—or dragged on, to Abby's way of thinking. The excess of wine had left her feeling dull and stupid. She longed to retire to her bed. But that was clearly impossible. She was asked to favor the company with a turn at the piano, obviously another test to see if she was suited to polite company.

To her benumbed mind the four faces looking at her seemed to *expect* her to fail. Almost to want-it. Her Dawson pride sprang to the fore once again.

She stiffened the shoulders that had been drooping and gave a glittering smile. "I should be happy to play. I must warn you that my skill is only moderate. I try to make up for it with enthusiasm."

As she walked to the piano, she saw Mrs. Drummond-Burrell lean toward the Dowager and mumble something about a "pretty-mannered chit." Abby played a pair of airs and a ballad, singing along in her light, pretty voice. She forced herself not to recoil as Longford leaned across her to turn the pages of her music, allowing his arm to brush lightly against her breast.

She was hard pressed to stifle an urge to give them a rousing chorus of "Yankee Doodle."

The tea tray was brought in, and Abby offered to pour. She did so with an acceptable degree of grace. When the guests finally rose to leave, she bade them a pleasant goodnight. She even earned a rather pleased nod from the Dowager before she mounted the stairs. She had acquitted herself beautifully.

She went to bed with a raging headache.

Chapter Nineteen

By the day of the Jersey Ball, the formal opening of the 1819 London Season, Abby was in a sad state indeed. She had not slept truly well since her arrival at Longford House. It was an unusual condition. How amazed her Aunt Sylvia would be, and how she would tease about "bride's nerves."

Abby tried to convince herself that that was all it was. Just nerves. Everything was so new, so different.

Charles had tried to warn her, to tell her there would be difficulties. She had blithely pooh-poohed the notion that anything about her new life in London could be less than comfortable, less than brilliant, less than completely perfect.

She looked around the bedchamber where she had been ordered to rest, reclining on a chaise in the acceptably languid fashion—a *very* uncomfortable pose, she found, that would require practice to look natural. She was thinking. How could she be so dissatisfied? What an unaccountable girl she must be. For here was everything she'd longed for since she was old enough to know that there was a London.

It was true that things were very different. Her room in the sprawling Pennsylvania farmhouse had been simple and uncluttered, with good if not elegant furnishings and hangings of flowered chintz. Light streamed everywhere. It had not a bit of the grandeur and opulence of this bedchamber.

But in this house that any sane girl would give her eye-teeth to become mistress of, Abby felt . . . she had to struggle for the right word. Yes, it was stuffed. She felt *stuffed*, as though a taxidermist had just completed her, rigged her out in stiff brocade and point lace, and placed her in the perfect position, the finishing touch in a tableau of elegance.

She couldn't help wondering what Charles would think of the picture. She didn't look at all the same with her feathery hairstyle and her new gowns.

Yes, everything was certainly different. But wasn't that precisely what she had wanted, what she had sailed over three thousand miles to achieve? She was being ridiculous to complain. Once she was comfortably adjusted to her new home and status, when she had made friends and carved a place for herself in the *ton*, she would be perfectly happy here. She *would*.

A scratching at the door pulled her from her circling thoughts. A moment later Betsey bounced in, steady, loyal, unchanging Betsey, an anchor in a swirling sea of change. She began chattering the moment her foot crossed the threshold.

"Sure hope I don't get too fat and lazy in this here England, Missy Abby."

"You, Bets? Lazy? Not possible," said Abby with a laugh.

"Well, one of the parlor maids, that Mary, jest told me quiet-like that I oughtn't to tend your fire. Nor I oughtn't to wipe up a spill, neither, nor even sweep out my own room. Did you ever?" She flitted about the room putting away some freshly pressed handkerchiefs and petticoats. "She says I'm to call a chambermaid for such jobs, for I'm a proper lady's maid and a lady's maid never does such low stuff."

Surprised though she was, and even a bit put off by such inefficiency, Betsey was terribly proud of her new status. "Why, do you know, Missy Abby, I'm not even to make up my own bed of a morning! Her ladyship's Winkle's even got her *own* helper to do the pressing and mending and suchlike." The bright-brown eyes closed a moment at the wonder of it. "When you get to be Countess, d'you s'pose I'll have one too?"

"I shall see to it," said Abby in her most regal manner,

her nose held high in the air. The effect was instantly spoiled by a burst of giggles. Betsey, the newfound dignity of a proper lady's maid forgotten, giggled with her.

If the last week or so had been difficult for Abigail, it had been hell for Charles. But it was not the same hell he had expected London to be.

He had dreaded the painful memories London would bring. He feared he would see Daisy's face around every corner, hear her light laugh with every breath of the English wind. He had braced himself for the pain.

How surprised he was then to realize he could scarce remember what Daisy looked like. She had been blond, he knew, and dimpled, with rosy cheeks. She had had blue eyes with long, golden lashes. Yes, he remembered all that clearly.

But when he tried to put the elements together in his mind, to conjure up a picture of the whole, the face that hovered before his mind's eye was a totally different construction. High cheekbones and a pointed chin. Coal-black lashes shading eyes like emeralds. A pair of lips sweeter than Daisy Hollings's could ever be.

It was not his love for Daisy that haunted him now. He laughed at the very notion of it, for the emotion was such a pale, shadowy reflection of what he felt for Abigail Dawson.

He could not run away this time. Difficult as it was to be near her, it would be impossible to stay away. She was like a sore tooth that he couldn't avoid sticking his tongue into to see if the pain was still there. It always was.

Some sort of painkiller was in order. Very much in the spirit of joining that which cannot be beat, Charles began to throw himself into the very sort of activity he had actively scorned for so long. He looked up old acquaintances and began joining in their revels. He sparred at Jackson's Saloon until his arms felt they would fall off, then he went shooting at Manton's or driving his new sporting curricle, with its team of perfectly matched greys, in the Row of an afternoon.

He posted huge sums on the betting books at Tattersall's and sat up till the small hours at Brook's or Watier's where the wine was good and the play was deep. Charles indulged freely in both.

There was more than a little desperation to all this activity. There must be some reason, he thought, why such pursuits were so popular with his cronies. Charles was looking for a reason, any reason, to smile again.

As the Longford carriage, an elaborate affair in antique style with the Earl's arms emblazoned on the sides, drew up before Jersey House, Abigail received the last of a long string of instructions and admonitions from Lady Longford.

"And you are to speak to *no one* without an introduction from me or from Longford. Sally Jersey is the highest stickler about Almack's. But where her own parties are concerned, she shows a deploringly catholic taste in whom she invites. I rather think she likes to shock. I am told she once invited one of Jersey's *chére amies* to her Christmas masquerade, though that does seem a bit much even for Sally."

Abby hardly heard her. She was too wrapped up in the scene outside the carriage. Flambeaux lit the front of Jersey House as if it were day. A plush red carpet covered the pavement from curb to door. Half a dozen liveried footmen stood at attention ready to assist with a carriage door or a lady's train or anything else that might need dealing with.

Golden light flowed from every window, carrying with it the soft lilt of music and the sound of well-bred laughter. It was all just as Abby had imagined it would be, and she was entranced.

She was also nervous.

Never had she felt so unsure of herself. She was uncomfortable in her gown, an elaborate concoction of Berlin silk and satin in jonquil yellow threaded heavily with gold. The dress had no movement to it and made Abby feel gauche instead of graceful. The profusion of orange silk flowers and green velvet leaves sprinkled across her bosom made her feel like a walking garden instead of the wood nymph she longed to resemble.

She tried to take pleasure in the fact that the gown was

a perfect rendering of the most fashionable gown in *Mr. Ackermann's Repository* for the month of March. The attempt was not entirely successful.

Unthinkingly, she fingered the pearl choker at her throat and found comfort and reassurance there. It brought memories of her father, and a real, if rather wan, smile crossed her face. Nothing second best for Abigail Dawson, she could almost hear him saying. If only Poppa could see her now. How proud he would be!

They were helped from the carriage and into the house, and Abby blinked in the light from a hundred candles. They climbed the mahogany staircase toward the ballroom.

It seemed like a mountain to Abby, but they reached the top at last. The butler intoned, "His lordship the Earl of Longford, her ladyship the Dowager Countess of Longford, Miss Abigail Dawson."

The buzz of conversation died on a hundred lips. Every head in the vast room turned to look at the disgustingly wealthy American chit that the Rake of London had managed to snare.

A youngish, handsome woman with brown hair and sparkling eyes fluttered up to them, gold gauze draperies billowing after her. "Longford, you scamp!" cried Sarah, Countess of Jersey, with a musical laugh. She tapped him playfully with a gold lace fan. It had been several years since Reginald Olney, Earl of Longford, had been welcome in her home. But she could forgive him almost anything, certainly something so small as a black reputation, for allowing her such a coup as being the first to introduce Miss Abigail Dawson to London Society. "Why did you not tell me what a pretty thing your American was?"

"I've no wish to encourage the competition, Sally," he drawled. Abby made a deep curtsy to the Countess, as graceful a one as her stiff gown would allow. Lady Jersey tinkled a laugh at the Earl. "Since when have you worried about the competition, Longford?" To Abby she said, "I hope you realize, my dear, that you have captured the greatest rogue in all London, with a string of conquests behind him." Her smile was arch, and her laugh was brittle, a perfect example of the art Charles had tried to instill in Abby. But behind the lady's eyes there seemed to lurk something very like sympathy. Of course that was ridiculous, Abby told herself. How could anyone possibly feel sorry for her? They were far more likely to envy her.

Charles Lydiard had just accepted a glass of champagne from a passing footman when the Longford party made its entrance. He froze, drank his champagne in one gulp, then exchanged the empty glass for a full one. He managed to sip this one more slowly, which was just as well. He'd already had more than was his custom.

He couldn't think why he had come to this deuced ball. He'd been afraid Abigail would be here. No, he had *known* she would be here. And the knowledge had made him come.

So here he was, full of champagne and melancholy. And here was Longford with his oily smile that was still able to bring a flush of anger and humiliation to Charles's face.

And here was Abby.

Charles saw at once that his lessons had not been entirely in vain. He had tried to destroy her spirit, her bubbling eagerness for life, and he had obviously done the trick. Gone was the impish smile, the impulsive laugh, gone all trace of the coltish awkwardness that so charmed him. He was looking at a well-turned-out and elegant young lady, the picture of sophistication. The look in her eyes would seem to most of the company one of fashionable *ennui*, with no trace of emotion.

But Charles knew better. He looked beneath the surface calm of the deep-green pools that were her eyes and saw a wariness like that of a small furry animal that stands very still in the bushes to take full advantage of its protective coloration while knowing full well its true helplessness.

The girl had lost artlessness—or rather had had it ripped from her—but had not yet learned artifice. That tenderness that she so easily called up in Charles welled and threatened to spill over as he looked at her.

He gulped the dregs of his champagne and disappeared into the cardroom.

Chapter Twenty

Abby saw Charles as soon as she entered the room, almost as though his very presence were a magnet for her eyes. She hadn't expected to find the likes of a mere Charles Lydiard at such a *tonnish* affair. Her already shaky equilibrium was threatened at sight of him. What the devil was he doing here?

She recalled Lady Longford's rather snide remarks about the Countess of Jersey's odd taste in friends. She supposed it might amuse the Countess to invite the penniless clerk of a shipping line to have a taste of the pleasures he usually could not afford. Well, perhaps not penniless. Charles was quite elegantly dressed, and he did know a great deal about the *ton*. It was clear that he had mixed with them in the past.

But Abby had been in London long enough to know the low opinion that members of the *ton* held of anyone engaged in "trade."

Abby sincerely wished that Lady Jersey were a bit less Republican in her choice of friends.

A wave of pure sadness swept over Abby as she saw Charles walk away from her. But it was replaced almost at once by an even stronger wave of pure anger. Turn his back on her, would he? Who did he think he was? She was the future Countess of Longford. She was Rupert Dawson's daughter. She would show him!

She was not precisely sure *what* she would show him. Or how. But she would do it nonetheless.

The ballroom was a fantasy, all draped in celestial blue silk and littered with a million white flowers. The scents of orange blossom, apple blossom, rosebud, and honey-suckle mingled with the heavier perfumes of the more exotic feminine flowers draped in petals of sarcenet and silk, tissue faille and gauze in every color of the rainbow.

A country dance was struck up, and Longford led Abby onto the floor. She was relieved that it was a simple dance, for she could still feel dozens of eyes watching her, judging her, and probably finding her wanting.

The pair of them must be quite an eyeful, she thought, as Longford took her down the dance. He was garbed in a plum-colored coat of cut velvet heavily laced with gold. His waistcoat glittered with diamond buttons—or paste buttons cunningly made to resemble diamonds, but Abby was not to know that—and his dancing pumps sported buckles of the same. His coiffed and pomaded hair gleamed in the candlelight, and he fairly reeked of the musk scent favored by the Prince Regent.

"You look a very tantalizing morsel this evening, my dear," he said in that oozing voice she was coming to loathe.

She tried to laugh off the absurd comment. "A tantalizing morsel, my lord? You make me sound like a piece of fruit."

He looked down at her through hooded eyes. "Yes," he drawled. "A nice juicy plum, I should think. And one ripe for plucking or I miss my guess." She gave a shocked stare and stumbled over her steps. He reached out a hand to steady her. When she had regained her balance, he did not immediately release her. "And I promise you shall very much enjoy being plucked. I will see to that."

The intensity in his watery blue eyes almost frightened her. She looked away only to catch the equally intense gaze of Charles upon her.

She felt herself grow pink. "I cannot think this a proper conversation for a ballroom, sir."

"True," Longford agreed with a lascivious look. "Perhaps we might find a more suitable place to discuss it. Your bedchamber perhaps? Tonight?"

The music ended, and, as she sank into a curtsy, she whispered, "I think we shall discuss it, if at all, my lord, after our wedding."

He bowed low and murmured in her ear, "Oh, but we shall do very much more than discuss it then, my plum. That I promise you."

She had never been so glad to have a dance end. She was even relieved by the hordes of people crowding about her for a closer look at "the American chit." She felt like some exotic bird in a menagerie, but even that was preferable to one more minute of conversation with her betrothed.

She heard him chuckle a throaty chuckle as she was led back onto the floor, and she shivered despite the heat of the overcrowded room.

Her next partner was a Sir Richard Something-or-Other—his drawl made him all but impossible to understand—and he was an awesome sight. He was a friend of Longford's and outdid even the Earl in sartorial splendor.

Sir Richard was dressed in an orange satin evening coat with balloon sleeves, skin-tight breeches of vermilion velvet which precluded much bending, and a heavily embroidered waistcoat. Knots of ribbons adorned his knees, fobs and seals by the score hung at his waist, and there were rings on his fingers. Abby wondered idly if there were bells on his toes inside his highly varnished dancing pumps.

"You are enjoying London," he said. It was less a question than a statement of irrefutable logic. He could not imagine anyone's *not* enjoying London.

"I have seen little of it as yet. I hope to visit the British Museum soon, however."

"Whatever for?"

"Why, to see Lord Elgin's marbles. Their fame has spread even to America, you see."

"Elgin," stated Sir Richard. "Has his coats from Stultz. Don't suit him. Do better to go to Weston. Ain't got the figure for a Stultz."

"I see," said Abby, stifling a giggle. They moved apart in the dance then, and when they rejoined, Sir Richard was silent so long that Abby felt the need to say something. "Perhaps you can advise me, Sir Richard. I hope to subscribe to one of the lending libraries. Which would you recommend?"

"Hookham's," he said immediately. "No one goes to Richardson's anymore. Wouldn't want to be seen there."

"Hookham's. Have they Mr. Scott's latest works, do you know?"

"Scott! Humph! Fellow doesn't know merino from kersey. Wears abominable trousers. Better stick to Byron. At least the fellow knows how to rig himself out."

Abby was quickly learning that Sir Richard's ruling passion in life was Fashion; to be known as a Man of Fashion was his one goal and only desire. He studied *The Gentleman's Magazine* religiously, carefully noting every minor nuance of fashion.

He pledged his credit at all the most fashionable shops, appeared at the most fashionable parties, and drove a most fashionable equipage in the park at the fashionable hour of five. He had been known to spend a whole morning deciding on which style of button should finish a new coat or whether an emerald or a sapphire should nestle in the folds of his exquisitely tied neckcloth.

But even Abby recognized that though his devotion to Fashion was complete, he was totally lacking in the one essential necessary to the truly fashionable gentleman. Sir Richard had not a speck of taste.

If yellow trousers were in vogue, his were the most vivid and sickening shade imaginable. When large buttons began to appear, his took on the dimension of saucers. And when Lord Byron had begun showing the slightest puff to the caps of his sleeves, Sir Richard's ballooned outward and upward until they threatened to make him an aviator if only he would fill them with some of the hot air he was continually spouting on every "fashionable" topic.

"Go to Bandon for parasols," he advised. "Got a way with a ruffle, Bandon. Trente for gloves. Makes the only ones worth wearing."

"Mmm," replied Abby for lack of anything more fashionable to say.

"So, you're American," he then said apropos of nothing that had gone before.

Choking back a giggle, she said, "Why, yes."

"Knew an American fellow once. Dressed like a peasant. Or a Republican. Comes to the same thing. Broadcloth and cotton. Dullest fellow you ever saw. But then, needn't tell you. You know what Americans are.''

"Have you met a great many Americans, Sir Richard?"

"Good heavens, no. Why should I want to do that? No, no. Wouldn't like it at all, I shouldn't wonder. Not good *ton*, Americans.''

"I see," she murmured through suddenly clenched teeth. It was lucky that the dance ended at that moment, for Abby turned and left the floor, leaving her partner to trail after her, thinking her very odd.

As she made her way back to Lady Longford, Abby's eyes covered the room almost involuntarily. But she saw no sign of Charles. She didn't care, she told herself sternly. She no longer needed him. Not at all.

Still, it was good to know that there was at least one person in the room who didn't care if Americans were bad *ton*. Also, it would be nice to have him observing her triumph. For bad *ton* or no, there could be no doubt that she was having a triumph. She was never without a partner, even if several of the gentlemen with whom she danced struck her as uninteresting in the extreme. The few who seemed to have a spark of humor or intelligence behind their eyes were deftly turned away by her ladyship. The rest, Lord Longford's dandy friends, spouted increasingly cloying compliments, blatant comments on her wealth, or vaguely disparaging remarks about Americans and how fortunate she was to be "out of all that."

Thanks to her many afternoons spent with Lady deForest in poring over the well-thumbed pages of her *Debrett's*, Abby knew almost more than she cared to know about the scores of people she made her curtsy to. She could have described his lordship of Greshington's coat of arms; she knew that Lady Drenton was half sister to the Duke of Favenham and sister-in-law to Lord Cholmonleigh; and she could state with accuracy that Lord Longford's title was older than Lord Petersham's, but not so old as Lord Jersey's.

"I hope you are enjoying my little party, Miss Dawson," said Lady Jersey during a lull in the dancing.

"Very much, my lady."

"I see you've had no lack of partners." There seemed to

be a spark of true warmth and humor in the woman's bright eyes, and Abby found herself liking the lady whom everyone called the Queen of Society. "But it occurs to me you might like to meet some young ladies." She gave Lady Longford an arch smile. "When you make your bow at Almack's you will want to have girlfriends to chatter with."

Almack's! Lady Jersey had said the magic word. The Dowager beamed approval upon Abby. If Lady Jersey gave her a voucher for Almack's, her position was assured. With a gracious and grateful nod from the Dowager, Lady Jersey led Abby across the room.

They approached a flower garden of young belles, all fluttering and laughing flutily and batting their lashes at the passing gentlemen. Each girl was a picture-perfect example of the *ton* belle. Their laughs were musical; their fans worked briskly. They were all elegant and fashionable, with perfect rosebud mouths and pert dimples in tea-rose cheeks. They all had golden ringlets.

Abby felt like a distinctly ugly duckling among such a bevy of swans. But she had so longed to meet some young ladies her own age. She badly needed a friend, someone she could really talk to.

She was doomed to disappointment. She quickly discovered that not one of the young ladies before her had a sensible idea in her head.

"My father, the Viscount, says . . ." began Miss Dunning's first sentence.

"My brother, the Earl, thinks . . ." was Lady Patricia's opening gambit.

"Well, my betrothed, the Marquis, expects . . ." were Miss Langston-Knowles's first words.

When they had done parroting the opinions of the various males in their lives, Abby asked politely, "And do you agree with the opinion of your betrothed, Miss Langston-Knowles?"

The sentence was greeted by dead silence and a sort of uncomprehending stare. Finally, the young lady in question replied, as though speaking to a rather dense child, "Well, of course I do."

"I see," said Abby with a sigh.

So much for the possibility of a mutually rewarding friendship with any of this lot, thought Abby, gratefully allowing herself to be led back onto the dance floor by some viscount or other.

Supper was eaten—through which she had to suffer more of Lord Longford's increasingly blatant innuendos—and a few guests had already taken their leave before Charles at last gave in and steeled himself for a dance with Abigail. He had been on the verge of leaving several times during the ball. He had spent few more miserable evenings in his life.

But he could see clearly the strain on Abby's face. He couldn't bear to leave her here alone without a single friend. True, she was exactly where she'd always wanted to be, perhaps even where she deserved to be. She was in the company of her noble betrothed. But he couldn't bring himself to abandon her entirely to her chosen fate.

Also he couldn't bring himself to take himself away from her.

So it was with a truly friendly, if slightly strained, smile that he solicited her hand for the quadrille.

"Why, thank you, Mr. Lydiard," she said with pleased surprise. "I should be honored."

The Dowager frowned after them as they took the floor. There was a look between those two she could not wholly approve. Still, she could not openly object to the girl dancing with someone as unexceptionable as Lydiard. He was Cumberley's heir, after all, well liked and respected by everyone even if he was not of Longford's set. But she would watch them with a wary eye.

They danced a few moments in silence, neither wanting to speak and break the spell of pure joy of being next to each other again. Whenever Charles's hand touched Abby's she felt its warmth flood through her and she felt somehow safer.

After a particularly complex movement of the dance, performed by Abby with flawless grace, Charles smiled down at her. "That was nicely done."

She returned the smile. "I thank you, sir. I had a good teacher."

"And I an apt pupil."

They danced some few minutes more in perfect charity with each other. Finally Charles spoke again. "No more whistling 'Yankee Doodle,' I trust?"

That seemed to give her pause, and it occurred to her with some surprise that not once since leaving the *Abby Anne* had she caught herself whistling or even humming softly to herself. She'd had no desire to do so. "Why, no," she said. "None at all. Does that please you?"

Oddly enough, it did not please him, though it was exactly how he had taught her to behave. He had loved her constant whistling. He felt guilty, as though he had helped to rob her of some vital part of herself. "Yes. Yes, of course," he said and put his thoughts to the dance.

When they came together again, Abby wanted desperately to say something clever, to hear his voice and see him smile. She sought for words. "How is your aunt? And your sister? I had hoped to see them again before this, but I haven't been allowed . . . that is, we have not been out visiting as yet."

"My aunt is well, but I'm afraid Sophie's come down with a nasty spring cold."

"Oh, I am sorry."

"Not half so sorry as she is, I'll wager, for you didn't have to miss the first ball of the Season. She was so determined to come she even got dressed, but her nose was still red as a cherry and clashed dreadfully with her new gown, so of course there was no question of putting in an appearance. But she'll be out and about by tomorrow, I daresay."

"Poor Sophie," said Abby, remembering how unlike the other young ladies she'd met this evening Sophie Lydiard was. She masked her surprise that a mere Miss Lydiard, daughter of nobody in particular, should have been invited in the first place. "And I'm sure you teased her about it unmercifully, Charles," she said.

"Of course. It is a brother's primary function, don't you know."

"Oh, male cousins do it just as well, I assure you."

How pleasant it was to banter with him as they had done those first golden days aboard the ship. They circled in the *grande ronde*, and she studied him with a sidelong glance. He certainly looked handsome. His coat of midnight blue was of the finest wool over a white piqué waistcoat and pearl-gray evening breeches. The blue of his coat turned his eyes the color of the endless ocean. She felt almost faint at the effect just looking at him could have on her.

She frowned. She was acting like a silly girl, as bad as her cousin Pru! It was Longford who was the embodiment of her dreams, in his elegant velvets and satins, with his flowery compliments and, more important, his ability to make her a countess. After all, who would a plain old Mrs. Lydiard be? No one.

Apparently he had also been thinking as they circled the floor. He was frowning as they moved together in the *glissé*. "So, you are a success," he said.

"Am I?" she asked, reacting to the sudden aloofness in his tone.

"Oh yes. Anyone can see it. If you're not careful, you'll find yourself invited to Carlton House before the month is out."

"And I shall go," she said more coldly than before.

"And make your bow to our illustrious Regent?"

"Of course. But I shouldn't have thought *you* would care about such stuff. It hardly seems in your style."

He smiled again, but this time the smile was a sardonic one. "Spoken like a true lady of the *ton*, my dear. Though it would come off better with a haughty snap of your fan for punctuation."

"Oh!" she exclaimed, snapping her fan in exasperation before she could stop herself. Chagrined at the move, she made an elaborate show of opening it again, daintily fanning her flushed face, and sank into a curtsy as the music ended.

He chuckled. It was not a pleasant sound. "No temper, please, my dear," he said softly as he bowed to her.

Through her teeth, she muttered, "I think you are hateful," before turning on her heel and leaving him in the middle of the floor.

It was not much later that Abby gratefully sank back

onto the squabs of the carriage for the short ride back to Longford House. The Dowager chattered her pleasure at their success, but the words washed over Abby. Her feet hurt; her head hurt. It seemed that her very *mind* hurt.

She was grateful that Longford had elected not to return to Piccadilly with them. He'd gone on to one of his clubs, undoubtedly to lose some of Rupert Dawson's money at the tables. But he would be home eventually.

After Betsey had helped Abby into a soft cotton nightshift, tucked her up in bed, and left the room, Abby arose again. She locked her door.

There had been something in his lordship's tone and looks all evening that told her it might be a good idea.

Chapter Twenty-one

It had well and truly begun!

The morning after the ball brought a veritable flood of invitations to Longford House. To Abby it seemed unbelievable, as though everyone and his wife were giving a party. Surely they would all be so busy hosting that no one would be left to attend as guests.

The Dowager attacked the pile with the thoroughness of a general planning a campaign. A calendar had been drawn up, each day marked off into blocks of time. These she began filling in with the function or activity appropriate to the hour and to their station. Abby could only watch awestruck.

Venetian breakfasts would precede afternoon musicales. The occasional ladies' tea—if the hostess happened to be *very* important—was also allowed, though most late afternoons were reserved for promenading in the park in the required fashionable ensemble before changing for the evening's festivities.

The Duchess of Clives was having a ridotto; Lady Berwick requested their presence at a masked ball. Routs by the score were planned. Two French galas and a dozen *fétes* were to be held. And Abby was invited to them all. Obviously being a member of the *ton* was full-time employment.

The Dowager was pleased. "It is not every matron of the *ton* who could introduce the daughter of a mere ship-builder without a qualm," she said with supreme arrogance. "*And*, bring it off so splendidly. But I saw at once last evening that I had done the trick."

Abby bit her tongue. It could serve no purpose to intimate that perhaps she'd had a hand in her own success. Perhaps she had not. Perhaps no one cared a whit about her except for the fact that she would soon be Countess of Longford. It was clear from their behavior that none of them cared what sort of person she was, how she felt about things, or whether she had a mind.

Charles had cared, once. During their early days at sea he had seemed to delight in getting to know her as she had him. But even Charles didn't wish to know Abby, the real Abby, anymore.

"Yes," Lady Longford mused, "I think I may rest easy on that head. Now if only Longford will agree to stop . . ." She bit off her words, looked briefly guilty, and went on with a little wave of one parchment-skinned hand. "That is neither here nor there. As long as you do exactly as I say, we shall come out all right."

For no particular reason Abby could name, she balked at that. She was beginning to face a somewhat startling and unattractive truth about herself. Or rather a pair of truths, and they didn't suit each other well. The first was that she had a temper. The second was that she was more than a little stubborn.

Abby had always thought of herself as easy-mannered, a basically obedient girl who liked to please. But so seldom in her young life had things turned out less than pleasantly, so infrequent were the occasions when man and fate seemed to conspire against her, that she'd had no idea she could be such a melancholy, unpleasant person when things did not turn out just so. It was a lowering realization.

And the irony of it was that things *had* turned out just so. Everything she'd ever wanted was pouring into her lap. All the elegance, the status, the parties and gowns and titled friends. She'd become a part of the elite world she'd always sought to join.

What an unaccountable girl she was! She would stop this mooning this instant and enjoy the miracle that had come her way. Sipping at her breakfast tea, she plastered a bright smile on her face and asked, "What are we to do today, ma'am?"

"There are calls we must pay," said Lady Longford, idly shuffling through the pile of invitations. "If your position is to be quickly cemented, you must be seen in the most important drawing rooms and other gathering places of the *ton*. This afternoon we shall make an appearance at Hookham's, where you can pick up a copy of Byron's latest scribblings. Oh, don't worry. You needn't actually read them. Only scan a page or two so you may speak of them if necessary. This afternoon Longford will drive you in the park. You can wear the green-striped mull with the ocher spencer. And the coal-scuttle bonnet. And do not forget your parasol. That horrid tan is finally beginning to fade."

"Yes, ma'am," said Abby. She really must try to be cooperative.

"Tonight we dine at Burlington House. Tomorrow is the theatre with the Drummond-Burrells. Later in the week, we shall go to the opera. That will be nearly as important as Sally's ball, for everyone will be there. Then . . . let me see." She read some more invitations. "An outing to Richmond with Miss Dunning and her friends. Unexceptionable. Dinner with the Duke and Duchess of Strall. We must accept that one, certainly. Tea with Lady deForest. DeForest? Who on earth is that?"

Abby brightened. "Oh, has she invited me to tea? How kind of her. I met her on the ship coming over."

"Hmmm. DeForest," mused Lady Longford, trying to place the woman in her proper niche.

"She was a Cumfrey, ma'am."

"A Cumfrey? Ah yes. She'd be the younger girl. Bettina? No, Beatrice. Beatrice Cumfrey. A silly goose, as I recall. Should have done much better for herself than a baronet. Well, we certainly shall not have tea with her."

"Whyever not, ma'am? I should like to see her again. She and Sir Geoffrey were very kind to me."

"Well, of course they were. If you insist, we might have her here one day next month. With several other ladies, of course. It wouldn't do to distinguish her too far. Normally, she could never hope to fly so high. An amazing piece of luck for her that she sailed on that particular ship."

Abby was piqued, but she did not press the subject. "If we are to make calls today, I should like to stop at Stevens's Hotel. I should have done so before." The Dowager stared. "The Stackpooles are stopping there. They were on the ship as well."

"Stackpoole?" said Lady Longford in a withering tone.

"Yes, ma'am. He is an import merchant from Boston. We became such good friends." She slathered a scone with butter and bit into it with relish. "Of course, one can hardly help becoming fast friends in such close quarters."

"One could certainly try."

"They're a very good sort of people. I look forward to seeing them."

"Out of the question," said the Dowager, patting her unsmiling lips with a linen napkin. "It wouldn't do to encourage their sort."

"What sort is that, ma'am?"

"Tradesmen, of course."

"My father is a tradesman."

"You needn't remind me of the fact. I am uncomfortably aware of it."

It was with difficulty that Abby kept a rein on her newfound temper. "I should like to visit the Stackpooles, ma'am, and I shall do so. It is only common courtesy." She spoke quietly but with determination.

The old woman studied her a moment. The girl was not so easily cowed as she should be. Clearly, she had been given far too much American freedom. Something must be done about it. But later. "Very well," she said coldly.

"You may call one morning. Early. It is not likely that anyone of consequence will know them, after all. Now go upstairs and change. The carriage will be ready in half an hour. Wear the red-and-yellow lampas walking gown with the lustring pelisse. Orange gloves. The yellow straw poke with the orange plumes." She rose from the table, magisterial even in a loose grey morning gown, and swept from the room.

The pace of activity accelerated at an incredible rate. Much as Abby had hated being cooped up in Longford House, she now found herself wishing for an hour, a minute even, to catch her breath. When she wasn't being rushed to this dinner or that party, she was being driven in the park by some sanctioned gentleman or receiving callers at Longford House. Or she was changing clothes.

Much as she loved having a huge, fashionable wardrobe, Abby was appalled at the amount of time she must spend each day in dressing, re-dressing, then dressing yet again. She couldn't wear the same gown to receive callers that she'd worn to eat breakfast. If she was to go out, she must put on a walking dress, then change into a driving habit for the Promenade. Finally, there was dressing for the evening, which seldom took under an hour what with all the petticoats, underskirts, overskirts, draped bodices, pins, hooks, tapes, and buttons. It seemed somehow decadent.

Her one true luxury was her ride in the park, the only time of the day she truly felt like herself. Although it meant yet another change of costume, she never missed a morning. Jacob had found himself an excellent gelding and happily accompanied her each day for a rousing gallop. Clearly, neither Lady Longford nor her grandson approved of the exercise, but they could do nothing to stop it.

If she entered the park each morning in some hopes of seeing Charles there, she did not admit it even to herself. Neither would she acknowledge that the dissipation of her hopeful mood as she headed home owed anything to the fact that he had not appeared.

The evening arrived when they were to attend the Italian Opera. Abby was rigged out in her most elaborate ensemble, a fanciful construction of melon-colored

marocain with an overskirt of lace. The whole was deco-
rated with French beading and gold floss. The pineapple
pattern around the hem was heavily embroidered in gold
threads. She wore silk slippers with rosettes of gold tissue. Her shawl was gold. Her fan was gold. Her headdress
was adorned with a pair of gilded roses and a gold-tipped
plume. She felt like King Midas's daughter.

The Royal Opera House was an awesome sight, and
Abby managed to forget herself in enjoyment of the splendor. The *créme de la créme* of English Society frequented
these hallowed halls. That much was clear. Their silks and
their jewels and their well-bred smiles fluttered all around
her.

Down in the pit were those who could afford a ticket
but not a subscription box, the newly emerging middle
classes, ogling the nobility and imagining the day when
they too would rise above the pit. There also were the
young gentlemen who wanted a closer look at the
singers—and the legs of the pretty opera dancers—than
the boxes could provide.

Among their numbers, Abby spied Ronald Dimmont.
His neckcloth had grown appreciably since he had touched
English soil, and it was stiff with starch. It was only with
difficulty that he studied the boxes through an enormous
quizzing glass. He spotted Abby and broke into a genuine
boyish smile before recalling himself and replacing it with
a vaguely bored look. He favored her with a grave bow of
recognition. She chuckled and nodded gravely in return.

Everyone seemed to be looking at everyone else, studying, judging, calculating the cost of a gown, the value of a
necklace. Many of them eyed Abby. They looked, they
took in every detail of her toilette and her behavior, they
nodded, then they let their gazes move on.

One pair of eyes, however, did not move on. Abby felt
the power of the gaze and turned to see a stunningly beautiful young woman staring at her. She sat in a box directly
opposite to the Longfords', and she was surrounded by a
sea of gentlemen. It was easy to see why.

Her hair was the color of a newly minted guinea and was
swept onto her head with *élan*. Her voluptuous figure was
unhidden by her gown of deep-rose *mousseline de soie*, so

low-cut as to leave bare an impressive expanse of a generous bosom and so clinging as to show clearly that the rest of her was just as alluring. She sparkled all over with diamonds, at her throat and her wrists, in her hair, even sewn onto her gown. The eyes studying Abby were a sparkling blue.

When Abby looked at her the woman smiled. It was a genuine smile, not the pinched movement of muscles that she usually got from women of the *ton*. Had they met before? Abby wondered. Surely she would have remembered. But then she had met so many people the past few days. She didn't wish to offend, so she smiled in return and nodded her head in greeting.

"Abigail!" hissed the Dowager.

"Ma'am?"

"You are *not* to acknowledge such people. Ever!"

"But who is she, ma'am? Do you know her?"

"Certainly not!"

Longford, who was standing behind Abby, chuckled. "Oh, everyone knows Desirée, Grandmama, though I'll grant you some few wish they didn't. Why, she's the tastiest little barque of frailty in all London, Abigail."

"Barque of . . ." began Abby uncomprehendingly.

"Reginald!" snapped the Dowager. "You will restrain yourself. Please to remember what we are trying to accomplish here."

"Oh, I remember, Grandmama. You are trying to make me respectable, which is a great bore. Besides, no one can hear. I shouldn't like to be leg-shackled to a milk-and-water miss who faints at the mere sight of a lady of the evening. Particularly such a fetching one as Desirée." He laid a hand on Abby's shoulder and squeezed. She clenched her teeth. "Abigail is made of sterner stuff, are you not, my dear? Why, you may even wish to learn a few tricks from one of the sisterhood. I know well how anxious you are to please your future husband." Abby was shocked by the malicious delight of his tone. He grinned and went on, "And Desirée has many tricks to teach, I can assure you."

"That will be quite enough, Reginald," hissed the Dowager.

Luckily, the opera was about to begin. As the first

notes of the overture were heard, Abby forced her attention to the stage. Lord Longford took the seat beside her but left his hand on her bare shoulder, one finger idly stroking her skin as if claiming it. Her eyes slid once more to the opposite box. Desiree was still watching her. The beautiful eyes flicked from Abby to Longford and back again. An intense, speculative look had overtaken them.

The opera had begun when Charles Lydiard ushered his aunt and his sister into their box. He had actually been looking forward to the evening, for he was fond of music, and Catalani, the ruling queen of sopranos, was singing. As it was, he heard but little of the superbly sung first act. One of the first sights to catch his eye was Abigail seated in a box to his right. With her was her betrothed touching her shoulder, stroking her, *manhandling* her in a way that enraged Charles. He turned away.

The next thing he saw, in a box to his left, was Daisy Hollings. There was no mistaking her, though she'd changed considerably. She now possessed a sophistication and an allure that would have been ludicrous in the green girl he'd met in the lending library. It was to be expected, of course. She was now a different person. He mustn't even think of her as Daisy anymore.

It had been Longford, one uncomfortable afternoon in Watier's, who'd told him of the change. "Calls herself Desirée now. Apt, don't you think?" he'd said, well aware that he was rubbing salt on old wounds and relishing it. "A perfect name for the most desired woman in London. You must call on her, Lydiard. Of course, Desi's terribly exclusive, but she might agree to see you. For the sake of old friendship." So saying, he'd laughed and walked away.

Well, Charles had no wish to speak to her, but neither did the sight of her cause him pain. She was laughing at something one of her many attendants had whispered in her ear, an engaging laugh. Perhaps she'd found what she wanted after all. She was decked out with splendor, and she did not look unhappy.

The same could not be said of Abby, and Charles wondered at it. She looked pale and drawn, as if she hadn't slept in a long time. She had none of the luster in her eyes that had first drawn him to her, the joy of life and eagerness for whatever it might bring. Instead, the green eyes, dulled somehow, stared at the stage from an unmoving countenance while his lordship stroked her shoulder. She might have been a statue.

Once, as the first act drew to a close, Abby turned. Her eyes met Charles's, and for one small moment neither was able to mask the hunger. Fortunately Longford did not notice that look. Lady Longford did not notice it. Neither did Sophia Lydiard nor her aunt. It was intense but fleeting.

But one person in the huge opera house saw the look quite clearly and read it quite clearly, brief though it was. The lovely Desirée, née Daisy Hollings, saw it, and she actually allowed a frown to mar the perfection of her alabaster brow.

Chapter Twenty-two

By careful management, Charles avoided speaking to Abigail at the Opera. But he did not sleep well that night. He could not banish that pale, drawn face, the strain evident in every look, from his thoughts. Clearly Abby, despite the seeming fulfillment of her every dream, was not happy. He had to know why.

And so next morning very early he mounted the gallant Pegasus and headed into the park. His instincts were not wrong. It wasn't five minutes before he saw Abby riding hell-for-leather across the green. Jacob was right behind her.

Charles was determined that for once he would not snipe at her. He could guess from her look the previous

evening that she badly needed a friend. It was not the role
he wished to play, God knew, but it seemed to be the only
one available. He would try to fill it.

She was approaching from an oblique angle and had not
yet seen him. Charles spurred Pegasus onto a parallel
course. She saw him then, noticed his grin of challenge,
and smiled. By silent agreement a race was on.

Clods of turf flew up from the pounding hooves as the
blood fairly flew through their veins. It was clear that neither of the great stallions liked to lose. Neither did either
of the riders. Jacob began to trail, unable to keep up the
spanking pace they set, but his white grin showed a determination to stick with it all the same.

Hunched low over Mr. Adams's flying mane, Abby
smiled with pure joy. She hadn't felt so free or so exhila-
rated in weeks. Charles had never seen anyone ride like her,
certainly no woman. She seemed to become one with the
horse, who responded perfectly to her every subtle command. It was all Charles could do to stay with her, and as a
horseman Charles was seldom bested.

They raced for upward of two miles. Bright March sun
glinted off the auburn lights in Charles's hair and made
Abby's eyes glisten. A dog barked and joined in the chase
but was soon left in the stallions' dust.

The racing pair elicited more than a few stares from
early-morning strollers and riders. Some few were frankly
shocked; one or two were merely curious. But most were
filled with evident admiration for such a beautiful pair.

On they ran, and the horses remained nose to nose.
Clearly, neither was going to give in. Finally, again by
unspoken consent, they called it a draw and reined to a
breathless stop under a giant willow.

"Oh, Charles!" exclaimed Abby in a happy, breathy
voice. Her eyes were sparkling like jade; her cheeks glowed
from the exertion. She looked lovelier than Charles had
ever seen her. "That was superb! I haven't had a good race
in I don't know how long." The jade eyes twinkled. "And
it has been even longer since I failed to win one hands
down. I congratulate you."

"And I you. A splendid bit of horsemanship."

"Oh, my darling here is up to anything, aren't you,

love?'' she said, stroking Mr. Adams's glossy neck. "He's not even winded.''

"Well, I am,'' said Charles, climbing down from Pegasus. Jacob finally caught up with them. "Come. Let's walk a bit. Jacob can take the horses, can't you, Jacob?''

"That I will, Mr. Charles,'' said the groom with a smile. He liked Charles Lydiard very much. "You know, Mr. Charles,'' he said in a conspiratorial tone. "You was right 'bout that other filly. I give her head, but she ain't gone far. An' I don't think she will, neither. She ain't all that impressed by London folk.''

"I'm glad to hear it, Jacob. Betsey's a good girl.''

A sentimental smile replaced the groom's usual insouciant grin. "She sure is,'' he said softly.

"What are you two whispering about?'' said Abby.

Charles laughed. "Nothing of the slightest interest to a mere female, my dear.'' He gave Jacob a wink. Abby felt herself thrill to the endearment, no matter how common it might be in the lexicon of the *ton*. "Now come down,'' he finished and walked to her horse to help her dismount.

She looked down at him with an odd, questioning look, but only for a moment. "Yes, all right,'' she said.

She rested her hands on his broad shoulders, and his fingers slid around her tiny waist. A jolt went through him, and he almost pulled back like someone burned. But he did not. In fact, he wanted never to let go of her.

He lifted her lightly to the ground. She scarce weighed anything at all, he thought. For a moment, they just stood there, touching each other and looking at each other and trying to read each other's thoughts. If they could have done so, they would both have read the same message: Why cannot the world just go away and leave only us two?

Jacob watched them with a very interested eye, speculating on the power of a look.

It was Charles who moved away first. He tried to keep his voice light when he spoke. "I was certain you'd be showing the effects of *ton* dinner parties by now, but I swear you'd blow away in a strong wind. Are they starving you?''

"Oh, dear me, no. I've never seen so much food in my

life. I cannot imagine what becomes of it all, for we cannot eat the half of it. I sometimes wonder if they aren't trying to fatten me up. Not that I should mind, of course. Rounded figures are all the vogue just now, and I look like a stick.''

''A very pretty stick,'' he murmured. By now she was used to the fulsome compliments of gentlemen of the *ton*. They had almost no effect on her. But those four little words, so simply said, were felt profoundly. Did he really think her pretty? Or was he just setting her up for another of his infamous snubs? ''Come then,'' he went on, breaking into her thoughts. ''Let's walk to the Dairy House and get you a glass of fresh milk. Very efficacious, I'm told, for the fattening up of young ladies who look like sticks.''

She laughed and took his arm, and they strolled off up the path. Jacob, following with the horses, looked vaguely disturbed as he watched them. He was slowly shaking his head.

They soon reached the thatched hut that was variously known as the Dairy House, the Cheesecake House, and Mrs. Richard's Cottage. The milk was fresh and cool. Abby, warm from her ride, drank it with relish.

''Ahhh,'' she sighed. ''How I have missed that particular treat. We never have milk at Longford House. I'm sure the Countess must think it very low-class. Chocolate is allowed, of course, and tea. And wine. A great deal of wine. But for a farm girl like me, nothing can ever be as delicious as a glass of fresh milk.'' She seemed not the least bit self-conscious about such an admission.

Charles smiled delightedly. Taking a clean white handkerchief from his pocket, he gently wiped a milky mustache from her upper lip. She laughed like a happy child. ''I'm sure my sisters would agree with you,'' he said. ''They like nothing better than to hang about the dairy yard at milking time. I shouldn't be too surprised to see Sophie milking the cows herself.''

''I was so pleased to see your sister was well enough to attend the opera last night. I did want to come and speak to her, but the Countess wouldn't let . . . that is, she thought we ought to remain in our box.'' She colored slightly and looked away.

Charles wondered at it. Why should Lady Longford keep such a tight rein on the girl that she wasn't even allowed to visit a totally unexceptionable girlfriend? He didn't like that.

"Did you enjoy the opera?" he asked.

"Oh yes, very much. Is not Catalani wonderful? And next Wednesday we are to go to Vauxhall for the gala. I have heard wonderful stories about it. Is it truly like a fairyland?"

"Very like," he said with only a touch of dryness. "Reality is locked out at the gates and only fantasy allowed within."

"Oh, Charles! I am not so very green as you think me, you know. Not anymore." Did he imagine a tiny note of wistfulness in her note? He made no reply.

The day was so fine they elected to sit on one of the rustic benches set about the Dairy House. They chatted of inconsequential things. They joked and laughed and generally reveled in being in each other's company. A young boy ran past rolling a hoop. Across the grass a nanny soothed a little girl whose doll had lost an arm. A pair of gentlemen tipped their hats as they rode past.

A dog came to sniff at their boots before loping off. Young lovers in servants' garb walked hand in hand. On a bench just to their left a man with a slouch hat pulled low on his head watched them. Or perhaps he was merely snoozing in the sun.

The trees were just beginning to glow with the first yellow-green of spring. Nearby a workman was scything the grass, and the heady new-mown smell was carried on the breeze that ruffled Abby's curls.

"It's so peaceful here," she said with a wistful smile. "I had nearly forgotten how that feels."

"Yes," mused Charles. "Being a part of the *ton* is many things, but it is seldom peaceful."

"You don't much like the *ton*, do you, Charles?" she asked as she had once before, a long time before.

"I don't much like it," he agreed.

"But why?"

This was dangerous ground. She was causing him to think of things—and people—he didn't wish to think of, not now when she was so near he could hear her breathe, feel her warmth. He didn't want to think of the *ton* or of Longford. He didn't want to think that this delightful girl would soon be married to that rogue. He could feel the old bitterness clutching at him and tried to push it away.

"Look there," he exclaimed to change the subject. "Isn't that Lady Berwick's carriage?"

"Oh Lord!" said Abby, reaching up to straighten her hat. "She and the Countess are bosom bows. I hope she didn't see us racing, or I'm in for a horrid scold. I had better be going in any case, or I shall be scolded for being late for breakfast."

They rose and started toward the horses. "Does she scold you often?" Charles asked.

"Oh yes," said Abby, but she laughed. "Nearly as often as you do, Charles. I am sure she finds me just as hopeless, too. She does not approve of me at all, you know. She would much rather I were a little mouse who only said 'Yes, my lady,' and 'No, my lady,' and 'Whatever you say, my lady.' I cannot think why, for then I should be a dead bore. Surely Lord Longford couldn't want such a boring creature for a wife. Would you?"

The words were out before she could stop them, though she immediately wished she had bitten her tongue instead.

"I've no idea what Longford wishes in a wife," he said through clenched teeth. All his joy in the morning had fled.

Abby hurried back to the original subject, for she could feel the conversation degenerating. Charles was no longer smiling. "I do try to please her. And the other ladies I meet as well. But I seldom seem to manage it. Oh, of course they do not scold me. They are all terribly proper." She mugged like a Society matron and laughed. But her face quickly became serious again. "But there seems to be so little warmth in them. I cannot think they really like me."

"Did I not warn you that liking has little to do with the *ton?* One doesn't choose one's friends on the basis of liking but on relative position and how one's standing may be enhanced by the relationship."

She wondered again at the bitterness he could not keep

from his voice. Was it because he had no position himself and so was not himself in demand? That seemed out of character for Charles. ''Why must you make everything and everyone out to be so cold-blooded, Charles? Surely true friendship, warmth of feeling, and mutual affection must count for something, even in the *ton*.''

''Do they?'' he snapped, and his black scowl, edged with contempt, overtook his face. ''And you, Abigail? Do those lovely attributes count with you? Is it *true friendship* with Sally Jersey that bought you a voucher to Almack's? Is it *warmth of feeling* that has everyone in London gossiping about Longford's rich American prize? Is it *mutual affection* that brought about your engagement to the man in the first place?'' He spat the words at her. ''Really, I had not thought even you could be such a hypocrite.''

She reeled from the verbal assault. To cover her confusion and her hurt, she motioned for Jacob to help her mount. The action gave her the moment she needed to blink back the hot tears gathering in her eyes. When she could speak, her voice was low and even. ''I do not know what I have done, Charles, that you should hate me so.''

''Hate you?'' he muttered, stunned by his own hasty words as much as he was wrenched by the hurt in her eyes, the hurt he had put there. ''But I . . .''

''But since you so obviously find my ideas, and no doubt my company, distasteful, I shall bid you good morning.''

She wheeled her giant horse and, calling to Jacob to follow, headed for Piccadilly, leaving her erstwhile lover in her dust.

Jacob, waiting a moment to stare at Charles in frustration, shook his head and said, ''I think you gotta be 'bout the stupidest man on God's green earth, Mr. Charles.'' Then he disappeared after his mistress.

Charles sat frozen on Pegasus looking for all the world like an equestrian statue. He stared after her for the longest time, the words ''Hate you?'' reverberating in his brain. Much as he might wish to, hard as he might try to, he knew he could never hate Abigail Dawson. Not when he loved her so much he thought he'd die of it.

He slowly turned his horse toward home, feeling a

deeper despair than he had ever known and looking like the very picture of the dejected lover.

He hadn't seen the man in the slouch hat stir himself and follow them from the Dairy House. He hadn't seen him watching them with great intensity. And he didn't see him now turn toward Piccadilly. If he had, he would have thought nothing of it.

Chapter Twenty-three

Abby wanted nothing more than to run to her room and hide when she got back to Longford House. She was not given that luxury. Crowther lay in wait in the entry hall, effectively cutting her escape.

"Her ladyship awaits you in the breakfast room, Miss," he said. His tone made it clear the summons was not to be ignored.

"Thank you, Crowther," she sighed, taking off her hat and gloves. She stopped to smooth her ruffled curls before the hall mirror and then entered the breakfast room.

"At last," said the Dowager, looking up from the remnants of her meal. "I must say, Abigail, these morning jaunts of yours get longer every day. If you must ride about like a common hoyden you might at least return in time for your engagements."

"Have I missed something, ma'am?"

"I have ordered the carriage for precisely ten. That gives you less than an hour to make yourself presentable. We are to have morning coffee with Lady Rusham. Absurd time of day to pay a call, I know, but she has grown decidedly peculiar in her old age. Still, she is terribly important.

You dare not offend her. *And* you may not call on her smelling of the stable.''

"I shall be ready, ma'am. It seldom takes me long to bathe and dress.''

"So I have noticed." The Dowager's tone said how little she approved of such *untonnish* behavior. To her mind, it denoted a lack of attention to detail she could only abhor in a future granddaughter-in-law. She finished her chocolate and set down the delicate Sévres cup with finality. "Well, you had better get to it." She patted her thin lips with a linen napkin. "I have instructed Betsey to lay out the persimmon faille walking dress and the yellow chip poke bonnet.''

Abby tried not to wince. The dress was an elaborate concoction with slashed sleeves puffed with yellow silk and edged with chenille. Its padded roll hem stood out like a tent, and there was an overgenerous amount of cotton wadding in the bodice, she supposed for the purpose of building up her bustline.

"Mary will bring you some tea and toast," the Dowager went on. "You haven't time for a proper breakfast now.''

Abby sketched a quick curtsy and left the room.

The day was not destined to improve. Lady Rusham was not only eccentric, she was a bore. A rude, disapproving bore. Worse yet, she somehow managed to wangle an invitation to visit the "newlyweds" at Long Meadow come summer.

From Lady Rusham's they drove to Messrs. Rundell and Bridges to make the final choice of wedding jewelry, a chore Abby found unnervingly depressing. This august establishment was the Dowager's single exception to her anti-shopping rule, for the premises were fine, the clientele extremely select, and the reputation awesome. While she was there she selected for herself an elaborate garnet-and-jet collar, adding it casually to the account of Mr. Rupert Dawson.

There were two more calls on *ton* matrons to be got through before they at last returned to Piccadilly and peace.

"I shall go have my rest now," said Lady Longford as they entered the house. "Madame Ruelle will be here at three to fit your wedding gown. I suggest you spend the interval going over those account books I had sent up from Long Meadow. You will need full understanding of them before we go down next month." The old woman took herself upstairs.

Thank God for her ladyship's afternoon rests. Without them Abby would never have had a moment to herself. And how she needed one now, one gloriously free moment of escape from the tyranny of Longford House and its family, from the dictates of fashion and the *ton*, from her own hopelessly tangled emotions. She needed to get out where she could breathe fully, where she could pull faces or giggle or scream or cry. In Longford House the air was too thin, the atmosphere too rarefied. There was no laughter, no sense of fun, and little human warmth. But there was nowhere to go, so she escaped to the garden. It was the one feature of Longford House she did not find stifling. Abby was beginning to harbor strong suspicions that she could never stand being mistress of this place. And she imagined she would like Long Meadow no better. In fact, she was beginning to suspect—very strongly to suspect— that she didn't want to live anywhere at all as the Countess of Longford.

She sat on a marble bench in the shade of a beautiful elm tree to consider this revolutionary thought. She sat there a long while. Doing away with the dreams of a lifetime is not the work of a moment. She had invested so much of herself, so many hopes and wishes and fantasies, in being the very thing now within her grasp. A noble lady, wealthy, stylish, accepted everywhere. As Countess of Longford it would all be hers.

And what of Poppa? He was so proud that his only child could rise so high. He had asked so little of Abby. How could she even consider disappointing him in the one thing sure to give him such pleasure?

She wandered to a small pond. A rustic fountain trickled water over stones to splash into the surface; fat goldfish glided about as languidly as the most bored member of the *ton*. Abby saw her own face reflected in the smooth water, saw the pinched look of unhappiness that had settled over her features.

Why was she so miserable? she demanded of herself. How could she be so ungrateful, so contrary, as to even consider throwing away a chance to have everything she had ever wanted?

And then she knew. She had left one vital element out of that rosy dream of her future. She had given little or no thought to love. Having always been surrounded by it, she simply took it for granted. To worry about finding it seemed of little importance, especially in the man so perfectly calculated to make all other elements of the dream come true.

Now here she was, poised for the final step, only to discover that nothing, *nothing*, was more important than this ephemeral, difficult-to-recognize, and terribly painful emotion, love.

Simply put, she did not love Reginald St. John Olney, the Right Honourable the Fourth Earl of Longford, Viscount Weede, Viscount Ragerton, Barons Tryon and Frome.

Just as simply put, she did love Charles Lydiard, gentleman. That he was a gentleman she could not question. That he could possibly be anything more never entered her mind. He had, after all, been in her father's employ. She'd been around London long enough to know that members of the aristocracy, even those as purse-strapped as Longford, did not do anything even remotely connected with work.

Yes, she loved Charles, and she always would. And she knew with the suddenness of a blinding light and the finality of a hanging that she would never, could never, marry anyone but him.

She looked at her reflection again. The glassy water showed perfectly the tears running down her cheeks. For a marriage to Charles was something that would never happen to her.

There were two things about this man she loved that she understood very well. He was proud. Far too proud to marry someone so far above him in material wealth, especially when she was the boss's daughter, so to speak. The second was more important and infinitely more painful.

Charles did not love her. He had shown it clearly on the ship. He had reiterated it at every meeting since. And this morning he had sounded the final knell of any hopes there might ever have been.

She could not have Charles, and she would not have Longford. And where did that leave her?

She could not simply go down to the harbor and take the first ship home to nurse her wounds. Poppa was even now on his way to London to dance at her wedding. She must at least wait for him, explain the situation. Poppa would understand. Poppa always did. But there would certainly be arrangements to be made, contracts to be broken. She fervently hoped it wouldn't be too horribly expensive to get her out of her entanglement.

But what could she do while she awaited Poppa? Where could she go? She could think of no one to whom she might turn.

Well, there was Mrs. Rustings, Charles's aunt. She had been so kind to Abby, given her such a warm welcome. And Sophie would be there as well, to laugh with, or cry with.

But it would not do. Although Charles did not live with his aunt, he would surely be about all the time, visiting, squiring Sophie to some affair or other, a constant reminder to Abby of her own unhappiness. Or worse, he would stop visiting his own family simply to avoid having to meet Abby there. That would be horribly unkind to the people who had been good to her.

She next considered the deForests. They had a charming house in Audley Street. It was large enough to house any number of guests, and nothing could be more respectable.

But Lady deForest had been working for years to improve her position in the *ton,* step by painful step. She would certainly do nothing to weaken that position such as alienating the powerful Dowager Countess of Longford.

The Stackpooles were in a very good hotel and would have been delighted to shelter Abby, she knew. And they would be jolly fun to stay with, too. But alas, they were leaving for Paris within the week, off on their much-anticipated second honeymoon.

That left no one to turn to. None of the Longfords'

friends were likely to take her in, and Abby had learned enough of London ways to know she couldn't just go to a hotel on her own, even if she could find one that would take her, which she doubted. Even with Betsey and Jacob to look after her, such a thing would cause a great scandal.

After much fruitless deliberation, dangling her fingers in the cool water of the pond, wandering aimlessly about the garden, and staring despondently at the great house, Abby realized she had little choice. She must stay here until her father arrived. Then Poppa would take her home.

She must say nothing to the Dowager or Lord Longford to let them guess she had changed her mind about the marriage. There would be no living with them. They might even throw her into the street. At the least, they would try to change her mind, harping and badgering and making her even more miserable than she already was.

No, she must become an actress of sorts, going on with the charade of her betrothal a little while longer.

But there would be some changes in her life, she decided. She would use her last days in London to good advantage. If she was to be locked forever into a life of loneliness and misery, a withered spinster, she might never again have a chance at excitement and glamour. She must store up memories enough to last all the rest of her dull days alone.

So she would stay at Longford House—she had no other choice—but she would run her own life. She would put Charles Lydiard from her mind as much as she could and enjoy herself if it killed her.

She strode purposefully back into the house. She would go to Bond Street this very minute and order that lovely rose pelisse Lady Longford had wrinkled her aristocratic nose at. Then she would pay calls on her own particular friends.

She almost ran up the stairs. She yanked on the bell for Betsey and reached for a white piqué bonnet with a beguiling blue ostrich feather. She was just setting it on her curls at a jaunty angle when Betsey came tripping in.

The maid's mouth formed a perfect O after the briefest look at her mistress's face. They had been together a very long time, and Betsey knew that mulish look.

"Get your bonnet, Bets. We are going out."

"Out, Missy Abby? But her ladyship . . ."

"Betsey," said Abby with deliberation softened by a slightly crooked smile, "as Poppa would undoubtedly say, 'Bedamned to her ladyship!' "

With a delighted giggle, Betsey followed Abigail out the door.

Life is full of little ironies, as Abby was to learn in the next few days. Had it not been for the unquenchable pain that burned in her heart, she would have found herself really enjoying London. For the first time in weeks, she felt free to truly be herself.

She decided straight off that she would no longer be bound by Lady Longford's limited and often silly notions of what was proper. She'd just trust to her own instincts and get by just fine. And of course she was right.

The first thing she did that first afternoon was head for the fashionable shops in Bond Street that had formerly been disallowed. Being a considerate girl, she stopped at Madame Ruelle's establishment to cancel her afternoon fitting. Then she moved on to a *modiste* whose taste more clearly reflected her own. She ordered a dozen new gowns to be made up at once with matching bonnets and parasols and all the other fripperies of fashion.

She flitted from shop to shop, buying every pretty trinket that caught her eye. "Oh, Bets, isn't this fun?" she said, turning back to the maid bustling along faithfully at her heels. "I feel like buying the whole of London."

"I thought that's what you was doing," said Betsey, a bit puzzled by her mistress's fervent activity.

"Oh, I've only just begun!" exclaimed Abby, popping into the next shop. She proceeded to purchase china and crystal and linens to ship home to New York. She chose gifts for the whole family: a Russian hat and gloves for Poppa, a beautifully tooled Spanish saddle for Uncle Roger, Dutch tulip bulbs for Aunt Sylvie's garden. For her cousins she chose French soap and fashion dolls for the girls, silk cravats and tin replicas of Lord Wellington's troops for the boys.

She discovered Hatchard's Book Shop and spent a blissfully forgetful pair of hours wandering among its shelves. Soon a huge crate of volumes was being readied for dispatch to Mr. Dawson's riverside warehouses for shipment to New York.

It was all great fun.

"I must find something for Jacob," said Abby. "What would he like, Bets?" She turned back to the maid. "Really, Bets, I do wish you wouldn't hang back so. I'm getting a crick in my neck from talking over my shoulder."

"Well, it don't seem right comfortable to me neither, Missy Abby."

"Then keep up with me, silly."

"They says I mustn't, Missy Ab— Oh, and I mustn't call you that, neither . . . miss."

"Mustn't? They? *Who* says you mustn't what? You're talking like a great goose."

"Mr. Crowther, and Miss Winkle an' all, that's who. They says I mayn't walk with you. 'A lady's maid remains three paces behind her mistress at all times. A lady's maid speaks only when spoken to. A lady's maid is not overly familiar.' " Her voice was such a perfect parody of Winkle's crisp, cold tones that Abby had to giggle.

"You are a goose. Who gives a fig what *they* say?"

"But Missy Abby . . ."

And right there in the middle of Bond Street Abby told her.

"I am not going to marry Lord Longford, you see. I am going home and take care of Poppa." Betsey's mouth fell open. "He needs a hostess. I shall be the most brilliant hostess in New York. It will be such fun." There was a slightly desperate note in her voice, as if she were trying to convince herself of something she did not really believe. But all Betsey heard just then were the magic words "I am not going to marry Lord Longford." The little maid almost whooped for joy. Instead, she contented herself with a flashing white smile.

"Oh, Missy Abby. I be glad of that. I be right glad of that."

"Well, I be right glad of that myself," said Abby with a giggle.

"Maybe I say it who shouldn't, Missy Abby, but I could

never much like his lordship. He don't seem near good enough for you, if you don't mind my sayin' so.''

"I don't, because you are right. He's not. Now get up here where you belong. *I* am your mistress, after all, and I say you *must* walk with me. Come, have I not given you a direct order, my girl?'' she said in her best Lady Longford voice. Betsey giggled, stepped forward to Abby's side, and the pair of them headed up the street. "This is ever so much more comfortable,'' said Abby.

It was not just her newfound freedom that Abby found so enjoyable. She began to enjoy people once again as well. On that very first afternoon, she encountered Sophie Lydiard in Burlington Arcade. With her were a number of lively young ladies who immediately invited Abby to join them at a nearby teashop. They devoured great plates of cakes and pots of tea, chattered continuously, and laughed a great deal. Abby had not enjoyed herself so much in a very long time.

All of the young ladies were pleasant and charming and refreshingly natural, and the conversation flowed easily. Abby laughed with the rest. But her determinedly sunny spirits dipped alarmingly when Charles's name came up. There was a great deal of talk about how handsome he was, and wasn't it fortunate that he'd chosen *their* Season to come home?

"Well, yes,'' said Sophie. "But today he was an absolute pickle. He *promised* to escort Aunt Lucy and me to the theatre tonight. But instead he's run off to Kent to see my Uncle George.''

"Charles is gone?'' murmured Abby.

"Oh, just for a few days,'' said Sophie. "But he might have given me some warning. I don't know what's got into Charlie lately. He's been grumpy as a bear with a sore head. Still,'' she added with an impish grin, "I shouldn't complain. Lord Braedon has agreed to take his place this evening.''

"Lord Braedon!'' squealed a dimpled blond. "Sophie! He's ever so handsome!''

Charles departed the conversation, though he did not leave Abby's thoughts. He never left Abby's thoughts.

She was surprised to hear Charles discussed so easily in

the same conversation as various young lords and baronets. But then, she was also vaguely surprised to find Sophie Lydiard so happily accepted into a group where conversation of young lords and baronets was commonplace. The Lydiards were clearly an exceptional family to have made a place for themselves in such high circles on the force of personality alone, Abby assumed.

Knowing that Charles was away and that she need not worry about running into him around every corner freed Abby even further from constraint. She bought a guidebook and took herself and Betsey on a tour of London. They visited the Tower, the Bank of England, the Royal Exchange, and the Menagerie, and they prowled about neighborhoods Lady Longford would faint at the mention of.

She danced with whom she liked and refused those she did not at the balls that Lord Longford still accompanied her to. She laughed and told jokes and was generally herself, and her success was greater than ever.

To her great surprise, she discovered that there were many people in London, even within the *ton,* that she liked. Oh, it was true that the ugly picture Charles had drawn of ladies of the *ton* was an accurate depiction of many. But there were others who were warm, friendly, and charming, who were sincere, not artificial, and who liked Abby for what she was, not for who she might become.

She was glad to have discovered this truth before she left London forever. Perhaps the aftertaste would be less bitter. She could go home knowing that she had made some true friends.

In short, for those few days, Abby began finally to realize her long-wished-for dream, the ideal life in London. She had friends, wealth, position. She danced and laughed and drank champagne. She rode in the park in elegant carriages beside pleasant, handsome gentlemen who laughed at her jokes and complimented her beauty. She would have a host of rosy memories to carry home to New York.

And every night she lay in her magnificent bedchamber and sobbed herself to sleep.

Lady Longford could hardly help being alarmed at the

changes she saw in Abigail's behavior. To be sure, the
chit had never been as biddable as one would wish. She had
a definite stubborn streak and an uncomfortable mind of
her own. But at least she had seemed anxious to please,
eager to adapt herself to her new role.

She had allowed herself to be guided by the Dowager's
superior judgment and firm hand.

But now, seemingly out of the blue, the chit's whole
attitude had undergone a distinctly unpleasant change.
Though she was never really uncivil, she made it quite
clear that she intended to do just as she chose.

Why, the chit was going off with that pert black maid
of hers to choose her own gowns, most likely highly
unsuitable ones. The Dowager found herself agreeing to all
sorts of excursions with all kinds of young people that she
could not at all approve.

She was being outfaced by a girl not one-third her age.

The Dowager Countess of Longford was not at all used
to such Turkish treatment, and she was not pleased.

There was more to the matter than injured pride, however. Much more. The Dowager had begun to entertain a
niggling suspicion that the girl might cry off from the
engagement. That was a disaster that must be avoided at
all costs.

Without Abigail Dawson, and her father's millions,
there was little hope for the future of the Longford name.
There was no money left to keep Long Meadow. They
might even lose this house. The Dowager would have to
retire permanently to the country, unable to show her face
in London again. Longford might well have to leave the
country at the rate he was going.

Such a fate must be avoided. The girl must be secured
permanently and irrefutably. The Dowager disliked the
idea of doing anything distasteful, but she liked even less
the idea of losing her. They must make certain, *absolutely
certain,* that she became the next Countess of Longford.

And the Dowager Countess knew just how to accomplish such a goal.

Her plan was certain to appeal to Longford, scamp that
he was. And it would not be so very bad. They would just

make quite certain that the girl *could* not change her mind.

She must speak to Longford about it at once.

Chapter Twenty-four

Vauxhall Gardens glittered and shone, twinkled and tinkled and charmed. Abigail was enchanted. The gardens seemed to epitomize all she had come to London to find.

In a strange way she also felt quite at home there, strolling the lighted paths on the arm of Lord Longford. But it was some time before she could understand just why.

Then it struck her. Vauxhall was perhaps the most egalitarian spot in all London. Ladies and gentlemen of the *ton* walked the same paths and listened to the same orchestra playing in the same rotunda as did the merchants from Hans Town or Clapham, the servants from Mayfair kitchens, and the cutpurses from the worst rookeries of London.

Ever since arriving in London, Abby had been strictly segregated, limited to genteel contacts with her own kind. But at Vauxhall everyone of every sort was thrown together and no one seemed much to mind. To Abby, the atmosphere was almost American and very refreshing.

As refreshing, that is, as any place could be when she was in the company of her so-called betrothed. By this time, she felt both uncomfortable and guilty in his presence, always wondering how much longer she must keep up her charade and whether or not she could pull it off. She was relieved that they were not alone at Vauxhall—

indeed, she was almost never alone in his company, for which she was truly grateful.

Their party that night consisted of Lady Longford, escorted by the equally aged Earl of Staines, Miss Langston-Knowles, and her betrothed, Lord Webberley. The entire group was terribly elegant, terribly proper, and, to Abigail's mind, a dead bore.

Still, she was resolved to enjoy herself, to extract all the magic Vauxhall had to offer and to savor one of the delights she had come so far to find.

At least she had the satisfaction of knowing that she was looking her best. The first of her new dresses, those she had selected herself, had arrived that very afternoon. For once, she wore a gown of her own choosing and her own taste.

It was a disarmingly simple creation of silver and white spider gauze draped over an underdress of violet silk charmeuse. The fabric flowed about her like a cloud. Ribbons of pale blue and lavender, royal blue and deep purple laced the neckline and trimmed the waist, fluttering about her as she walked. Betsey had woven forget-me-nots and violets through her hair. They wafted their delicate scents about her.

Lady Longford had been scandalized by the gown, as much by its daring simplicity and the fact that Abigail had chosen it for herself as by the amount of creamy shoulder it left exposed. But Abby no longer cared a whit for the Countess's opinion. She suspected the Dowager sensed as much.

The evening began well enough. Lord Staines had reserved a box where they could sit in splendor, gossiping about each acquaintance that passed and nibbling the paper-thin shavings of ham and sipping the arrack punch for which Vauxhall was justly famous. Music from the orchestra in the Pavilion swirled about them. Scores of people nodded greetings or stopped to pass a word. It promised to be a pleasant enough evening, and for that Abby was grateful.

But scarce half an hour after they entered their box, her peace was rudely shattered. Directly opposite them another elegant party entered a box. Mrs. Rustings,

Sophie Lydiard, and Viola Wyngate, all chattering happily, were accompanied by three gentlemen. Two of them Abby had never seen before. The third was Charles Lydiard.

She was sipping her punch when she saw him. The delicate cup stopped halfway to her mouth, trembling, as a jolt went through her. Charles here! Charles leaning tenderly over Viola Wyngate, helping her with her wrap. Charles actually smiling in that wonderful way he never smiled at Abby anymore.

Her trembling caused her to spill a drop or two of the punch. Longford saw it, looked at her face, then looked at Charles. He gave a rather amused smile. "You are cold, my dear," he drawled to Abby. "Let me help you with your shawl."

Before she could protest, he draped the bit of Norwich silk about her nearly bare shoulders, allowing his hand to linger there, stroking her skin. Slowly stroking and all the while moving his pale eyes back and forth between Abby and Charles. And smiling the languid smile of a jungle cat. "Now drink your punch, my dear," he went on, refilling her cup from the steaming bowl. "It will help warm you."

She was much in need of the sustenance of the hot punch and did as he bade her. It burned her tongue, but she was glad of it. It gave her something to think about, something to focus her attention on besides the spectacle of Charles and Viola Wyngate. When the cup was empty, she felt sufficiently in command of herself to smile across the green and wave lightly to her friends. Sophie and Viola returned warm, happy smiles. Charles nodded.

Lord Longford refilled Abby's empty cup.

Since no one ever went to Vauxhall merely to sit in a box nibbling ham and drinking hot punch, no matter how strong and famous it might be, it wasn't long before the younger members of the Lydiard party decided to stroll the walks, which were subtly lit by Chinese lanterns hanging in the trees. Their path took them directly past the Longfords' box.

Abigail took another deep gulp from her punch as she saw them approach. Longford's reptilian smile grew more pronounced and distinctly less pleasant.

Greetings and introductions were made all around. Abby was more than a little surprised to learn that the handsome young man to whose arm Sophie was clinging so comfortably was none other than Lord Braedon, an earl with a title older than Longford's. What a coup for a mere Miss Lydiard!

Abby had not seen Viola Wyngate since leaving the *Abby Anne*. Under other circumstances, she would have been most pleased to see her again. Her enthusiasm on this occasion, however, was severely diminished by the sight of the onetime governess on Charles's arm. *And* looking so serene and perfectly at home there!

Of course there was no reason Charles should not escort Viola, or any other young lady, wherever he wished, Abby told herself sternly. No reason at all. In fact, he and Viola were eminently well suited. Both were Quality, but both were of modest means and family. Both were intelligent, well read, sober-minded. Who could possibly object to the union of such a perfect pair? Certainly not Abigail Dawson!

"Was it not famous of Charles to bring us to Vaux-hall?" said Sophie. "We were to have gone to a lecture on steam power. Terribly educational, I'm sure, and a perfect bore. How pleased I was when he told us we were to come to the gala instead."

Abby wondered why he had changed his plans when he knew she would be here. She had told him herself. Surely he had not *wanted* to encounter her. Their meetings, always so acrimonious, must be as painful for him as they were for her. Or did he mean to taunt her? Or simply show her how inadequate he found her by flaunting the perfect Miss Wyngate in her face?

The perfect Miss Wyngate cut into her thoughts. "I confess I was most glad of the change. I fear I've had enough of lectures, both the giving and the receiving of them, to last me a lifetime. But I have not had nearly enough dancing."

Charles, tearing a hungry gaze from Abby, answered lightly, "Then you shall have some. There is to be dancing in the Pavilion at ten. It is nearly that now."

Abby was greatly relieved when they said goodbye and

started toward the Pavilion. But her relief was short-lived. To her horror, Lord Longford said, "Shall we not join your friends, my dear? You will want to see the Pavilion, I feel sure."

"Oh, but I . . ." she began, but he was already pulling her to her feet.

"Oh yes, let's do!" said Miss Langston-Knowles. "And then we can walk to the Knoll. We shall see the fireworks ever so much better from there."

"Quite," said Lord Webberley, almost his first comment of the evening.

It was decided before Abby could say another word, and off they all went, leaving their elders to the quiet of their box and the solace of the arrack punch.

Two cups of the strong punch drunk in rapid succession had made Abby less than perfectly steady on her feet. She almost tripped as they left the box. Longford seemed amused, but his grip on her arm was like a vise. He steadied her almost against her will.

All Abby's delight in the evening was now gone. She had seldom felt so wretched in her life.

And things were destined to get a great deal worse.

The Pavilion was crowded. The music swirled about them, too loudly, and the smells of heavy perfumes and wilting flowers increased the headache that had begun to niggle at Abby's temples. The brimming glass of iced champagne that Longford put into her hand almost as soon as they entered helped somewhat, though it tickled her nose and made her sneeze.

The orchestra began a waltz. Longford took Abby's glass, already empty, set it aside, and slid an arm about her tiny waist to swing her into the dance.

"I have been looking forward with great anticipation to waltzing with you, my love," he murmured in her ear.

"But my lord," she said as playfully as she could, "you know I may not waltz. Not until the Lady Patronesses of Almack's say I may."

"Almack's be damned," he said. "I think I may waltz with my affianced wife if I wish." His lordship had also had a bit more punch and champagne than was good for him.

"Her ladyship will be angry."

"Grandmama is often angry," he countered lightly. "Never comes to anything." He pulled her close, enjoying the resistance he could feel in her muscles. His pale eyes glittered into hers. "And besides, I don't think in this case Grandmama will mind. And if we do not waltz, *I* will be angry. I know you would not want that."

There was more menace in his tone than Abby had ever heard. She was learning that his lordship did not like being thwarted, even in so small a matter as a dance. She shuddered to imagine his reaction when she ended their betrothal.

She had little choice. Hoping no one of consequence would see her—or report on her—she let herself be waltzed onto the floor.

Charles was waltzing with Viola, a graceful and competent partner, but she benefited from little of his attention. He observed every detail of the scene between Abigail and Lord Longford. He also misinterpreted a great deal of it, since he could not hear the dialogue. It never occurred to him that Longford would have so little regard for Abby's reputation as to force her to waltz in public before she had been approved. The Patronessess of Almack's were adamant on this point, and breaking the rule could ruin a young lady's chances before she had even begun.

The whole thing must have been the idea of the impetuous Abigail, he decided. She was so deuced headstrong. He took her hesitation for petulance and her rigidity in his lordship's arms for anger at his reluctance to satisfy her every whim. For surely Longford had tried to dissuade her from such a course.

Still, the fellow had given in to the plea of those big green eyes, and for that Charles could not forgive him. He ought to have a greater care for her good name, even if she did not. And need he hold her *quite* so close? Need he bend over *quite* so intimately to whisper in her ear?

He could no longer watch. He must force his attention away. Viola found herself swept into a series of dazzling swoops and turns that almost took her breath away. The rest of the company looked on with admiration.

When finally she was given the chance to speak again,

she said, "You know, Mr. Lydiard, I really think you must decide on one of two courses of action, if only for the sake of your dancing partners." He looked at her questioningly. "You must either stay entirely away from those places where you are likely to encounter Miss Dawson, or you must resolve to take her away from his lordship."

So surprised was he that he stopped in his tracks, causing her to step on his foot and causing several other dancers in the crowded room to step on hers. "It is either that or give up dancing. I doubt many of your partners could stand up to the strain." Though the words were teasing, her voice was very kind.

He flushed and apologized and got them moving again. He huffed and puffed a moment, preparing a spirited denial, then finally gave in under the influence of her sympathetic smile. "Is it really so obvious?" he asked finally.

"Not to all, I am certain," she said gently. "You must remember that I spent a great deal of time with you both on the crossing. And I like and admire you both a great deal." She looked at him as if weighing how much to say. "You know, I must say she doesn't seem terribly taken with the Earl."

"Nonsense. Why, she has him wrapped right round her thumb. Besides, he can give her everything she wants."

"Can he?" she said steadily. "And you cannot?"

He had to look away from her steady gaze. They waltzed a few moments in silence. Finally he said, "We do not wish for the same things from life, Abby and I. We could never make each other happy."

"And yet you are both so adept at making each other miserable," she said matter-of-factly. The music ended before he could think of a suitable reply, and Lord Braedon appeared to dance her away for the next set.

Charles was left to ponder her cryptic comment.

Abigail had never been so glad to see a dance draw to a close. It was only the second time in her life she had waltzed. How very different it was from the first! Not only was she afraid someone would notice and ruin her only chance to shine at Almack's. There was also the problem of her feet. The punch had apparently gone to her toes.

They seemed unwilling to obey her commands, wandering off on their own. Also, her head was buzzing. She would have fallen had not Longford been holding her much tighter than she could like. His touch made her feel cold all over, and his hands felt as though they were all over her.

And then there was Charles. And Viola. They danced together with a beautiful grace, a lovely couple that seemed to belong together. She couldn't watch.

As Longford assuredly steered her through the crowd after the music ended, Abby felt she was being watched. That in itself was not unusual. She was always being watched in London, like some scientific exhibit, she sometimes felt. But this particular gaze felt different, more intent.

She turned and saw a pair of beautiful blue eyes trained upon her. She had seen them before. They belonged to the elegant Cyprian she had seen at the Opera, the one who went by the name Desirée.

In fact, she had seen the woman several times. At least twice while riding in the park she'd noticed her. Once she had seen her carriage pass in Piccadilly. And always the woman watched her.

"Ah," murmured Longford, following her gaze. "The Divine Desirée. Would you care to meet her, my dear?"

His voice brought Abby from her reverie. "I . . ." she began.

"No. I do not imagine even I dare go quite so far as that. Not just yet." He studied her face. "Not when you are yet so innocent, and with everyone watching, too." He laughed an awful laugh and brought his face close to hers. "But perhaps later, when you are a bit riper . . ."

She was afraid he was about to kiss her and jerked her head away from the hand he held to her chin. He only laughed the harder. How grateful she was to see Lord Webberley approach, a polite request for the next dance on his rather vacuous lips.

As he led her to the floor, she looked back at Desirée Hollings. A frown marred the woman's lovely face. It was not an angry frown precisely, nor a jealous one. It was pensive.

Abby moved mindlessly through the cotillion, offering

perfectly inane answers to Lord Webberley's remarks. He didn't seem to mind; he was perfectly inane himself.

A country dance came next. Abby was partnered by the handsome Lord Braedon. His smile was friendly, and she began to relax a bit under his benign influence.

"I always thought Longford an uncommonly lucky dog," he said as they waited to go down the dance. "Now I see just how lucky."

It was a refreshing change from the more fulsome and less sincere compliments she usually received. She smiled. "I thank you, sir."

"Lucky for the rest of us, too."

"My lord?"

"It's my opinion we could do with a lot more like you, Miss Dawson."

"Like me?"

"Outsiders, you know." He smiled a totally disarming smile. "You are lovely and charming. For that alone we welcome you. But if I may speak frankly—and you make one feel that he may—even were you an antidote, I, for one, would welcome you. We need fresh blood. Good God! The English aristocracy has been marrying itself so long it's a wonder we don't all have four heads by now or haven't all ended up in Bedlam."

She grinned. "I suppose I am to take that as a compliment. And I can assure you that not one member of my family, as far as I know at least, has even two heads, much less four."

The dance moved them apart, and when they came together again, they spoke of other things. When the music ended, he offered her a courtly bow softened by a twinkle of the eye.

What a pleasant fellow he was, she thought. And she quite liked his enlightened attitude. She had heard one or two others say the same in the past pair of days. It had made her feel less of an outsider. Of course, she could never imagine Lady Longford offering any such remark, even though she was willing to allow the blood of her own grandson to mix with Abby's. Grudgingly.

Perhaps Lord Braedon's attitude explained his interest in Sophie Lydiard, or at least his willingness to succumb to her considerable charms. He cared not a whit that she was Nobody.

Abby did not ponder the thought long, however, for another thought, stronger than any other and much less comfortable, invaded her mind. It was Charles's turn to dance with her. She had been partnered by every other gentleman in their group, and he had danced with every other lady. He could not in all civility neglect to ask her.

She trembled in anticipation while she shuddered in dread. Oh, why had he come here tonight? She had been doing so well, holding her head high, even managing to enjoy herself a bit. She saw him approach.

Charles had been berating himself for a fool almost from the moment of entering the Gardens. He had arranged this party deliberately, knowing Abigail would be here. He could not seem to stay away from her.

And yet the sight of her on Longford's arm was well nigh unbearable.

Now he must dance with her. Good manners demanded it. She clearly expected it, as did everyone else in their party. But how could he do it? How could he hold her in his arms without telling her that he loved her? How could he get through a whole dance without broadcasting his emotions to the world?

He approached her. Then he was standing before her. Her huge green eyes were on his face. Everyone was watching. He opened his mouth to speak.

No, he could not do it. It was too impossible. "Miss Wyngate," he blurted out, "it is grown so warm here. Shall we stroll outside?"

Viola stood shocked for the smallest moment and stared at him. Then she gave a small, exasperated sigh. "Very well, Mr. Lydiard," she said, and Charles hustled her away.

If the others were somewhat shocked by this unaccustomed breach of manners in Charles, Abigail was mortified. He had snubbed her! It was practically a cut direct. Like Lot's wife, who for one tiny moment of curiosity was doomed to an eternity of saline immobility, she stood rigid as stone, pillared to the floor. So unyielding had her whole being become that there was no longer even enough movement to her imagination to wonder if Lot's wife had also tasted salt as tears poured down her frozen face.

Sophie saw her friend's stricken face and rushed to her defense. "It is terribly warm here, is it not? Why do we not all stroll?" she said brightly. "They will be starting the fireworks soon. We'll want to find a good spot to view them."

It was quickly agreed, and off they all went.

Their departure, as well as the scene leading up to it, was again closely observed. The lovely Desirée was frowning in earnest now. Leaving an adoring duke stranded on the floor, she walked purposefully to one corner of the Pavilion, her heels clicking over the polished floor and her closed fan snapping thoughtfully against one gloved hand.

Near one open wall, a shadow detached itself from a clump of bushes just beyond the dance floor as she approached. A man in a wide-brimmed slouch hat stepped forward, Desirée spoke to him quickly and quietly. He listened, nodded once or twice, pulled his hat lower on his head, and disappeared back into the shadows.

Vauxhall Gardens had been laid out with a little something for every taste, with constant changes of vista to delight the eye and many secluded nooks to delight a few of the other senses.

The Knoll, a hillock generally accounted the supreme spot for viewing the fireworks that always climaxed a Vauxhall gala, stood near the center of the Gardens. It was here that the four young couples headed. Abby scarcely knew or cared where they were going. Lord Longford, with a strong hand on her elbow, led her through the throng along with the others. She could hardly take her eyes from Charles and Viola several feet ahead of them. She had managed to stem her tears—she would not allow herself to be so humiliated by *him*—but it was all she could manage to put one foot in front of the other. She went where she was led.

The Knoll was already crowded with revelers jockeying for position. To the north, the little hill was edged by an outcropping of rock dusted with old trees. Here shopboys and apprentices and the more adventurous of their female counterparts could perch on rocky ledges or climb into the branches of elms, breeches and petticoats dangling and laughter rippling among the newly budding limbs.

To the east, paths led off to circle a small lake, and to the west the Dark Walks brooded. Here lovers and others could hide from curious or censorious eyes, shaded by kindly hedges and branches.

As the crowd grew, those on the fringes were already being elbowed and shouldered away from the Knoll.

Abby looked about the thickening throng. She suddenly realized that she and Lord Longford had become separated by the crowd from the rest of their party. She did not mind. In fact, she was glad of it. She couldn't bear to be near Charles another moment.

Longford steered her along the edge of the crowd. There were so many of them! She was beginning to feel she couldn't breathe. She desperately wished she had not drunk that last cool glass of champagne.

She was relieved when they suddenly broke free of the throng and stepped onto a gravel path. She breathed deeply. She thought she heard Longford chuckle, but he continued to lead her along the path as though he had a definite destination in mind.

She heard the gravel crunch beneath her feet just as the first thunderous boom of the fireworks split the sky overhead. She jumped in surprise and looked up at Longford. His face was wreathed in a thoroughly unpleasant smile.

She looked about her and realized they were quite alone on the path they'd taken. It was bordered by high hedges broken every few yards by a small alcove. From these issued the muffled sounds of giggles and grunts and strange rustlings.

They were deep within the Dark Walk.

A rocket showered overhead, bathing the scene in blue light. She looked at him again. It was not a smile that covered his face. It was a leer.

"My lord . . . ?" she began, only to be cut off by another great boom. Scarlet and crimson flashed. He pulled her roughly to the left, toward one of the secluded, almost hidden alcoves. In another moment they were inside.

The high hedge shaped an ell vaguely illuminated by lanterns in the trees. In the short arm, completely hidden from the view of the path, was a wide, cushioned bench.

"At last, my dear," said Longford in a throaty voice. "We have a chance to get to know each other more . . . intimately. Without interruption."

The booms and flashes overhead came louder and faster. Abby took a step back from him. "Surely, my lord . . ."

Boom! Boom!

"Come, my dear. Relax. Just feel the champagne. It feels delicious, does it not?"

"Lady Longford . . ." she began desperately.

Crash!

"Ah, yes. Grandmama. Quite a brilliant idea of hers, really. Can't imagine why I didn't think of it myself." His words were slightly slurred, but the hands moving over her arms and shoulders were firm.

She managed to pull free from his grasp. "No! I . . ." But he reached easily out and caught her again, holding her firmly.

Boom!

"Really, my love," he drawled, but there was a hard edge of determination to his voice. "Why must you make something so pleasurable be so tedious? You should not be surprised. I am a shrewd shopper, and a shrewd shopper never seals a bargain before personally inspecting the merchandise." *Boom!* "The inspection is about to commence." He looked at her with hooded eyes, the icy blue reflecting the light of the explosions blossoming overhead. "You needn't worry. I am well disposed to like the merchandise. Very well, indeed."

He reached for the delicate ribbons that laced the bodice of her flimsy gown.

Crash! Boom!

"Please, my lord," she whimpered. She had to think what to do. But she couldn't seem to think at all. Her mind was all fuzzy, her thoughts muddled together.

"Relax, my love. You shall find the inspection a delightful experience." His teeth flashed in a mockery of a smile. "A small taste of the myriad pleasures to come once we are man and wife."

Boom! Boom!

"But why?"

"Why? Really, I had not thought you stupid, Abigail. I need you. Rather badly, in fact. You don't seem disposed to stay around. So I must make you stay. Once you are my wife in fact, you cannot object to becoming so in name. You will have no choice. Insurance, I think it is called."

Boom! Boom! Crash!

His hands moved over her. She could feel his hot breath as his face came close to hers and he spoke again. "I shan't mind if you try to resist. Adds zest to the experience, you know. But it will do you no good. I have seen to that."

He was right. She could not resist. She could scarce move. The wine had robbed her of all strength, all clarity of thought.

He pushed her back onto the bench with one hand. She collapsed. His other hand slid past the loosened ribbons at her neck to close on her soft flesh.

Her skin screamed at his touch. Her mind screamed. She did not know if any sound actually came out. It would not have mattered, for no one could hear her. The thunderous crash of the fireworks was now continuous.

Time seemed to slow down; details magnified. Above the din she could hear his heavy breathing as his lips closed on hers. She could smell the acrid odor of the exploding blossoms of light. She could taste champagne and punch rising up in her throat as his hands, more urgent now, moved across her crawling skin.

She was about to be sick.

Boom! Boom! Crash! Boom! Boom!

Suddenly, his insistent lips tore away from hers. The groping hands disappeared from her breast. The demanding body pressing her down so immovably flew up and away, releasing her to struggle to her feet.

Lights flashed, yellow and green and red. She saw a man, a slouch hat pulled low onto his head, pick Longford up by the collar of his exquisitely tailored coat. A beefy fist connected with his lordship's aristocratic jaw, blood spurted from his aquiline nose, and his noble backside connected with the ground.

He slumped. The Earl of Longford was out cold.

Without a word, the stranger took Abby's hand and

rushed her from the alcove. She was not reluctant to go. Out on the path she could hear the delighted squeals of the crowd on the Knoll. Fiery rainbows continued to burst overhead.

The man in the slouch hat hurried her along the path. She'd lost all sense of direction. She didn't care where she was going as long as it was away. Away from the cold, groping hands and the hot, winy lips. Away from her own helplessness and humiliation. Away from Longford.

She tripped and fell. The gravel cut through her thin gown, scratching her knees. The stranger helped her to her feet with a solid hand and guided her farther along the path.

They ran until she was out of breath, then they walked for several moments more, twising to and fro through the pathways. Abby realized that the sound of the fireworks had become fainter. They were moving *away* from the others.

Abby's relief changed to renewed alarm. Was she running from one madman into the arms of another? she wondered. She stopped short and dug in her heels.

By that time, they had reached a road that skirted the Gardens. The man in the slouch hat stopped too and tried to catch his breath. Before Abby could think clearly or turn to run away, an elegant dark-blue carriage rolled along the road and stopped just before them.

The door swung open as Abby shrank back. Eyes wide with fear, she looked up to see Desirée Hollings smiling out at her.

"May I offer you a lift, Miss Dawson?"

"You?"

"Yes, me. I rather suspected you might need a bit of help. Come."

"Oh, but I . . ."

"You don't really wish to go back to Longford House, do you?"

"No! I mean . . . that is . . ."

"Please," she said in a voice amazingly gentle. "I know Reginald very well, and I understand perfectly. That is why I am here. You cannot go back to Longford House tonight, and I rather suspect you've no place else to go just now. I will be happy to take you home.''

The woman's voice was so gentle and understanding, her eyes so kind, and Abby was so very, very tired and confused that without another word she climbed into the carriage.

The door swung to behind her.

Desirée set to tucking a warm fur carriage rug about her knees. The man in the slouch hat climbed up beside the coachman, and Abby was driven away from her first visit to the famous Vauxhall Gardens of London.

Chapter Twenty-five

As the carriage rolled toward the river, Abby began to shiver. Shock, champagne, and the chill night air were combining for an unpleasant effect. Desirée tucked another carriage rug around her.

"Here," she said. "This will make you more comfortable." She sounded more like a mothering matron than a fashionable lady of the evening only five years Abby's senior. "In a few moments now we shall be at home, and you shall have a nice cup of tea to warm you. We need not talk now. Just relax."

Relaxation, of course, was out of the question, but Abby did manage to still the shivering, burrowing deep into the fur of the rugs. Her heartbeat slowed almost to normal as they crossed the river. And by the time they pulled up in front of a fashionable house in Cadogan Place, she was sufficiently in command of herself to try speaking.

"I'm sorry, Miss . . . Miss . . ."

"Just call me Desirée. Everyone does."

"Desirée. I very much appreciate your assistance tonight. I really do. But now I think . . ."

"Please, Miss Dawson. Or may I call you Abigail? It is Abigail, is it not?"

"Yes, but I . . ."

"Good. Now we will go inside and have some tea. Surely you will not object to a cup of tea, and we really can talk so much more comfortably inside, don't you think? I promise no one will know."

Abby reluctantly agreed to this. Firstly, because she did in fact owe this strange, beautiful woman a great debt. And secondly, she really didn't know what else to do. She soon found herself comfortably ensconced in a chair before a cozy fire sipping gratefully at a cup of strong tea. And almost before she knew what she was about, she was pouring the whole sordid tale of her evening's adventures into her young hostess's ears.

"Reginald really can be incredibly stupid at times," said Desirée, sounding almost amused. "But then he isn't terribly bright at the best of times. Oh, please don't misunderstand. I quite like Reginald. Perhaps because we are two of a kind. But I knew from the first moment of setting eyes on you—at the Opera, you may recall—that you were not at all the wife for him, or rather that he was not the husband for you." She might have added that she had also seen at the Opera exactly who *was* the husband for Abby. Instead she sipped her tea.

"Well, you were right," said Abby in a remarkably strong voice. The tea had worked wonders, and there was something about this odd young woman that made Abby want to trust her. "I *shan't* marry him. Or anyone. Ever."

"Oh dear," said Desirée softly. "Things are in an even worse muddle than I suspected."

Abby gave her a curious look. For the first time it really dawned on her how fortuitous was her escape, how precipitate the appearance of her strange rescuer. "But how could you suspect anything at all?" she asked. "How could you know he. . . ?"

"It was no great feat, really. I assure you I am no mind reader. But did I not tell you I know Reginald very well? When I saw the way he looked at you tonight, *and* the amount of champagne he filled you with, I felt fairly certain he would try something of the sort. Especially if he feared you were about to cry off. And it was obvious from the way you looked at him that you were."

"I tried not to let him know," said Abby in a small voice.

"I'm sure you did. But there is no pretense in you, Abigail. One can see everything quite clearly on your face. I've known only one other person in my life quite as transparent."

"Yes," Abby sighed. "Charles used to berate me for it too."

Now Desirée sighed. "Charles would. Anyway, it was quite clear you were going to need help at some point. I've been expecting it for days. That's why I've had Jamey watching you."

"Jamey? Is that your . . . your . . . ?"

"Hmmm, I don't suppose there really is a title for what Jamey is. He just does things for me when I need them. I was able to help him once, so now he often does the same for me. He is very loyal."

"But why? I mean, why did you send him after me? You don't even know me, and I shouldn't have thought you'd have much reason to like me. Did you wish to spite Lord Longford?"

"Good heavens, no. I owe Reginald a great deal." She paused, and a gentle, almost wistful smile crossed her face. "But I owe Charles Lydiard even more."

Abby's eyes flew to hers. "Charles?"

"I think perhaps I had better go back to the beginning of the tale. It is not a pretty story, though I'll not say I'm ashamed of anything I've done or anything I am. Still, I am certain it's not a tale your mother would wish you to hear."

"My mother is dead."

"Well, there you are then. In any case, you've a right to hear it."

And hear it she did, from that very first morning when ambitious little Daisy Hollings first batted her blue eyes at Charles Lydiard in the lending library all those years ago.

"Poor Charles," said Abby when the tale was told. "How terribly hurt he must have been."

"I'm sure he was, poor dear," said Desiree. "But not nearly so badly as he would have been if I'd married him. I really had intended to, you know. Right from the first. But when it came right to it, I couldn't do it. I would have made him miserable."

"And so you gave Charles up for Longford?" asked Abby, not believing anyone could be such an idiot as that.

"Not at all. I gave him up for a different world, a world for which I was very much better suited. Reginald was merely a door into that world."

Abby shook her head. Her eyes were heavy, and her mind was fuzzy. "I'm not certain I understand."

"Of course you do not," said Desirée in a kindly voice. "You are much too innocent, and you've had too much punch and champagne and too much fright and too many unanswered questions to be expected to understand anything at all tonight. What you need now is sleep." She rose gracefully and went to pull the bell. "There is one more thing I think we must deal with tonight. At once, in fact. Reginald is not one to accept defeat gracefully. He will certainly be looking for you very soon. He might even call out the Runners. You shan't be safe from him until the whole world knows that your betrothal is at an end. Shall we tell them?"

"How?"

"It's quite simple, really. The editor of the *Morning Chronicle* is a . . . uh . . . a friend of mine. If I send him the notice at once and tell him I'd like it in tomorrow's edition, I'm sure he'll oblige me. Shall I, Abigail?"

Despite her weariness, a look of determination crossed Abby's face. She was still uncertain why Desirée was involved in her problems, but there was no question in her mind of how she felt about her betrothal to Lord Longford. "Yes," she said firmly.

"Good. I'll send Jamey straightaway. And now here is Emmy to show you to your room."

A chambermaid appeared at the door, and Abby gasped as a thought struck her. "Betsey!" she said:

"Betsey?"

"My maid. She'll be worried sick."

"Oh dear, I'm sure she will. Well, she must get through the night somehow, I'm afraid. We shall find a way to spirit her away first thing in the morning. Now go up with Emmy and get some sleep. She will bring you anything you may need."

Abby was almost asleep on her feet, too tired to consider the impropriety of spending the night in the house of such a woman, too tired to worry further about Betsey, too tired for anything but sleep. "I don't know how to thank you," she mumbled as she rose to go.

Desirée gave a secret smile. "I believe I will find a way for you to do that, Abigail. Sleep well."

Abby did sleep well and long, her dreams surprisingly untroubled by visions of cold, grasping hands and demanding lips. She awoke with her head feeling twice its normal size and her eyes burning like a pair of coals in her head. But the welcome smell of fresh coffee teased at her nose from just beyond the flowered chintz hangings surrounding the soft featherbed in which she lay.

The sound of the curtains being yanked back sounded like a cannon shot into her ear, and the bright morning sunlight felt like lightning flashing in her eyes. She pulled the coverlet over her head with a groan.

It was gently but firmly pulled back down. "Now, none o' that, Missy Abby," came the stern, affectionate voice of Betsey. "It's coffee and exercise you be needin', not sleep. Why, it be near noon!"

Abby sat up with a start at the sound of that beloved voice, then groaned at the pain shooting through her head from the movement. She forced her eyes open. Slowly. "Bets? What are you doing here?"

"An' jest where'd you expect me to be? I *am* your personal maid." She did not sound too pleased by the fact. "Even though you don't see fit to inform me of where you be goin' off to of a night." This last was punctuated by a definite sniff.

"Well, I could hardly tell you I'd be coming here when I didn't know it myself," said Abby after she'd swallowed some of the coffee. "One doesn't usually know in advance when one will need rescuing, you know."

Betsey was muttering, "Shoulda knowed we'd come to no good in that house."

Abby slid lower into the bed. "But I am *so* glad you're here, Bets. I feel perfectly wretched."

"Good. What you put us through, you ought to."

"Was Longford House in an uproar?" she asked sheepishly.

Betsey laughed. "Never saw such a tizzy in your life. The old lady carryin' on fit to be tied, callin' his lordship a perfect dolt. An' him sittin' there with a piece of raw beef on an eye black as I am an' whinin' that it weren't his fault an' he was jest doin' like she told him. An' nobody knowin' where you was nor what to do next. Couldn't make no sense out of it atall. An' only Mr. Charles doin' anything sensible."

"Charles was there?"

"There? He was everywhere! Showed up right after the others got back from that Vauxhall place. An' when he couldn't get no answers from his lordship 'bout where you was, Missy Abby, he blackened his other eye." Betsey interrupted herself with a hearty giggle at remembrance of the scene. "Then he off an' called the Runners. Been back to the house three times this morning afore I left to see if maybe you'd come back."

"Charles?" Abby repeated, both amazed and thrilled at such a show of concern on his part.

"An' *then*, when the newspaper came with that there notice in it! Well! No one knew what to make of it, but I never seen anyone so angry as his lordship. His face turned redder and purpler than his black eyes. I knew enough to start packin' your things. Quick!"

Another stab of pain brought a groan from Abby. Betsey looked up from a tray where she was mixing some sort of concoction. "Humph," she sounded and went back to her mixing.

"What are you doing, Bets? I couldn't possibly want anything but coffee this morning."

"Shouldn't think you would, but you'll have it all the

same. Miss Desirée says you're to drink this right up. Says it'll put you back to rights quick as a wink.''

"Wh-what is it?''

Betsey looked at the dark liquid in the glass. "Don't rightly know. Drink it.''

Abby was still too weak to argue. She took the glass, grimaced, and drank it off in one gulp. Surprisingly, it wasn't at all vile. It was rather sweet and a bit fizzy, a bit lemony and a bit . . . well, it was tasty. She sank back onto the pillows and sipped the rest of her coffee while Betsey bustled about. In an amazingly short time, she did begin to feel much more the thing, as if she might live through the day after all.

"Oh, Bets,'' she sighed. "How glad I am to be away from that awful place. I shall never go back there. Never.''

"No need to, Missy Abby. I brought your pearls an' your momma's wedding gown an' everything else that matters.'' She was hanging away Abby's newest gowns. "I left the ones the old lady chose behind.''

"Good,'' said Abby. "Soon Poppa will be here and we shall be on our way home.'' She lay there a moment, trying to feel happy at the prospect of leaving London. Then another thought struck. "Mr. Adams!'' she exclaimed.

"Safe in Miss Desirée's stable,'' said Betsey.

"Jacob came with you?''

Instead of the pert reply Abby might have expected, she got a vivid blush and a softly murmured, "I won't be goin' anywheres without Jacob anymore.''

Abby grinned. "Does that mean you've finally agreed to put the poor man out of his misery?''

Then Betsey grinned. "Well now, I wouldn't go so far as to say that. But I did agree to marry him. If you don't mind, Missy Abby.''

"Mind? You goose, of course I don't mind.'' And she jumped out of bed to give her maid a joyful hug and dance her about the room. "Oh,'' she groaned finally, collapsing onto the bed. "I'm not up to dancing yet. I can't think why I should have such a horrid headache this morning.'' Betsey just arched a brow at that. "Anyway, I must say it's about time you and Jacob came to the point. Anyone can see you belong together.''

"There be a lot anyone could see if anyone had eyes in her head," muttered Betsey.

"What?"

"But some people do be awful blind," she muttered some more.

"Betsey!"

Before Abby could make any sense of these dark mutterings, Desirée floated into the room on a cloud of pink China silk and rose scent. She seemed even lovelier than the night before.

"Good morning," she said cheerfully. "I do hope your headache is better."

"How did you know. . . ?"

Desirée arched a brow. "You really must learn to stay away from the arrack punch at Vauxhall. It is deadly, as I have reason to know."

"Oh," said Abby, both understanding and embarrassment dawning.

"I shall have to warn Charles to keep a wary eye on you," Desirée teased with a twinkle in her eye.

"Charles? What does Charles. . . ?"

"I have brought you the *Chronicle*. George was good enough to oblige me. I thought you'd like to see for yourself the announcement of your freedom."

Abby took the paper eagerly. In but a moment her eye found the welcome words:

> Miss Abigail Dawson wishes to have it known that her betrothal to the Earl of Longford is at an end. Henceforward no tradesmen's or other bills submitted to Miss Dawson for goods or services rendered to his lordship will be honored.

"I imagine that's set the cat among the pigeons," said Desirée. "Poor Reggie." There was genuine regret in her voice, but she pushed it quickly away and smiled. "And now you really must dress. We are expecting a visitor soon." She turned to Betsey. "Have you brought your mistress's prettiest frock?" Betsey curtsied a yes. "Good. Put her into it and fluff her hair. And you might put just a *touch* of rouge on her cheeks. She's still rather pale.''

With a smile that had devastated many a Peer of the Realm, Desirée floated out of the room.

Something more than an hour later, Abby was seated in Desirée's pretty drawing room, sipping tea and feeling melancholy. The grand adventure was nearly at an end. Soon she would be going home, home to a life of hostessing for Poppa, a life of good works and charity and loneliness, a life without Charles.

Desirée was chatting inconsequentially about her life and how well it suited her, though of course it wouldn't do for everyone. ''I think I always knew, you know, that I was cut out for the role of courtesan. I think I need the admiration. And the pay is quite wonderful if one is good at one's work. I happen to be very good at mine. I have a wonderful degree of independence, and I am never bored. And you would be quite amazed at the interesting people I meet. *And* at the tidy nest egg I've already put by for my old age. Yes, I am really quite satisfied with the life I've fallen into.''

Abby, looking pretty as the proverbial picture in a muslin round gown of ice blue sprigged with violets, barely heard her benefactress. Occasionally, she nodded glumly. She was too sunk in gloom to be very attentive.

From the hall outside the drawing room, the sound of loud voices interrupted Desirée's monologue. ''At last. I think our guest has arrived. It has certainly taken Jamey long enough to locate him, but then I imagine the man *has* been having a busy morning, poor dear.'' She started toward the door just as it burst open.

''Really, Daisy,'' said Charles Lydiard, nearly exploding into the room. ''I wish you'd tell me what you mean by having that fellow of yours practically drag me here.''

Abby could not see him with Desirée blocking her view, but the sound of that beloved voice froze her to her chair. What on earth was Charles doing here?

''Charles,'' said Desirée, flowing toward him with outstretched hands. ''How very good to see you again. Thank you for coming. Do come in.''

It dawned on him that he was being uncivil. He had not, after all, spoken to her in more than four years. "Yes, well, it is good to see you too, Daisy. You are looking wonderful, as always. But the thing is I'm rather busy today. Perhaps I . . ."

"Oh, do be still, Charles, and for heaven's sake come in! There's someone here to see you." And she stepped aside to offer him a full view of the only thing in the world he wished to see at that moment.

He still wore the black evening coat he'd sported the night before, but it somehow lacked the polish it had had at Vauxhall, accompanied as it was by a sadly crumpled neckcloth and an overnight stubble of beard. His auburn locks were too disheveled even to qualify for the popular Windswept look, and it was evident from his reddened eyes and the purple shadows beneath them that he hadn't been to bed all night. He looked more than a little crazed.

And Abby had never seen anyone or anything more beautiful in her whole life.

She rose slowly to her feet, and the two of them just stared at each other a long moment. Then Charles crossed the room with three long strides and scooped her into his arms, almost squeezing the breath from her with the strength of his embrace. She didn't seem to mind. "You're all right! Thank God, Abby, you're all right!"

She sighed into his shoulder, saying, "Oh yes, now I really am all right."

"Well," said Desirée brightly. "If you two will excuse me I really must confer with my housekeeper. I would like to say one thing, however, before I leave you." She paused and waited for them to give her their attention, which they did reluctantly. "I have been put to a great deal of trouble to bring you together today. Do at least try not to muddle things up this time." Then with a beneficent smile she floated away.

As relief flooded through Charles at seeing Abby safe and well, the frustration and panic he'd been suffering exploded into anger. He took her by the shoulders and shook her like a recalcitrant child. "Look here, my girl. Just what did you mean by it, running off like that without a word to anyone? Have you any idea what you've put me through in the past dozen hours?''

She managed to pull free of him. "You needn't rip up at me, Charles. What about what *I* have been through?''

His eyes took in the comfortable drawing room with the remains of a nice tea, her fresh gown and her cheeks glowing pink from the rouge Betsey had carefully applied. "You don't look to me as though you've had a particularly trying morning,'' was his sarcastic response.

"If you had my head this morning, you wouldn't say that," she muttered. "And I had a *damnably* uncomfortable night, I can tell you!'' The profanity from those sweet red lips was so unexpected that it shook a hearty laugh from Charles. "And if you *dare* to laugh at me, Charles Lydiard, I shall . . . I shall . . . well, you won't like it in the least, I can promise you.'' Her hands had balled into fists, and for some reason the sight enchanted him. She hadn't had *all* her spirit wrenched from her, he was glad to see.

He left off laughing and merely smiled. It was that old wonderful smile that could always turn Abby into something akin to a plate of jelly. She sank onto the settee. "Oh, Charles," she sighed. "It was horrid, and I wanted you so, and where *were* you?'' She sounded as though she was about to give way to tears.

He sat beside her and took her hand. "Tell me now. All of it.'' And she did, all of it. Well, almost all of it. She couldn't tell him why she'd decided not to marry Lord Longford. She couldn't tell him that she would never marry anyone but him.

When the story was done, Charles was again shaking with anger, even though he had suspected something of the sort had happened. "Damn the blackguard!'' he said, practically exploding from his chair. "I should have killed him. I *will* kill him. I'll call him out for this, the swine!''

She ran to him in alarm. "Charles, you mustn't! You could be hurt.'' She grabbed his arm with the fierceness of terror. "You could be *killed*, Charles!''

He stared down at her, wanting desperately to believe that the worry he saw on her lovely face and the concern he heard in her voice were genuine. He almost whispered, "Would that matter to you, Abigail?"

Without thought and without embarrassment, she said, "Nothing could matter more. Please, Charles. Promise you won't do anything so foolish as to call him out."

His smile had grown until he was positively glowing. He wanted to whoop for joy. Instead he laughed. "I can't. He's gone!"

"Gone? Gone where?"

"The Continent would be my guess. Wouldn't be the first fellow to head that way when the money well dried up. And for a man like Longford, I imagine such banishment is a fate far worse than death in a duel."

"So soon?"

He laughed harder. "My love, it wasn't half an hour after the *Chronicle* appeared with that blessed announcement that the first tradesman was at the door. When I was last there, the bailiffs were all over the house. Even the old lady's skipped, gone down to the country, I imagine, and I doubt she'll be back for a very long time, if ever."

"Poor Lady Longford. It was all so important to her."

"Save your sympathy. Your pretty little love scene last evening was her idea, you know. Reggie's not bright enough to think of it on his own. And she'd have tried it again if you'd given her the chance."

Abby shivered at the memory of that horrid scene. She could still feel Longford's groping hands on her. "Oh, Charles, is he really gone? Truly?"

"Yes, truly," he said tenderly. "He'll never touch you again." Then he pulled her into his arms, squeezing her close. "By God, *no one* will ever touch you again!"

"But Charles," she whispered into his shoulder. "What if I *wish* to be touched?"

Her head lifted slightly to gaze up at him; her green eyes were shining, mirroring his own bemused gaze. "Well then," he whispered in a throaty way, "I think perhaps that can be arranged." And then he lowered his eager lips to hers.

It was a feather of a kiss, light as a dream at first. But the two pairs of lips grew quickly warmer, less fluttery, more demanding. Soon the kiss grew in intensity, billowed, mounted, and quickly overtook them both until nothing remained in the whole world except each other, the warmth of each other, the magic of each other, swirling into one quivering being.

When Charles finally broke free with a gasp, he held Abby to him till she could scarce breathe. "I cannot let you go this time, Abby," he said in that throaty voice. "I cannot!"

"Don't, Charles. Please, don't ever let me go. I don't ever want to be let go of again." And before he could give her an answer to this heady, wonderful request, she pulled his head down to hers and kissed him again.

As they swirled about their magic world, Abby thought how different her life would be as Mrs. Lydiard than it would have been as the Countess of Longford. She didn't care anymore. The mere touch of Charles's hand on her skin sent a wave of excitement racing through her whole body, an excitement she knew the Earl could never have caused. The ugly memory of his cold hands and his awful kisses fled entirely from her mind, replaced by the wonder of Charles.

But did Charles wish to marry her? She thought she would die if he did not.

In answer to her thought, he broke the embrace to murmur into her ear, "Marry me, Abby. Oh, God, you *must* marry me!"

"Of course I must," she murmured before he kissed her again.

This sort of thing went on for some while longer—it was not an activity they were likely to grow bored with anytime soon—but they did eventually feel the need to speak rationally again. So they finally found themselves seated decorously beside each other on the settee. Well, not *too* decorously, for Charles's arm was wrapped about her, and Abby's head rested comfortably on his shoulder. But at least speech was again possible.

She sighed with contentment. "Now I know why I came to England."

"I thought you came to England to be a countess."

"Well, yes I did, and I didn't. I mean, I came to find my dream. For a while I just had the dream a bit mixed up. But now I really have found it. So you see, I didn't really wish to be a countess at all.''

''Good.''

''But I must say, Charles, that I think you are wrong about the *ton*. Oh, certainly there are some, many even, who fit your very negative description of them. The sharks, I think you called them. But there are others who are quite wonderful. I almost didn't have a chance to learn that. I'm glad I did learn it, though, before leaving the *ton* forever. I wouldn't want to have bitter memories about the whole affair.''

''Leaving the *ton*? What are you talking about? Oh, I know I've spouted a lot of nonsense about them, but I have seen the past few weeks that I was not entirely correct. If I hadn't been so miserable over you, I should have quite enjoyed being back in the thick of it, I think. And the Viscountess Cumberley will always be a part of the *ton*, like it or not.''

''Viscountess. . . ? Charles, what are you talking about? I don't wish to be a viscountess. I just wish to be a . . . a missus. Mrs. Lydiard!''

''And so you shall, my darling, for I'm not letting you off the hook. But I'm afraid you will eventually have to become Viscountess Cumberley whether you will or no. Oh, not soon. My Uncle George has many years in him yet, I hope.''

''Viscountess Cumberley,'' she murmured to herself. ''But Charles, I . . .'' Understanding began slowly to seep in. ''Charles Lydiard, do you mean to tell me that all this time you've had a title up your sleeve and you let me think. . . ? Well, of all the shabby tricks!''

Charles looked confused. ''Tricks? I assumed you knew. I . . .''

''And I suppose you're not penniless, either,'' she accused.

''Penniless? Of course I'm not penniless. Would I have asked you to marry me if I were? Do you want a penniless husband? Don't you want to be a viscountess?''

''Well, of course I . . .'' she began.

''I suppose I could give it away. The money, I mean. Of course we should still have yours, so we couldn't be quite

penniless. I don't know about the title. I'm not quite sure
how that's done, giving it away, I mean. I'll have to ask
Uncle George. If you really insist, that is."

"I don't insist!" she screamed, then she noticed the
growing twinkle in his wonderful blue eyes. "Really,
Charles! I think you are quite impossible. Perhaps I shan't
marry you after all." She squirmed away from him and pre-
tended a huff.

But he was after her in a trice. He grabbed her by the
shoulders and shook her again, but gently this time, very
gently. "Now you listen to me, my girl. You shall marry
me, and you'll be disgustingly wealthy, and you'll be the
toast of the *ton*, and you'll be a viscountess, and you'll
like it! Do you understand me?"

She smiled a dreamy smile, the green of her eyes dancing
like emeralds in the sun. "Yes, Charles," she said docilely.
"I rather think I shall like it. Especially if you will kiss me
again."

Which he did.

And she did like it. She liked it very much indeed.

About the Author

Megan Daniel, born and raised in Southern California, combines a background in theater and music with a passion for travel and a love of England and the English. After attending UCLA and California State University, Long Beach, where she earned a degree in theater, she lived for a time in London and elsewhere in Europe. She then settled in New York, working for six years as a theatrical costume designer for Broadway, off-Broadway, ballet, and regional theater.

Miss Daniel lives in New York with her husband, Roy Sorrels, a successful free-lance writer. Her other Regency novels—*Amelia, The Reluctant Suitor, The Unlikely Rivals* and *The Sensible Courtship*—are also available in Signet editions.

SIGNET Regency Romances You'll Enjoy

⊘

SIGNET Regency Romances You'll Want to Read